Sincerely Yours

*Also by Al and Joanna Lacy
in Large Print:*

Secrets of the Heart
A Time to Love
Tender Flame
Blessed Are the Merciful
Ransom of Love
Until the Daybreak

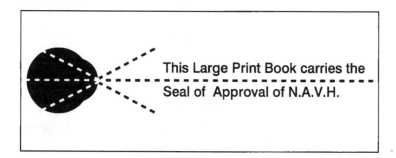

This Large Print Book carries the
Seal of Approval of N.A.V.H.

Sincerely Yours

Mail Order #7

Al & Joanna Lacy

Thorndike Press • Waterville, Maine

Published in 2001 by arrangement with Multnomah Publishers, Inc.

Thorndike Press Large Print Christian Fiction Series.

The tree indicium is a trademark of Thorndike Press.

The text of this Large Print edition is unabridged. Other aspects of the book may vary from the original edition.

Set in 16 pt. Plantin by Elena Picard.

Printed in the United States on permanent paper.

Library of Congress Cataloging-in-Publication Data

Lacy, Al.
    Sincerely yours / Al & JoAnna Lacy.
      p. cm. — (Mail order ; 7)
    ISBN 0-7862-3615-9 (lg. print : hc : alk. paper)
    1. Mail order brides — Fiction. 2. Women pioneers — Fiction. 3. Montana — Fiction. 4. Large type books.
I. Lacy, JoAnna. II. Title.
PS3562.A256 S59 2001b
813′.54—dc21   2001053469

With deep affection we dedicate
this book to our special friend
and "adopted daughter,"
Karen Denson.

Your sweet words of encouragement
and acts of Christian love
have been a rich blessing
and inspiration to us.
In your profession as a nurse,
we are sure you have touched many lives,
even as you have touched
and brightened ours.
We love you, Karen!

"Papa" and "Mama" Lacy

2 TIMOTHY 4:22

Prologue

The Encyclopedia Britannica reports that the mail order business, also called direct mail marketing, "is a method of merchandising in which the seller's offer is made through mass mailing of a circular or catalog, or advertisement placed in a newspaper or magazine, in which the buyer places his order by mail."

Britannica goes on to say that "mail order operations have been known in the United States in one form or another since colonial days but not until the latter half of the nineteenth century did they assume a significant role in domestic trade."

Thus the mail order market was known when the big gold rush took place in this country in the 1840s and 1850s. At that time prospectors, merchants, and adventurers raced from the East to the newly discovered goldfields in the West. One of the most famous was the California Gold Rush in 1848–49, when discovery of gold at Sutter's Mill, near Sacramento, brought more than 40,000 men to California. Though few struck it rich, their presence stimulated economic growth, the lure of which brought even more men to the West.

The married men who had come to seek their fortunes sent for their wives and children, desiring to stay and make their home there. Most of the gold rush men were single and also desired to stay in the West, but there were about two hundred men for every single woman. Being familiar with the mail order concept, they began advertising in eastern newspapers for women to come west and marry them. Thus was born the name "mail order bride."

Women by the hundreds began answering the ads. Often when men and their prospective brides corresponded, they agreed to send no photographs; they would accept each other by the spirit of the letters rather than on a physical basis. Others, of course, did exchange photographs.

The mail order bride movement accelerated after the Civil War ended in April 1865, when men went west by the thousands to make their fortunes on the frontier. Many of the marriages turned out well, while others were disappointing and ended in desertion by one or the other of the mates, or by divorce.

In the Mail Order Bride fiction series, we tell stories intended to grip the heart of the reader, bring some smiles, and maybe wring out a few tears. As always, we weave in the gospel of Jesus Christ and run threads of Bible truth that apply to our lives today.

Introduction

During the bloody and devastating Civil War that took place in this country from April 1861 until April 1865, the pendulum of the War swung both ways for the first three years. By the spring of 1864, however, the better-equipped and larger forces of the Union army began to wear down the Confederate forces, and the Yankees were capturing more and more strategic cities of the South.

In early May 1864, General William T. Sherman led three Union armies south from the federal base at a subjugated Chattanooga, Tennessee, into Georgia. His mission was to destroy the Confederate forces led by General Joseph E. Johnston and to capture Atlanta — the strategic manufacturing and railroad center of the Deep South.

Though greatly outnumbered, General Johnston led his fighting men in a string of shrewd, well-executed blocking actions before finally being forced back to Atlanta in the second week of July. There, Johnston was replaced by General John Bell Hood, whose aggressive tactics kept Sherman at bay.

Infuriated at the losses his armies sustained in repeated attempts to seize Atlanta, Sherman knew that Hood was being supplied with ammunition and other needful items by Confederate forces at Jonesboro, several miles to the south. He decided to conquer Jonesboro first, then march full force on Atlanta.

The Rebel forces at Jonesboro gave Sherman a battle he would never forget. But finally, in the latter part of August, Jonesboro fell into Sherman's hands, which left Atlanta alone and vulnerable. The crafty Union general knew he would still have a fight on his hands with Hood at the helm in Atlanta, but he could smell victory as he moved his massive force toward the city he was determined to conquer and seize.

On Tuesday morning, August 30, General Hood was told by his scouts that Sherman had devastated the Confederate forces at Jonesboro and was preparing to march toward Atlanta. The scouts estimated that Sherman and his armies would arrive by Thursday.

General Hood alerted his troops to the impending attack and had men on horseback ride through the city, blowing bugles to get attention, and shouting out the warning to Atlanta's citizens that Sherman was coming. Fear spread throughout the city, and it was all Hood could do to keep the people from going into a frenzied panic . . .

1

Clarence and Edna Taylor and their twenty-year-old daughter stood on the front porch of their two-story frame house and listened to mounted soldiers in the street shout: "Sherman is coming! Sherman is coming! General Hood says he will be here by Thursday! Friday, at the latest! You will be warned when the Yankees are drawing close. At that time you must stay off the streets and inside your houses!"

The Taylors scanned the street in both directions and watched their neighbors react with the same fear that made their own blood run cold. For the past four months the Yankees had been bent on capturing Atlanta. General John Bell Hood had done a good job fending them off until now, but there would be no help from Confederate forces outside the city this time. Jonesboro had fallen.

Hood's troops were preparing as best they

could, but everyone in Atlanta knew their gunpowder supplies were low and there was no way to replenish them.

Edna Taylor took hold of her husband's arm with a trembling hand and said, "Dear? Some people have been talking about evacuating."

"And going where?" Clarence replied. "There's nowhere to go. General Hood warned us that Sherman might fire on civilians if he finds them out in the open. We're better off staying right here in our house."

While Clarence was speaking, the soldier rode on down the street. Another rider, who was not in uniform, came toward him. The two men exchanged a quick greeting and the soldier rode into the next block to shout out his news once again. The civilian rider kept his horse at a trot.

Annamarie Taylor's eyes widened. "Why, it's Pastor Darnell!"

The pastor guided his horse up to the porch and touched the brim of his hat. His features were drawn and void of color. "Hello Edna, Annamarie, Clarence. I see you've just heard the bad news."

"We did," Clarence replied glumly, his features drawn and void of color.

"I learned about it half an hour ago myself. I'm calling a special prayer meeting for seven o'clock tonight at the church."

"We'll be there," Clarence said.

"Are you going to work today?"

"Yes. I know Mr. Whitmore will keep his crew digging in the quarry while the Yankees are still at least two days away. If we want to be paid we have to dig out the rock."

"And how about Peterson's Clothing Store?" said Darnell, setting his eyes on Annamarie. "I haven't gotten to the Petersons yet. Do you think their store will be open today?"

"I've heard nothing to the contrary, Pastor," Annamarie said, "so I'll be heading for work in an hour as usual. I would imagine that Mr. Peterson will keep the store open both today and tomorrow."

"I'm glad we're having the special prayer meeting, Pastor," Edna said. "If Atlanta is going to survive, we're going to need God's help."

Darnell nodded. "Well, I'll see you folks this evening. I've got two more stops before I get to the Peterson home. I'd like to catch them before they leave for the store." With that, he wheeled the horse and trotted away.

Harry and Lila Peterson watched their pastor ride away, then Harry embraced his

17

wife and said, "We're in God's hands, honey. We have to trust Him to take care of us."

There were tears in Lila's eyes as she nodded. "Even as we have to trust Paul to the Lord's hands."

"Yes, especially since we haven't heard from him in four months."

"And poor Annamarie," said Lila, wiping tears from her cheeks. "This is so hard for her."

"I know. But she's ever the optimist. You heard her at the store yesterday. She's so sure he's all right and we'll be getting letters from him any day now."

Harry loosened his arm from around Lila's shoulder. "Well, my dear wife, we'd better head for the store."

Humidity already hung in the air as Annamarie walked toward downtown Atlanta. It was only eight-thirty in the morning, but the blazing Georgia sun was punishing the city with its heat. Annamarie tried to maintain a cheerful attitude and spoke to people along the street as usual but received only dismal responses. The Yankees were coming and the fear and dread in the hearts of Atlanta's citizens showed on their faces.

Annamarie's thoughts went to Sergeant Paul Peterson. Certainly when she returned home this evening, a letter would be waiting for her.

She and Paul had met at church when the Petersons came to Atlanta in the fall of 1860. By the end of March 1861, the two young people had found themselves falling in love. Before they could make any serious plans for the future, the Civil War exploded in early April and Paul had enlisted in the Confederate army. After a brief training period of less than two weeks, he was sent to Virginia, where the Confederates were battling daily with the Yankees.

Paul had not been home since leaving Atlanta to fight in Virginia, but he had sent letters to Annamarie, though of necessity they had come quite irregularly. Each time a letter had arrived, she hung on every word. Paul was made a corporal in late 1862, which he wrote about. In that letter he had also asked her to marry him when the War was over and he came home. Annamarie had written back an affirmative reply. Two months passed before his next letter came, but in it he told her he was the happiest man in the whole world because the most wonderful and beautiful woman in the whole world had said she would be his wife.

Believing that any day now the War would be over and Paul would be coming home, Annamarie had begun planning the wedding right down to the most minute detail. She sent letters to Paul at the rate of at least three a week and kept him apprised of her desires concerning the wedding. In his return letters he had assured her that he was happy with whatever she wanted.

Annamarie thought of the last letter she had received from Paul, which told of his promotion to sergeant. The letter had arrived the first week of May — almost four months ago. Neither she nor Paul's parents had heard from him since.

When Annamarie entered the store, Lila was already behind the counter. They greeted each other and went to work, preparing for the day's business. They talked about the special prayer meeting that evening, then Lila looked at her future daughter-in-law and said, "Honey, I know the prayer meeting is about the coming attack by the Yankees, but I'm more concerned about Paul. We need to ask Pastor if he will encourage the people to pray harder for him. The longer we wait for a letter from him, the more concerned I become."

"I'm having the same problem, Mrs. Peterson, but somehow I believe there's going to be a letter from him real soon."

Lila laid a hand on Annamarie's shoulder, cocked her head to one side, and said, "You never cease to amaze me, honey. I wish I had your optimism."

Annamarie smiled. "You sound like Mother. I won't say it's always easy, but I try to let the Lord help me to see the bright side of things."

Lila kissed her cheek. "I'm so glad you're going to be my daughter-in-law!"

The air was still humid that evening when a brilliant sunset adorned the Georgia sky. The sun had disappeared on the western horizon about twenty minutes earlier but had left its colorful light and oppressive heat behind.

Dressed in summery clothes, the Taylors left the comparatively cool comfort of their house and stepped out into the heavy evening air.

No letter had come that day from Paul. With their minds on what might be his plight and on their own desperate situation with the enemy forces marching from Jonesboro, their hearts were burdened with fear and uncertainty.

The church was just over two blocks' distance from the Taylor home. By the time they were within a half-block of the church, Annamarie's spirits had risen above the disappointment of still no word from Paul. Never one to be depressed for long, she swung her gaze to the west, marveled at the golden hue of the sky that was turning purple around the edges, and said, "Mother, Daddy, look at that! God has painted a lovely masterpiece for us to feast our eyes upon. It reminds me that He is always in control and can give beauty even in the midst of chaos."

A gentle smile crossed her features as her parents turned their eyes toward the western sky and spoke their agreement.

When they entered the churchyard, a silent prayer wended its way heavenward as Annamarie prayed for Paul's safety and thanked the Lord that she could entrust their lives to Him.

At the crack of dawn on Friday morning, September 2, buglers rode through the streets of Atlanta, blasting their horns. Some people opened their doors, their weary stances indicating the sleepless night they had endured; others only pulled back window curtains, revealing pale, frightened faces.

The Taylors huddled in the open door

and listened to the words of the rider who was warning the citizens to stay inside. The Yankees had camped on the outskirts of the city last night on all four sides and would be attacking at any time.

When the soldier finished his message and trotted his horse further down the block to proclaim it again, Edna said, "Clarence, I'm afraid." Her voice sounded strangely flat and hollow.

Clarence pulled her back into the house, saying, "Let's go sit down in the parlor."

"I'll get you some water, Mother." Annamarie hurried away.

Just as she entered the kitchen, the popping sound of rifle fire met her ears. Her hands trembled as she dipped water from the bucket on the cupboard and poured it into a cup. By the time she reached the parlor door, the sound of rifle fire was coming from every direction.

Clarence was standing at the window when Annamarie entered the room. She glanced at him, then went to her mother, who was seated on the couch.

"They're fighting all around the perimeter of the city," Clarence announced, glancing over his shoulder.

Annamarie hurried to her father's side. She could see puffs of blue-white smoke lifting toward the morning sky and riding the breeze as the firing continued.

Edna began to whimper. "We're going to die! We're going to die!"

Both father and daughter turned from the window and went to comfort her. Clarence knelt down and took her trembling hands in his own.

"Honey, we'll be all right," he said, attempting to keep his own fear from showing in his voice. "General Hood is a brilliant tactician. With God's help, he'll fight off those Yankees."

Suddenly, another sound rose above the crackle of rifle fire. It was a deep rumbling like thunder.

Clarence's head came up. "Cannons."

Seconds later, they heard cannonballs exploding, and it seemed that each boom grew louder.

Edna's breathing began to sound like that of a frightened animal. "Clarence, we've got to get out of here!" she wailed. "We've got to get out before —"

When they heard the next explosion, both Annamarie and her father dashed to the window.

"Oh no!" Clarence said. "John and Clara Benson's house has been hit!"

"We've got to get out!" Edna screamed,

bolting for the door. Clarence stepped in front of her and took her firmly by the shoulders. She was screaming for him to let go of her when another explosion shook the house.

Annamarie ejected a fearful cry. "It landed in the Everlys' yard!"

"We've got to get out of here!" Edna wailed. "We've got to get out now!"

The rumble of cannon fire continued to fill the air.

Another cannonball struck directly across the street, exploding the house as if from the inside out. Shattered glass and splintered wood flew in every direction. The impact made the Taylor house shake. Windows rattled and articles fell from a whatnot shelf.

Edna wrenched herself from her husband's grasp and lunged for the door.

"No!" shouted Clarence, seizing her by both arms and pulling her to himself. "It's more dangerous out there!"

When Edna continued to struggle, Clarence wrapped his arms around her and said to Annamarie, "Go mix her a sedative! We've got to settle her down!"

Annamarie was almost to the hallway when a deafening explosion shook the house, blowing a huge hole in the parlor wall and sending broken glass, wood splinters, and a shower of hot shrapnel in every direction. Annamarie found herself flat on the floor, stunned by the impact of the explosion. Her head was reeling as she opened her eyes and began to cough. Smoke surrounded her, tinged by red flames on the other side of the room.

When she tried to get up, dizziness claimed her and she fell down once more. "Mother!" she cried out. "Daddy-y-y!"

The room was beginning to fill with blinding black smoke. Annamarie crawled in the direction she had last seen her parents. Her eyes smarted and watered as she called out to them in a hoarse voice. She could feel the searing heat of the flames engulfing the front wall of the house.

Suddenly her hand brushed against a body. She wiped a sooty hand across her eyes, leaving dark smudges where tears had been. As she blinked and focused on the form, she saw that it was her mother. She bent over the prostrate body and cried out in despair, pressing an ear over her mother's heart. There was no heartbeat. She placed her fingertips on the side of Edna's neck, but there was no pulse.

"No, Mother!" Annamarie gripped her mother's limp body and pulled her close as if to put life back into it.

Suddenly, above the crackling of the flames, Annamarie heard a moan. Her head jerked around, and through the curling smoke, she saw her father lying on the floor.

She gently released her mother's body and crawled through the black soot and rubble. The smoke seemed to thicken and she found herself groping for her father as she crawled toward him. Her right hand felt his solid form. She fanned the smoke from her face and saw that his pant legs were soaked with blood.

She put an ear to his chest and heard an erratic heartbeat.

"O Lord, help me," Annamarie whispered. "I can't do this on my own. My strength is gone."

The weariness she felt made her want to do nothing more than just lie down beside her father and close her eyes. But she fought her way to a standing position, then leaned down and grasped her father's wrists. One glance at the wall of fire and smoke at the front of the house told her she would have to find another exit. There was a side door in the sewing room, two doors down from the parlor.

Annamarie was aware of male voices outside. They were shouting excitedly as she began dragging her unconscious father toward the hall door. She thought she heard water splashing on the front porch.

With a tenaciousness she didn't know she possessed, Annamarie dragged her father's limp body into the hall and headed for the sewing room. All the while, the smoke was growing thicker. Grunting and coughing, she dragged him toward the side door, pausing only to fling it open, then pulled him outside.

The fresh air assailed her senses and she drew in one deep breath after another. When she had dragged her father across the lawn some thirty feet from the house, she knelt down to assess his wounds. She heard more shouts and in her peripheral vision saw at least a score of men in front of the house. They had formed a bucket brigade and were throwing water on the flames.

One of them spotted her and called out for the man next to him to keep moving the buckets, then he ran and knelt beside her. She recognized him as neighbor Walt Candler.

He checked Clarence's breathing, then said above the noise, "What about your mother, Annamarie?"

Her face twisted with grief. "She's dead, Walt. But I'm going back in and bring the body out! You stay with Daddy. I'll be right back!"

He grasped her arm in a gentle but firm grip. "No! It's too dangerous for you to go back in there!"

"Let me go!" Her words came out hoarsely. "I have to get Mother's body out of there, Walt! Don't you understand?"

"I do understand, Annamarie, but it's too dangerous! That front wall could collapse any minute. You could get trapped in there!" Looking down at Clarence, he added, "Your daddy's coming around. He's bleeding badly. Do what you can for him!"

Before he finished speaking, the front porch and the wall behind it collapsed in a fiery heap. For a brief instant Annamarie was mesmerized by the sight, then she heard a voice calling her name and realized it was her father. He extended a shaky hand toward her and she dropped to her knees to lean over him.

"Wh-where's your mother?"

Tears welled up in Annamarie's eyes. "Daddy," she said hoarsely, "Mother didn't make it. She . . . she's gone to heaven."

Clarence began to weep. "No! She can't be dead! She just can't be!"

Annamarie began ripping her petticoat into strips. "Daddy, you've taken a great deal of shrapnel in both legs. I'm going to bind you up as good as I can till we can get you to a doctor. Okay?"

Clarence continued to weep as he watched his daughter wrap the strips of cloth around his bleeding legs. Before she had finished, he slipped back into unconsciousness.

When she tied the last strip, Annamarie sat down on the ground and lifted her father's head into her lap and caressed his smoke-streaked face.

On the morning of September 8, General William T. Sherman prepared to move his army northward out of Atlanta. He would leave a sufficient number of troops behind to occupy the city, as well as many wounded men — one of them was one of his best officers, Major Derek Logan.

Logan, who lay in Atlanta's hospital under the care of Sherman's favorite Union army physician, young Dr. Quint Roberts, had fought beside the general in many a battle for the past three years and twice had saved Sherman's life at the risk of his own. In the attack on Atlanta, Logan had taken a bullet in his chest.

Sherman left his army at the north edge of the city, telling them he was going to check on Major Logan and pick up three of their five doctors to take with them. There could be many more battles before they reached Washington, D.C., and he wanted all three doctors with his army.

Upon entering the hospital accompanied by Captain Derold Carpenter, the stone-faced general entered the room where he had last seen the wounded major.

Quint Roberts was barely out of medical school, but his physician skills had quickly gained Sherman's respect. Roberts was standing over Derek Logan when Sherman and Carpenter entered the room. Two other Union physicians were there — Dr. Judson Smith and Dr. Howard Poston. Sherman knew they were excellent physicians, but both had told him that Roberts seemed to have the energy of two men and had been able to give aid to many more wounded and dying soldiers than they had.

Roberts turned and smiled at Sherman. "Good news, General," he said. "Major Logan has come through the surgery quite well. He will live."

Sherman moved toward the bed and took note of the Bible in Roberts's hand, then looked down at Logan and said, "That's plenty good news, Major. I'm so glad you're going to be all right."

Logan managed a weak smile. "That's because of this fine young doctor, General. He's good."

"I agree. We're about to pull out and I'm taking these three doctors with me, Major. But you and these other wounded men will be in good hands with the doctors we're leaving here."

After spending a few minutes with Logan, General Sherman told him he would see him again one day and then turned to the others. Running his gaze between Drs. Smith and Poston, Sherman said, "Did you tell Dr. Roberts about what's going to happen in Washington?"

"No, sir," Poston said. "We thought it would mean more to him if he heard it from you."

"What's that?" said Roberts, who at six-two stood taller than the other men.

Sherman grinned. "Dr. Smith and Dr. Poston have told me of your ceaseless care for our wounded men. I've seen plenty myself, but they came to me and said they feel you should have a public commendation when we return to Washington. So, it's going to happen in front of a few dozen high-ranking army personnel, plus whatever enlisted men we can gather for the occasion. Drs. Smith and Poston will also be given a chance to speak on your behalf. They're prepared to testify that many of our soldiers' lives would have been lost had you not been assigned to our unit."

Roberts's face flushed. "I don't deserve any more recognition than these doctors, sir."

Sherman chuckled. "Well, you're outvoted. It's going to be done as planned."

"Another thing, General," spoke up Dr. Smith, "do you see what's in his hand?"

Sherman nodded, glancing again at the Bible. The general was known for his profanity and made no pretense of being a Christian. But on occasion he had spoken his admiration for men in his army who read their Bibles and prayed before going into battle.

Dr. Smith continued speaking. "Dr. Poston and I plan to commend Dr. Roberts for the way he prays with his patients and encourages them by reading the Bible to them."

"Well, you just do that," said Sherman. "I know it helps the men a lot."

Major Logan's voice was weak as he smiled faintly and said, "Dr. Roberts helped me, General. He showed me in the Bible how to be saved. I'm a Christian now and I know I'm going to heaven."

The tough general choked slightly, his facial muscles stiffening. "That's . . . ah . . . that's nice, Major."

2

Even though Atlanta was still under occupation by the Union army, by mid-September the people of Atlanta were beginning to rebuild houses and buildings destroyed in the September 2 attack. Many of the streets where cannonballs had left deep holes were also being repaired.

Annamarie Taylor and her now invalid father were living in the back part of their house, which had been spared from the fire by the bucket brigade. They had not been wealthy people; still, the Taylors had a nice home and were glad the second floor was intact and that the kitchen, sewing room, and one bedroom on the ground floor were still livable. Clarence Taylor, now confined to a wheelchair, occupied the ground floor bedroom, which had been a guest room before the Yankee attack.

Annamarie disliked leaving her father each day to go to work, but neighbors checked on him throughout the day and she made a hurried trip home at noontime to fix his lunch. Although there were days he was in extreme pain, he never complained, and she did everything in her power to make him comfortable. Father and daughter only had each other now.

One day in early November, Annamarie was waiting on customers at the clothing store. Owners Harry and Lila Peterson worked alongside her.

One of the ladies from their church approached the counter and laid two new dresses in front of Annamarie. "I'll take both of these," Althea Connors said.

"Oh yes," Annamarie replied, "these are both attractive. I'm sure they will look very nice on you."

"Thank you, dear." Althea ran her gaze to both Lila and Harry, who were busy with customers, then set kind eyes on Annamarie. "Honey, how's your daddy doing?"

"Quite well." Annamarie folded the dresses and began wrapping them in paper. "He has accepted the fact that he will probably never walk again. I take him for walks just about every evening, and he's learning to handle the wheelchair better all the time. I think in another couple of weeks he'll be able to go back to church."

"It will be nice to see him again. I . . . I'm sure he misses your mother terribly."

"We both do," said Annamarie, placing the dresses in a box.

Althea paused for a moment, then said, "Pastor Darnell said from the pulpit on Sunday that there still has been no word from Paul. Anything come since Sunday?"

Annamarie flicked a glance at Lila standing just a couple of feet away. "No, ma'am. Nothing yet."

"I see. Well, those Yankees make it pretty hard for the mail from our soldier boys to get through."

"Yes, ma'am."

"It probably works both ways, Althea," said Lila. "No doubt there are a lot of Yankee wives, parents, and sweethearts who have to wait and wonder just like we do."

"I suppose . . ." said Althea, her voice trailing off.

Harry Peterson was waiting on a man named Cliff Waters, who captured everybody's attention when he said, "I don't think the Yankees will stay here much longer."

"Why not?" Harry asked. "General Sherman came here for the express purpose of occupying the city because of its importance with railroad connections and factories."

"Well, I overheard two Yankee soldiers talkin' yesterday, and they were agreein' that they would probably only be here another couple of months."

Harry chuckled as the others looked on. "Cliff, I think they were talking about themselves. No doubt, the occupation troops will be rotated from time to time. But I can't see General Grant pulling his army out of Atlanta till this dirty ol' war is over."

"Harry's right, Cliff," said a woman customer standing in front of Lila. "Those Yankees are going to be here for the duration of the war. And I pray the Lord will bring it to an end real soon."

"We all do, Louise," Lila said.

After a few minutes, all the present customers were taken care of and were exiting the store, packages in hand. Harry glanced up at the clock on the wall. "Well, ladies, only forty-five minutes till closing time."

Lila ran the back of her hand across her forehead. "Can't come too soon for me. It's been a busy day."

Annamarie started to add a comment, but her attention was drawn to the Union soldier coming through the door. The insignias on his coat identified him as a lieutenant.

Face grim, the man in blue said, "I need to talk to the parents of Sergeant Paul Peterson, Confederate army in Virginia. I'm Lieutenant Ronald Nelson."

"We're Paul's parents, Lieutenant," Harry said.

The man pulled a white envelope from his coat pocket. "We intercepted a message wired in from Confederate army headquarters in Richmond, Mr. Peterson." As he spoke, he placed the envelope in Harry's hand. "Now, if you will excuse me, I'll be going." Without waiting for a reply, he hurried out the door.

Harry stared at the envelope.

Annamarie bit her lip, and her fingernails dug half-moons into the palms of her hands.

Lila looked at her husband with a questioning frown. "Harry, open it."

He swallowed hard, then tore the envelope open and took out the folded sheet of paper. His eyes grew round and rheumy and his skin took on a pallor. He looked at Lila, then Annamarie and said, "Paul was killed in a battle on the banks of the Shenandoah River on May 11."

"No!" Lila wailed. "No-o-o-o!"

Tears welled up in Annamarie's eyes, but she moved up to put an arm around Lila. At the same time, Harry put his arms around both women and the three of them wept together.

Clarence Taylor was accustomed to his daughter's daily routine and was surprised when he heard her footsteps at the back door. He had been resting on his bed for about an hour, and as always, had planned to be up and in his wheelchair before she arrived home from work.

He sat up quickly, reached over, and pulled the wheelchair to the side of the bed. He heard the kitchen door open and close.

When Annamarie stepped into his room, he eased into the chair and said, "How come you're home so early? It's only — Honey, what's wrong?"

"We closed the store early, Daddy. We . . . we got some bad news. A wire came from army headquarters in Richmond about four-fifteen. Paul —" She choked up, putting her hands to her face. "Paul was killed in battle on May 11." Her last words came out with a sob.

Clarence opened his arms and Annamarie rushed to him, leaning her head against his.

When her weeping came under control, she clung to her father and said, "Daddy, Paul and I were so sure the Lord wanted us to marry and live our lives together. Why,

Daddy? Why did He let Paul die?"

"I can't answer for God, honey. I know He never does wrong, but I can't tell you why Paul died."

As Annamarie broke down and sobbed again, Clarence held her tight.

The next day, Pastor James Darnell appeared at Peterson's Clothing Store to talk to Annamarie. The Petersons had gone to the parsonage the night before to let him know about Paul's death. Darnell found Annamarie so withdrawn that he could do little to comfort her.

In the weeks that followed, he and his wife tried to counsel Annamarie, but her grief was so deep that they made little progress.

New Year's Day came, and as 1865 grew older, still Annamarie carried the anguish over Paul's death like a cold stone in her heart.

One evening in February, Clarence and his daughter were just finishing supper when he looked into her pain-filled eyes and said, "Honey, you can't go on like this. I haven't seen you smile since you learned that Paul had been killed."

Tears misted Annamarie's eyes. "Daddy, how can I smile when my whole life has been shattered?"

"Listen to me, sweetheart. You're very young. The Lord has a young man all picked out for you, and you've got plenty of living to do yet. I know you're hurting because Paul was taken, but God doesn't make mistakes. He could have spared Paul's life if He had chosen to, but He took him to heaven instead. The Lord left you in this world because He has a different plan for your life than what you thought it was. You must allow Him to work it out."

Annamarie's voice was tremulous as she replied, "The Lord allowed Mother to be killed when the Yankees attacked Atlanta, Daddy, and He allowed you to be crippled for the rest of your life. I don't understand! I just don't understand!"

"Honey, I've thought about this over and over. I've prayed about it in earnest — many times a day — and I've come to the conclusion that we don't have to understand. The Lord doesn't expect us to understand everything He does; He only wants us to accept His will and believe that 'all things work together for good to them that love God.' He didn't say that all things that come our way are good. I know you love Him, Annamarie, and I know you want His will done in your life."

"Of course I do, Daddy."

"Would you go get my Bible, please? I've been doing some study on this, and there are some Scriptures I want to show you. All of the answers God wants us to have for our questions are going to come from His Word. Let's see if we can get some help for you."

While Annamarie was out of the room, Clarence entreated his heavenly Father for wisdom to be able to help his heartsick daughter.

Annamarie returned to the kitchen with her father's worn Bible and placed it in his hands, then pulled her chair up next to his and sat down.

Clarence flipped the pages to Psalm 34, where he had recently marked several verses, and said, "Listen to these, honey. Verses 4 through 10, first:

I sought the LORD, and he heard me, and delivered me from all my fears. They looked unto him, and were lightened: and their faces were not ashamed. This poor man cried, and the LORD heard him, and saved him out of all his troubles. The angel of the LORD encampeth round about them that fear him, and delivereth them. O taste and see that the LORD is good: blessed is the man that trusteth in him. O fear the LORD, ye his saints: for there is no want to them that fear him. The young lions do lack, and suffer hunger: but they that seek the LORD shall not want any good thing.

"Think about this, honey. David doesn't say here that God's saints will never face troubles, but the Holy Spirit did tell him to say that the Lord saved him out of all his troubles. Verse 17 carries the same truth: 'The righteous cry, and the LORD heareth, and delivereth them out of all their troubles.' And look at verse 19: 'Many are the afflictions of the righteous: but the LORD delivereth him out of them all.' "

Annamarie nodded as she dabbed at her tears. "Then He won't leave me in this brokenhearted state, will He? He will take me out of it."

"That's right, sweetheart. You must look unto Him and it will turn out all right. Notice verse 5 again: 'They looked unto him, and were lightened.' You must keep your eyes on the Lord."

"Yes, Daddy," she said, sniffling.

Clarence flipped the well-worn pages again and stopped at Isaiah 43. "Look here, honey," he said, pointing to the first two verses. "Listen to what God says: 'Fear not; for I have redeemed thee, I have called thee by thy name; thou art mine.' He's talking about you, isn't He? You are one of His redeemed."

"Yes, Daddy."

"Now look here at verse 2: 'When thou passest through the waters, I will be with thee; and through the rivers, they shall not overflow thee: when thou walkest through the fire, thou shalt not be burned; neither shall the flame kindle upon thee.' I've emphasized the word *through*, Annamarie. Do you see it?"

Tears flowed down her cheeks as she nodded. "Yes, I see it, Daddy. God's children have to go into the waters, into the rivers, and into the fire . . . but it's always temporary because He says we will not stay there, we will pass through them!"

"Yes, honey. That's it! The Lord is telling you that you won't always be in the grief and heartache you've suffered over losing Paul. You will get through this."

Annamarie laid her head on her father's shoulder. While he stroked her long black hair, she wept tears of relief. When her weeping subsided, she sat up and said, "Daddy, the Lord is so good. I'm so glad I belong to Him! I noticed verse 3 back there in Psalm 34 while we were looking at it. David said, 'O magnify the LORD with me,

44

and let us exalt his name together.' "

"Yes, my precious daughter." Clarence lifted his eyes heavenward and spoke softly: "Dear Lord, Annamarie and I do magnify You, and together we exalt Your wonderful name. Help us to do as You said in Psalm 46:10: 'Be still and know that I am God.' "

When he finished, Annamarie gave him a watery smile. "Thank you, Daddy."

She rose and wrapped her arms around his neck. They wept together, giving their sorrow to the Lord, knowing He would give them His peace that passes all understanding.

Later, when the dishes were done and Annamarie was cleaning up the cupboard, Clarence looked at her from his wheelchair and said, "You have a light in your eyes I haven't seen in a long time."

She turned to look at him. "Yes, praise the Lord. And I can smile now too. See?"

"Oh, that's wonderful! I think you should go see Pastor and Mrs. Darnell tomorrow and let them know what the Lord has done in your heart."

"I will, Daddy. I'll stop by the parsonage on my way home from work."

The next afternoon, in the parlor of the parsonage, Annamarie told the Darnells how the Lord had spoken to her through

His Word and brought her peace that she hadn't known since learning of Paul's death.

They were relieved and happy to hear it, and when the pastor lifted a Bible from a side table, Annamarie listened intently as both he and his wife gave her examples of people in the Old and the New Testament — people whose lives had seemingly been ruined by their hard times. Yet they loved the Lord all the more as He worked out His plan in their lives. And they became better servants to Him because of their heartaches and tragedies.

When the session was over, Annamarie had an even better outlook on her Christian life, a clearer understanding of how God works in the lives of His children, and a fresh optimism about her future.

As time went on, she happily filled her life with taking care of her father, working her job, and serving in the church.

The Civil War ended in April 1865. Toward the end of May, Dr. Quint Roberts told his medical colleagues good-bye in Washington, D.C., and boarded a train for Chicago.

He took a seat by the window on the port side of the coach and watched people on the depot platform bidding friends and loved ones good-bye.

As passengers boarded his coach, Roberts looked up to see a sour-faced man of sixty enter. The man ran his gaze around the immediate area. When he spotted the empty seat beside Roberts, he elbowed his way to it, placed his small valise in the overhead rack, and sat down.

Roberts smiled at him and extended his hand. "Good morning, sir. I'm Dr. Quint Roberts."

The man met his grip hesitantly, and without smiling in return said, "Rudd Romaine."

"Glad to meet you. Do you live here in Washington?"

His response was a grunted, "Yeah."

"What do you do, sir?"

Romaine gave him a mild scowl. "Up until this semester came to an end, I taught biology at a local university. They just retired me, so I'm going to Chicago to live with some relatives."

"I see. Well, I hope everything works out for you. You certainly look too young to be retiring."

"I said *they* retired *me*, Doctor. I had no say in it."

"Oh. I'm sorry, I —"

47

"Don't be." With that, Rudd Romaine turned his head to scan the rest of the coach.

Soon the train was rolling, and when it was away from Washington and racing across open fields of grass dotted with clumps of trees, Roberts picked up the small satchel at his feet and pulled out his Bible.

About half an hour later, the young doctor was engrossed in the book of 2 Samuel when he happened to look up and find Rudd Romaine staring at him. Roberts smiled.

Romaine said, "You're a fool to waste your time reading that ridiculous collection of fairy tales and myths."

"Why do you say that?"

Romaine chuckled as a sneer curved his upper lip. "Because it was written by a bunch of starry-eyed men who invented God. He only exists in the minds of fools."

Roberts's voice stayed level as he said, "Tell me, Professor, how do you know God doesn't really exist?"

Romaine stared straight ahead, was silent for a moment, then replied, "I just know it."

"You *know* God doesn't exist?"

"That's right." Romaine turned to give him a cold look. "I'm an atheist."

"Well, do you have all the knowledge there is?"

"Pardon me?"

"Within the confines of your intellect, Mr. Romaine, do you hold all knowledge in this universe?"

"Well, of course not."

"So there are some things that lie outside your realm of knowledge?"

"Certainly."

"Then, sir, couldn't God be one of those things that lies outside your realm of knowledge?"

Romaine glared at him in silence. The steady rhythmic click of the steel wheels beneath them seemed to grow louder.

Still the biology professor remained silent.

"Well?" Quint said.

Romaine's eyes were sharp, black points. "What kind of doctor are you?"

"Medical."

"Then as well educated as you are, you ought to know that the idea of a God who created this universe is utter foolishness."

"On the contrary. When I study the human body, I see just how wonderfully it's made. Only a self-blinded person could say it came from some explosion billions of years ago. It's easy to see that an intelligent mind far beyond anything we humans could ever grasp designed and created the human body, as well as animals and the rest of the earth and the universe, for that matter."

"Well, Doctor," said Romaine, "that's your opinion."

Roberts met the man's mocking gaze. "You still haven't answered my question, Professor."

"What was that?"

"Since you do not possess all knowledge that exists, couldn't God be one of those things that lies outside your realm of knowledge?"

Romaine gave him a long, glowering look. "Yeah," he grunted reluctantly.

"Then, Professor Romaine, since this is true, you need to be honest. Don't call yourself an atheist. You are an agnostic. You just don't know whether God exists or not. But you certainly cannot positively say there is no God."

"I can't say it with my mouth without you manipulating the words, but I can sure say it in here." He thumped his chest.

Quint opened his Bible, turned to Psalm 14, and said, "Look here in verse 1, Professor. I mean no ill will toward you, but you need to see this. The true and living God says right here: 'The fool hath said in his heart, There is no God.' "

Romaine's eyes were riveted to the page. He began breathing heavily and suddenly stood up, muttering, "I don't have to sit here and take this! I'm going to another car!"

He yanked his valise from the overhead rack and stomped to the door. When he had stepped through, he slammed the door with a bang.

Quint Roberts shook his head sadly, closed the Bible, and put it back in the satchel. Just as he eased back on the seat, he looked up to see a young man approximately his own age smiling down at him.

"Dr. Roberts, I've been sitting in the seat right behind you. I couldn't help overhearing your conversation with Professor Romaine. Do you mind if I sit down?"

"Of course not. Be my guest."

When he was seated, the young man extended his hand. "I'm ex-lieutenant Tom Stafford, Doctor, Union Army of the Potomac."

"And you already know my name."

"Yes, sir. I have to say that a man who can handle an atheist like you just did has to know the Lord."

Quint grinned. "Well, I don't know if I handled him correctly, but I do know the Lord Jesus Christ as my personal Saviour, yes."

The two men hit it off immediately and

had a wonderful time of Christian fellowship as the train rolled westward.

After some time, Roberts asked, "Are you going to Chicago?"

"No, sir. I'll be getting off at Akron, Ohio. That's my home. I have a precious Christian girl there who's been waiting for me to come home ever since I went away to the War. Her name is Glenna Porter. Glenna and I are getting married in two weeks."

"Well, congratulations! I have a wonderful Christian girl waiting for me too. Her name is Susan Bedford. Susan and I haven't set a date, but we'll be getting married soon. I've had a hard time getting mail through to her for the past year, and as a result I haven't heard anything from her in that time. Being in the medical corps, I've moved around continuously, and since she apparently hasn't been receiving my mail, she hasn't known where to send her letters."

"That was one of the tough things about the War," said Stafford. "Glenna and I had problems with the mail at times, but during the last six weeks since the War ended, we've been able to correspond quite well. You're from Chicago, are you?"

"Yes. Susan lives in Chicago too. I have family in Aurora, Illinois. Actually all of my family is there — my father lives with my

52

brother, Philip, who's four years older than I. Philip and his wife, Elaine, have gotten a few letters through to me."

"You say your father lives with your brother and his wife?"

"Yes. My mother died almost six years ago. She was a wonderful Christian and the best mother I could ever ask for."

Quint went on to explain that his father was not a Christian. He did construction work and had lived with Philip and Elaine for just over a year in a nice spare room in their house. The main reason they wanted him close was to try to win him to the Lord. So far it hadn't worked — George Roberts had hardened his heart against the gospel years ago and it seemed his heart was getting harder all the time.

"Don't give up on him, Doctor. Keep witnessing to him and keep praying for him."

"We'll do that," said Quint, "but it gets so hard, sometimes — especially for Philip and Elaine. But we've agreed that as long as Papa is alive, we'll show him all the love we can and do everything we can to win him to the Lord."

Hours later, when the train rolled to a halt in the Akron depot, the two men shook hands, and Tom Stafford got off the train. Quint watched Tom's progress across the platform and smiled to himself when he saw a lovely young woman step into Tom's embrace.

Easing back on the seat, he said in a whisper, "Susan, that makes me even more eager to have you in my arms."

MAIL ORDER BRIDE SERIES

NO. 7
1876
USA

AL & JOANNA LACY

3

When the train chugged out of Akron's depot, Quint Roberts stretched out his legs, scooted down, and laid his head against the back of the seat. He thought about the telegrams he and Philip exchanged two days ago. Philip had said that he and Elaine would be at the Chicago depot to meet him and they would bring their children too.

A smile curved Quint's mouth. He was anxious to see Alex, who was three, and little Gina, who was two. The steady click of the wheels and the gentle sway of the coach soon lulled Quint to sleep.

He woke up when the conductor came through the car announcing the train would arrive at Chicago's railroad station in twenty minutes.

The young doctor sat up straight, stretched his arms and yawned. The train was on a wide bend and he had a clear view of downtown Chicago with its tall buildings silhouetted against a clear blue sky. He had heard that the tallest building so far — twenty-two stories — was under construction.

The full view of downtown Chicago was soon gone, but only moments later the train began to slow down. When the train rolled to a halt, Quint scanned the depot platform before rising from the seat. His heart skipped a beat when he saw his brother and sister-in-law, holding their children in their arms. He thought he and Philip were looking more alike than ever.

He stepped out of the coach, satchel in hand, and Philip and Elaine hurried toward him, threading their way through the crowd. When they reached him, Philip and Elaine embraced him, and Alex and Gina both gave their uncle hugs.

Quint held one child in each arm and studied them. "Alex," he said, "you've grown a lot since I last saw you! What a fine, husky boy you are."

Though Alex had no memory of his uncle, he liked him immediately and laughed at his words. Quint kissed little Gina's chubby cheek and said, "I wondered if you'd be as pretty as your mother, and I'd say it's an even match as to who is the prettiest!"

Gina giggled and Quint kissed her cheek again.

As they walked toward the parking lot, Quint said, "Philip, would you mind taking me by the office where Susan works before we head for Aurora? I'm dying to see her."

Quint noticed the glance between Philip and Elaine. Before he could ask what was wrong, Philip said, "Susan doesn't work there anymore."

"Oh? Where is she working now?"

"I don't know. She no longer lives in Chicago. Last I heard she was in Pittsburgh."

Quint shook his head, his frown deepening. "Pittsburgh, Pennsylvania?"

Elaine hurried a few steps ahead and drew up to their buggy. While Philip was trying to work the words past the lump that had risen in his throat, Elaine said, "I'll take the children, Quint."

He released the children to their mother's arms and studied his brother's face, waiting for him to speak.

Philip cleared his throat and nodded. "Yes. Pittsburgh, Pennsylvania."

"What on earth took her to Pittsburgh?"

"I've dreaded telling you this, little brother, but Susan married another man seven months ago and they moved to Pittsburgh. Elaine and I have known it for some time, but we wanted to be with you when you heard the bad news."

"I . . . I appreciate that," Quint said, his face pallid.

Quint sat in stunned silence as the buggy pulled out of Chicago and headed west for Aurora. Both Philip and Elaine tried to comfort him.

"I thought Susan would at least have written to tell me she was marrying someone else," Quint said. "No wonder she didn't respond to my letters this last year. I don't know how I could ever give another woman a chance to cut my heart out like this. Maybe I'll just be a bachelor all my life."

Elaine, who was in the backseat of the buggy with the children, leaned forward and patted his shoulder. "When the initial shock is over and the pain leaves your heart, Quint, you'll feel differently about it."

"I don't know, Elaine. How can I ever give another woman a chance to do this to me?" Fighting tears, he said, "I wish Mom were still alive. I need her voice in my ear right now."

After a few minutes, Quint took a deep breath, ran his gaze over the fields around them, and said to Philip, "What about Papa? Anything different with him?"

"Not spiritually," Philip said. "He still hasn't weakened one bit in his aversion for

God and the Bible. Elaine and I both make opportunities to speak to him and quote Scripture so it will sink into his mind and heart, but he resists us every time."

Quint nodded. "And physically?"

"His health continues to fail. He still does part-time construction work for a contractor in Aurora. His boss gives him light work so he can handle it."

"Well, I'm glad he can still work some."

"Yes." Philip paused, then said, "What are your plans, now that you're a civilian again?"

"I've been thinking that I'll either go to work in one of Chicago's hospitals or maybe see if I can get into a clinic with some other doctors. Now that Susan is gone from my life, I'll just concentrate on my medical career. Someday I'd like to have my own private office."

"That would be good. I hope you can."

George Roberts was sitting on the front porch, looking down the street toward the east. He had worried a great deal about Quint caring for wounded soldiers right there on the battlefields with bullets flying and cannonballs exploding.

A smile spread across his wrinkled face when he saw the familiar bay gelding with

59

white face and stockings pulling the buggy. He marveled at how his sons were exactly the same size, with the same coloring, and even held their heads and shoulders the same as they sat on the buggy seat together.

George made his way down the porch steps as Philip pulled rein. Quint slipped from the seat, opened his arms, and father and son embraced.

"It's so good to have you home, son," George choked out.

"It's mighty good to be home, Papa."

Quint was somewhat taken aback by how much his father had aged in the last two years. He put an arm around the older man's stooped shoulders and walked up the porch steps with him.

Looking up into Quint's dark blue eyes, George said, "I'm sure that by now you know about Susan."

"Yeah."

"What are you gonna do now?"

Quint guided his father to an overstuffed chair in the parlor. The rest of the family came in behind them.

"I'm considering two things. Either getting into a clinic with some other doctors or maybe going to work in one of Chicago's hospitals."

"Sounds good. I s'pose this thing with

Susan has hit you pretty hard."

"Yes . . . very hard."

Elaine walked toward the kitchen with the children in her arms and paused to say over her shoulder, "You men sit down and relax. I'll have supper ready in a little while."

Quint spent most of the evening answering questions about his work in the War. Periodically, his father attempted to bring up Susan, but either Philip or Elaine would politely cut him off.

The next morning, after breakfast, Philip had gone to work and Quint and his father were sitting at the breakfast table having an extra cup of coffee.

George took a sip of the hot brew, looked across the table at his youngest son, and said, "Quint, I need to ask you somethin' about this Susan thing."

"What's that, Papa?"

"Well, if your God is as great as you've told me He is, why did He let this happen to you? Couldn't He have kept Susan from fallin' in love with that other fella?"

"Of course He could."

"Then why didn't He do it?"

Quint thought on it a moment, then said, "Well, you see, God has a plan for my life and it's obvious that Susan isn't in it."

George's bushy eyebrows knitted together. "You really figure He cares about you that much?"

"He cared enough to die on the cross for me. And for you, too. He watches over the lives of His own and is with them at the hour of their death. Those who don't know Him go through life without Him and they die without Him. That means they go into eternity without Him . . . into the flames of hell forever."

George shook his head. "I can't believe that, Quint. There's no hell to worry about because there's no eternity to worry about. When a man dies, he dies like a dog. That's the end of it. There's no heaven and there's no hell. The grave is the end."

"Not so, Papa. God's Word says it is appointed unto man once to die, and after this the judgment. After *this*, Papa. The grave is not the end. Every one of us has to stand before God . . . including you. Lost people, like you, will face Him at the great white throne judgment, and because you have rejected His Son, you will be cast into the lake of fire. Philip and I have shown this to you in the Bible many times before."

George shoved his chair back and stood up. A deep scowl lined his brow. "And I've told both of you before that I don't believe it!" With that, he wheeled about and stomped out of the room.

As time passed, Quint Roberts established himself in a clinic in downtown Chicago. Still carrying the pain of Susan Bedford's betrayal, he took up residence in an apartment building located near the clinic and threw himself into his work.

On his days off, he often traveled to nearby Aurora and spent time with his father and his brother and family. He took time to play with Alex and Gina and to take them on buggy rides. To George, Philip, and Elaine, it was evident that Uncle Quint had stolen the hearts of his niece and nephew.

4

Ten Years Later

In November 1875, Dr. Quint Roberts was living in Bozeman, Montana, and working with an older Christian physician, Dr. Obadiah Holmes. Holmes was planning to retire within two or three years and turn the practice over to thirty-three-year-old Dr. Roberts.

Quint was quite comfortable in the large two-story five-bedroom house he had purchased, though he hadn't wanted a house that large. However, the price was good and there had been nothing smaller for sale in the whole town.

It was sold to him furnished, and nicely so. He had added some of his own furniture, along with some personal mementos.

He had gotten over Susan's jilting within a couple of years, and though he dated many women in his church in Chicago, he had not found one he felt led to pursue as a possible wife. He hoped the Lord would bring the one of His choice into his life when the time was right. Often he pictured laughing children playing in the yard. Maybe someday . . .

Winter came early in Montana, and on a cold November night, Quint sat in his parlor close to the glowing, crackling fireplace, reading his Bible by the light of a kerosene lantern. The wind howled around the eaves, driving crystals of snow against the windowpanes.

Quint's head came up when he thought he heard a knock on the door. The sound came louder this time, and he could hear a loud voice calling his name. He laid his Bible aside and hurried toward the door. A gust of snow-filled wind rushed in when he opened the door.

"Harvey, come in here out of the storm," he said to the man who was covered with snowflakes. "Has Laura gone into labor?"

Harvey Spencer wiped snow from his eyes. "That she has, Doc. Early stage yet, but I didn't want to wait any longer to come and get you. This is number six, as you know, and with each labor the time has been shorter between labor and birth." As he spoke, Harvey removed his hat and shook the snow from it.

"You look half frozen," said the doctor. "Come into the parlor and stand by the fire. Thaw out a little bit. I've got some coffee on the stove. Be right back."

A minute later, Quint entered the parlor, carrying a steaming cup of coffee. Harvey had taken his coat off and now stood as close to the fireplace as he could get and rubbed his hands together.

"Drink all of it, Harve," Quint said, handing him the coffee cup. "I'll get my coat and hat and medical bag."

"Okay, Doc, but hurry, won't you?"

"Be back in a flash."

When they reached the Spencer ranch about ten miles west of town, Quint Roberts timed Laura's pains and quickly assembled everything he would need to assist the birth. Just an hour later, the Spencers welcomed their third daughter.

After mother and baby had been cleaned up and were resting well, and the other children were in bed, the two men sat down at the kitchen table. Harvey made a pot of coffee, wanting to get some warmth in the doctor before he went back out into the storm.

While they drank the brew, Harvey said, "Doc, you've been here in Bozeman for

66

nearly two years now, but we've never had a chance to learn much about you. How about filling me in? I know you're from Chicago, but that's about it."

Quint told him about having graduated from the Chicago University Medical School, his internship at University Hospital, and of his service as an army doctor in the Civil War. Upon returning home when the War was over, he took a position in a downtown Chicago medical clinic. After three years, he was offered a partnership with two other doctors in a private practice and took it.

While Harvey was refilling Quint's cup, Quint told him about his disappointment in love and that he hadn't yet found a woman he wanted to marry. As the years passed, he began to hear a lot about the great migration to the western frontier. It caught his interest and the more he read about it the more interested he became. He also felt an increasing desire to have his own private practice.

"In '73, I learned from another doctor at Chicago University Hospital about Dr. Obadiah Holmes way out in Bozeman, Montana. Holmes wanted a young physician to eventually take over his practice. So I wrote to Dr. Holmes, and you know the rest of the story."

Harvey grinned. "Yes, and I like it. I'm mighty glad you're here, Doc, and so is Laura." He eased back on his chair and said, "Now tell me about your family."

Quint was in no hurry to face the storm, so he took Harvey back to when he was born in Chicago and raised in the home of George and Eva Roberts. His father was a hardworking construction worker. He told Harvey that his mother became a Christian after he and his brother Philip were born.

"When she got saved, my father became very angry and told her to forget about Jesus Christ. But my mother, in her always loving way, explained that she had never been so happy or felt such sweet peace in her heart.

"Even when my dad told my mom she could never go to church again, she remained sweet and kind to him, and through much prayer on her part, it was only a matter of a few weeks until he gave in and told her she could go to church again.

"My father could find no answer for the change in her life, but still he wanted nothing to do with the Lord or with church. Without fail, Mama took us to Sunday school and church. Both of us were saved in Sunday school within two weeks of one another — Philip was ten and I was six.

"My father was very upset when he

learned that Philip and I had become Christians. He told us we could not be baptized. But once again, Mama prayed, and it was only a few months before my father gave in. However, he refused to come to church to see us baptized."

Harvey shook his head in amazement. "Your father must be one stubborn man, Dr. Roberts."

"Yes, and even when Mama died of pneumonia at the age of thirty-six, my father said that she had gone out of existence, in spite of the pastor saying during the funeral service that she was in heaven."

After their mother was buried, their father did all he could to persuade his sons to forget their foolish beliefs and be sensible. As the years passed, both Philip and Quint remained steadfast in their Christian faith and continued to witness to their father of the truth of God's Word and of salvation in the Lord Jesus Christ.

Quint explained to Harvey that his father's health had been failing since he was in his late thirties. He had declined even more since the last time Quint had seen him, just before coming to Montana. Letters from Philip and Elaine told him that his father's health was getting worse. And though Philip and Elaine continued to talk with him about his soul, George Roberts would not budge from his position of unbelief.

Wiping a tear from his eye, Quint said, "Harve, I still can't give up on seeing Papa saved. But his health is failing, and I have to admit that at times I've been tempted to just throw up my hands and say it can never happen."

Harvey set his cup on the table with a thump. "Doc, don't ever give up. As long as he's alive, God is able to bring that father of yours to Himself."

"I know that, Harve. In spite of my lack of faith at times, I know the Lord is able to bring forth fruit from the seed of the Word planted in my father's heart and watered faithfully all these years."

"That's right. You just cling to Genesis 18:14: 'Is anything too hard for the LORD?' My paternal grandfather was just like your pop, but he got saved shortly before he died. He lived long enough to show that his testimony of salvation rang true. Don't give up."

"That's a real encouragement, Harve. Thank you for telling me that."

"You're welcome, Doc. Tell me, how's your brother and his family?"

"They still live in Aurora, about twenty-five miles west of Chicago. They have three children. Alex is thirteen, Gina is twelve, and Melissa is three — they call her Missy."

"Sounds like a nice family, Doc. Any plans to go back for a visit?"

"Nothing solid. But one of these days this Montana doctor will find time to go back home for a visit." A smile spread over Quint's face. "Once in a while, when they write, they stick in a note from Alex or Gina — or one forged by Elaine signed 'Missy' — telling me to hurry back to see them."

"Sounds like you're pretty close to that nephew and those nieces."

"Yes, sir. I sure am. Of course, Missy doesn't remember me, but those three are the most wonderful children in the whole world."

In Bozeman, Dr. Obadiah Holmes and his wife, Maggie, were sitting by their fireplace, staring into the dancing flames and listening to the howling wind beat the snow against the house.

Holding Maggie's hand, the doctor said, "Sounds like we're getting a lot of snow in this storm."

"I would say so, dear. It could be a big one."

At the sound of a knock on the door, the doctor let go of his wife's hand and stood up. "I hope somebody hasn't gotten sick to-night."

On the porch stood the snow-crusted form of Bozeman's Western Union agent, Chet Utley.

"Come in, Chet," said the doctor. "What brings you out on a night like this?"

The agent stepped inside and removed his hat. "A wire just came through from Dr. Quint Roberts's brother in Illinois. I went to his house to deliver it, but there was no answer when I knocked. So I came here."

"He's probably at the Spencer ranch. Laura's baby is due any time now. Does the telegram have anything to do with Dr. Roberts's father?"

Chet hesitated, then said, "Ordinarily I couldn't reveal the contents of the wire, but in this case I'll make an exception. Dr. Roberts's father has taken a turn for the worse and his doctors are giving him, at best, three weeks to live. Philip is asking if his brother can come before his father dies."

The silver-haired physician closed his eyes and pinched the bridge of his nose. "Chet, in spite of this raging storm, Dr. Roberts should get the telegram right away."

"I agree, Doctor, but company rules are that I can't leave the office but for a few minutes at a time."

Maggie, who had joined the two men,

said, "Obie, what about Lenny Hartman? He loves Dr. Roberts so much and is so devoted to him for saving his life last spring. I'm sure Lenny would ride out to the Spencer ranch and take the telegram to him."

"I should have thought of Lenny right off. Of course he would. He's a fine Christian boy, and you're right. He does have a special love for Dr. Roberts. Lenny lives right next door, Chet. I'll go with you to ask him."

When Lenny and his parents were told the message in the telegram, Lenny was eager to go out to the Spencer ranch. The Hartmans were concerned about their son riding in the storm, but on the condition that he would carry a lantern, they gave their consent.

When the doctor and the Wells Fargo agent spoke their appreciation to the youth, the slender, straw-haired boy grinned and said, "I'm more than glad to do this for Dr. Roberts. After all, if it wasn't for him, I wouldn't even be in this world."

Chet handed him the envelope. "Lenny, tell Dr. Roberts that the afternoon stagecoach from Billings arrived late this evening. It will head back to Billings as soon as the storm lets up. He'll need to be on it so he can catch the first train east."

The doctor spoke up. "Of course, if Laura

hasn't given birth to her baby by the time you get there, he won't leave until she does."

Mrs. Hartman went to the hall tree where the coats and hats hung. "Let's get you bundled up good, son," she said.

A few minutes later, Lenny rode away into the night with the lantern held high.

He pushed his horse through the storm toward the Spencer ranch. The circle of light given off by the lantern penetrated the blizzard enough to help guide him, but twice he found himself taking a wrong turn and had to backtrack. Determined to get the telegram to the doctor, he pressed on.

At the Spencer house, the fierce wind moaned under the eaves as Harvey and the doctor were finishing another cup of coffee.

"Doc," said Harvey, "that storm sounds pretty bad. We have a spare room. How about staying overnight? Maybe it'll ease up by morning."

Quint cocked his head. "It does sound bad, but if I'm not there in the morning when it's time to open the office, Dr. Holmes will wonder where I am. I've really got to get back. I'll check on Laura and the baby, then I'll head out."

"Well, if you insist. But I want you to carry

a lantern with you. I'll get one for you."

Just then there was a knock on the front door.

Lenny Hartman was hardly recognizable for the snow that coated his face.

"Lenny, what are you doing here?" Harvey said. "Come in, quick!"

When Lenny stepped inside he saw Dr. Roberts and grinned. "I'm sure glad you're here, Doctor. If you weren't, I wouldn't have had any idea where to find you." He reached into his coat pocket and took out an envelope. "I'm here as a substitute for Chet Utley."

Harvey and Lenny looked on as Quint read the message.

"What is it, Doc?" Harvey asked.

Quint set misty eyes on him. "My father is dying. I'll have to hurry if I'm going to get there in time."

Lenny spoke up. "Mr. Utley said the stagecoach crew would be ready to head back to Billings as soon as the storm lets up."

"Tell you what, Lenny," said the doctor, "you go in there by the fireplace and warm yourself while I check on Mrs. Spencer and the baby, then we'll head for town."

Lenny nodded, then looked at Harvey. "Congratulations, Mr. Spencer. Boy or girl?"

"Girl," said the proud father.

"Hey! Wonderful! Now you have three of each!"

"We sure do. Let's get you out of that coat and in front of the fire."

A half hour later, Harvey watched the doctor and his young friend ride away into the storm.

It was two hours past midnight when Dr. Quint Roberts and Lenny Hartman arrived back in Bozeman. By this time, the storm was easing.

When they approached the Hartman house, they saw lantern light burning in the windows. As they turned into the yard, there were four figures at the parlor window.

"Looks like we've got some people waiting up for us," said Quint.

"Sure enough," Lenny said.

"Let's put your horse in the barn before we go in."

When Lenny's horse had been unsaddled and given oats to eat, Quint laid a hand on the boy's shoulder and said, "I really appreciate your riding all the way out there in this storm to deliver the telegram." He took a ten-dollar gold piece from his pocket and pressed it into Lenny's hand.

Lenny glanced down and said, "Dr. Roberts, I did it because of the importance of the telegram, not for pay."

"I know that, but I want to show you my appreciation."

"But I —"

"No arguments. It was a mighty unselfish thing for you to do. I want you to keep the gold piece."

Lenny studied the doctor's eyes for a moment. "All right, sir. If you insist."

"I insist. Now, let's go in the house and tell everybody about the Spencers' new little girl."

At sunrise the Montana sky was cold and clear.

The stagecoach crew made sure their three passengers were as comfortable as possible, with blankets covering their legs. The driver leaned through the door and said, "I know all three of you are wanting to catch the eastbound train leaving Billings at one o'clock. Ordinarily I could assure you we would make it with no problem, but with this three-foot depth of snow to plow through, all I can say is that we'll sure do our best."

"That's all we can ask of you," Quint said. The other two men agreed.

Moments later, the stage rolled out of

Bozeman and headed east toward the long, steep pass that stood between Bozeman and Billings. All around the slow-moving coach was a frozen landscape of white and shadow. Long, tedious hours passed. But when the stage arrived in Billings, it was after two o'clock and the train had already gone.

Quint stayed in a hotel until the next day, praying that the Lord would let his father live until he could get there.

When he arrived in Cheyenne City, he went to the Western Union office and sent a wire to Philip and Elaine, telling them when he would arrive in Chicago.

As the train carried him across the snow-covered plains of Nebraska, Quint stared through a frost-edged window and told himself it seemed like a hard cold had fallen on the whole country. He watched gusty winds scatter glittering snowflakes over the prairie and prayed earnestly, pleading with God not to let his father die until he was saved.

The words Harvey Spencer had quoted from Genesis 18:14 kept running through his mind: "Is anything too hard for the LORD?"

Night fell as the train was rolling across western Iowa. Quint was stretched out on his seat with his arms folded across his chest and his hat tipped over his face. He was about to sink into slumber when he felt a hand touch his shoulder and a male voice say, "Dr. Roberts . . ."

Quint lifted his hat and looked up into the face of the conductor. "Yes, sir?"

"Doctor, we have an elderly man in the next car forward who just collapsed. His wife is hysterical. Would you come?"

"Of course. I'll get my medical bag out of the rack."

When they entered the next coach, a silver-haired woman was kneeling over a man, crying, "Edgar! Wake up! Please, darling, wake up!"

While wide-eyed passengers looked on, Quint examined the man. After a few seconds, he looked up and said, "Ma'am, it's heart failure. Has he had heart trouble before?"

"Yes, Doctor. He's seventy-two and has been suffering with his heart for several years. Please don't let him die, Doctor. Please."

Quint's palm was pressed flat against the man's chest. He pressed harder on the chest, but could feel no heartbeat. Feeling for a pulse on the old gentleman's wrist and then the side of his neck, he found none.

He looked back at the woman and said quietly, "Ma'am, I'm sorry. Your husband just died."

Two women passengers tried to help the grieving woman while Quint Roberts administered a sedative to her. The conductor asked a couple of male passengers to help him carry the body to the baggage coach.

When the sobbing widow was seated with the two women beside her, Quint returned to his own coach and eased onto his seat. The man's sudden death sharply brought the truth to him that his father would soon die. Again he prayed, asking God to keep George Roberts alive until he could be led to Jesus.

Clouds darkened the afternoon sky and a sharp, brisk wind whipped through the Chicago railroad terminal as Quint's train chugged to a halt. He clamped his hat tight on his head and smiled at the young family hurrying toward him, their coat collars pulled up tight against the raw wind. Little Missy was in the arms of her father. Alex and Gina broke from their parents and ran to meet their uncle.

Quint set his hand luggage down and waited for them to reach him. Alex, who outran his sister, was quickly folded into his uncle's arms. Quint hugged him good while Gina waited impatiently, then he folded her into his arms.

"I love you, Uncle Quint," she said, pressing her head against his chest.

"I love you too, sweetheart."

Gina eased back in his arms and said, "Uncle Quint, Grandpa Roberts is going to die, and he's still not saved."

By this time, Philip and Elaine had drawn up and heard Gina's words. Quint smiled at them, then looked down into Gina's sad eyes. "As long as he's alive, honey, there's still hope. We mustn't give up. The Lord can save him."

Quint turned to embrace Elaine, who said, "Oh, Quint, I'm so glad you could come!"

"Me too, sweet sis." He kissed her on the cheek.

Missy, who was in her daddy's arms, was taking in the scene with wide eyes and watched her father wrap his free arm around his brother and say, "It's so good to see you."

Quint returned the embrace. "You too," he breathed, "in spite of the circumstances. I know Papa is still alive, but how's he doing?"

"Still hanging on to life," Philip replied,

"but he's looking worse each day. I'm glad you could come this soon."

Quint nodded, then set loving eyes on the three-year-old. "Hello, precious little one. You don't remember your Uncle Quint, do you?"

Though normally not shy, Missy ducked her head against the side of her father's neck. Reaching a hand toward her, Quint chucked her under the chin and tickled her.

Missy giggled.

Tickling her under the chin again, he said, "Maybe if I tickle you enough, you'll give Uncle Quint a big hug."

The little girl giggled again and soon the ice was broken. Still giggling, she reached out her arms for him. Quint took her from Philip's hands and folded her close to him. He kissed her cheek and said, "How about a hug, cutie?"

Deciding that her Uncle Quint was as nice as her family claimed him to be, Missy wrapped her arms around his neck and completely won his heart.

He kissed her chubby little cheek again and said, "I sure do love you."

"You have any other luggage, little brother?" Philip asked.

"Nope. Just what I carried off the train."

"Well, then, let's head for the buggy."

Missy said, "Unca Quint carry me?"

Elaine smiled at her brother-in-law. "Better be careful, Unca Quint. She might pester you more than you want."

"Oh no. That couldn't happen."

Alex and his father gathered up Quint's hand luggage, and the small group headed out of the terminal toward the parking lot.

When they climbed into the buggy, Missy asked if she could sit on Unca Quint's lap. Gina sat on one side of him and Alex on the other.

As they pulled into wagon and buggy traffic on the busy street, Philip said, "Little brother, we're going to let Elaine and the children off at the home of some friends who live here in Chicago, then I'll take you to the hospital."

5

A cold wind off Lake Michigan whipped through the city as the Roberts brothers, their heads bent against the wind and their collars pulled high, drove away from the house on East 23rd Street and headed for Mercy Hospital.

Quint said, "I've prayed hard all the way from Bozeman that God would do a work in Papa's heart and give him a glimpse into eternity that will shake him good."

"We've prayed that way too," Philip said. "Seems it's going to take something like that to get him to listen." Philip paused a few seconds. "Oh! I need to tell you about Papa's roommate before we get to the hospital. His name is Homer Watson. He's about the same age as Papa and he's of the same opinion about spiritual matters. Homer has butted in on Elaine and me a couple of times when we were talking to Papa about the Lord."

"He and Papa are two of a kind, eh?"

"Mmm-hmm. The first time he butted in, Papa was arguing that the Bible is only an old worn-out book that is no more than a collection of fairy tales. When I started to defend it, Homer took Papa's side and told us what fools we were to actually believe that the Bible is the Word of God and that every word in it is true."

Philip swerved the buggy around a wagon stopped in front of them, then swung back on his side of the street and proceeded with his story.

"The second time was when Papa and I were arguing about the existence of heaven and hell. Homer cut in while I was trying to persuade Papa of his error and said he agreed with Papa — that there is no existence beyond a man's last breath."

"Well, if Homer butts in this time," said Quint, "one of us will have to divert him so the other one can talk to Papa."

"Let's plan for me to divert Homer since you haven't been able to talk to Papa for a couple of years."

"Fine with me."

Philip slowed the horse as they approached the hospital, then turned into the lot where wagons, carriages, and buggies were parked. He drew rein and guided the horse into a spot, then set the brake and said, "Let's pray before we go in."

As the Roberts brothers bowed their heads with the icy wind plucking at their hats and upturned coat collars, Quint prayed, "Lord, I remind You that You once said to Abraham, 'Is anything too hard for the LORD?' Now, dear God, Philip and I have prayed all these years for Papa to be saved, and You know we've faithfully witnessed to him. I think of all those years Mama witnessed to him. He's heard enough gospel to save a thousand men like him. Lord, You know that Papa is now on the very edge of eternity. He's about to step through death's door . . . and he's still lost."

Quint paused to thumb the tears from his eyes, then said, "Lord, we're going in there to give him the gospel again. Indeed nothing is too hard for You, not even breaking down the wall our father has built up in his heart against You and Your gospel. By faith, Philip and I are laying Your own question before You and asking You to bring Papa to Yourself before it is too late. In the name of Jesus, amen."

Philip's voice was full of emotion as he said, "Dear God, I hadn't thought about Your question to Abraham in this light, but yes, Quint and I are asking You to demonstrate in Papa's case that nothing is too hard for You."

The Roberts brothers dried their tears and walked into the hospital together. Philip led Quint through the hospital lobby and into the hall, where they approached a wide staircase and made their way to the second floor.

"Papa's room is 112," Philip said.

As they neared the room, they could hear a strained female voice calling their father by name. The brothers looked at each other fearfully and dashed into the room.

George Roberts was gasping for breath. His eyes were wild with terror and his face was ashen.

The nurse glanced at the two men, settled her line of sight on Philip and said, "Oh, Mr. Roberts! I'm glad you're here! Please help me! He's in a terrible state."

George Roberts blinked and focused on Philip's face, then Quint's. "N-nurse," he stammered, "these are my sons! I . . . I want to talk to them!"

"All right, Mr. Roberts, but first let me explain to them what has happened. You're in no condition to tell them."

George nodded. He looked at Quint as Nelda Stone said, "The man who was in the other bed over here — Homer Watson —

died just an hour ago. Mr. Roberts," Nelda said to Philip, "you remember I told you when we first met that I'm a Christian."

"Yes. Before you go on, Nurse Stone, this is my brother, Quint. He's a Christian too. He's also a doctor."

Nelda extended her hand. "I'm more than glad to meet you, Dr. Roberts."

The handshake was brief, then Nelda said, "Mr. Watson died a horrible death — screaming that he was dropping into hell. Your father has been terribly upset ever since."

"I can understand why," said Philip. "You may recall, Mrs. Stone, that Mr. Watson said just a few days ago that the Bible was nothing but a book of fairy tales."

"Yes, I remember." As she spoke, she looked down at George.

He averted his eyes from hers for a brief moment, then looked at her again and said, "Mrs. Stone, I'll be all right now. Thank you for trying to help me. I would like to talk to my sons in private, please."

"Certainly." When she reached the door she looked back over her shoulder. "Let me know if you gentlemen need me."

The brothers thanked her, and she stepped into the hall.

As soon as the door closed, George Roberts looked up at his sons and said, "Quint, Philip knows that Homer and I shared the same feelings toward the Bible and what it says about eternity."

"Yes. Philip told me."

"When Homer and I were alone here in the room, we talked about it a lot. We both agreed that born-again people are empty-headed fanatics who need some kind of crutch to lean on, so they foolishly cling to the Bible and the 'mythical Jesus Christ' for hope and help. We also agreed that there is no hell for people who aren't born-again, and those poor fools don't have a heaven to go to either."

Nodding, Quint said, "The same thing you used to tell Mama and us boys."

George bit his lip. "Anyway, a little more than an hour ago, Homer was lying quiet in his bed. Suddenly he began to choke and gasp as he clutched his chest. I rang my little bell over here on the table. When Mrs. Stone came in, she took one look at Homer and hurried out into the hall. She called for help, and a doctor and two other nurses came in to work on him. Homer began to scream that his feet were on fire — that he was slipping into hell. He was begging the doctor and the nurses to pull him out of the fire when he died."

By this time, George was trembling from head to foot. Breathing shallowly, he looked at his sons with tears glistening in his eyes and said, "Boys, I've been so wrong. So terribly wrong. I realize that everything your mother told me, and everything you two and Elaine have told me is true. There is a heaven and a hell, and this fool of a father of yours is on his way to hell — just like Homer Watson. I know that the Bible is the Word of God and is true in everything it says. Jesus Christ is truly the Son of God — the only way of salvation. I want to be saved if . . . if it isn't too late. I'm afraid Jesus won't want anything to do with me after the way I've been all my life, and especially the way I've treated Him."

Quint took hold of his father's frail arm and said, "Jesus loves you, Papa, and He still wants to save you no matter how bad you've been and no matter how you've treated Him."

George blinked and said through quivering lips, "Really?"

"Really. He died on the cross for every sinner."

"Even sinners as bad as me?"

"Even worse than you," said Philip.

George weakly rolled his head back and forth on the pillow. "There isn't anybody worse than me. Besides, if I asked Him to save me, He would probably think it's just because I'm about to die and I'm looking for a fire escape. He wouldn't think I meant it."

"He knows your heart, Papa," said Quint. "He knows if a person is sincere or not."

George closed his eyes and pulled his lips into a thin line. "It's too late for me, boys. Too late. I've heard about deathbed religion. It doesn't mean a thing to God."

Philip leaned closer to his father. "For you to call on Jesus and ask Him to save you has nothing to do with religion."

"Well, you know what I mean. It's too late. Too late!"

Quint reached into a side pocket of his coat and pulled out a Bible. He moved back to the bed and said, "Papa, it's the devil who doesn't want you to be saved, so he's putting these thoughts in your mind. You said a few minutes ago that everything that's in the Bible is true. Right?"

"Yes."

"Then listen while I read to you about a man who was dying — a man who had been what you would call a real bad sinner, a low-down thief. But in spite of his past, he called on Jesus to save him just before he died, and Jesus did save him."

Philip looked on with a prayer in his heart as his brother opened the Bible to Luke chapter 23. "Papa, you know what a malefactor is, don't you?"

George nodded. "A criminal."

"Right. Now in this passage I'm reading from, the Lord Jesus is brought to Calvary by the Roman soldiers. He is about to be nailed to a cross. Two malefactors are also about to be crucified at the same time."

George fixed his eyes on his youngest son as Quint read verse 33:

And when they were come to the place, which is called Calvary, there they crucified him, and the malefactors, one on the right hand, and the other on the left.

"You get the picture, Papa? Jesus was crucified between the two thieves."

"Yes."

"All right, I'm going to drop down a ways to when the malefactors began to talk to the Man who was hanging on the cross between them.

And one of the malefactors which were hanged railed on him, saying, If thou be Christ, save thyself and us. But the other answering rebuked him, saying, Dost not thou fear God, seeing thou art in the same condemnation? And we indeed justly; for we receive the due reward of our deeds: but this man hath done nothing amiss. And he said to Jesus, Lord, remember me when thou comest into thy kingdom. And Jesus said unto him, Verily I say unto thee, Today shalt thou be with me in paradise.

George stared blankly at Quint, then said, "I . . . I never knew that story was in the Bible."

"So what do you think of it?" Philip asked. "The repentant thief was told by Jesus that they would be together that very day in paradise. The thief was dying, yes, but Jesus looked into his heart and saw that he was honestly repentant and was putting his full faith in Him to save him. They both died that day. Do you suppose the thief went to hell?"

"Not when Jesus had told him He would meet him in paradise."

"Good. I'm glad you see that."

"That thief got saved the same way Mama, Philip, and I got saved," Quint said. "In repentance of sin, by grace through faith. I remember showing you in the Bible many times that Jesus said in Luke 13:3, and repeated it in verse 5, 'Except ye repent, ye shall all likewise perish.' In Ephesians 2:8 and 9, it says, 'For by grace are ye saved through faith; and that not of yourselves: it is the gift of God: Not of works, lest any man should boast.' "

"Do you understand, Papa?" Philip asked.

George blinked back the tears and set his eyes on his oldest son. "I understand. Only God knows how many times over the years my Christian family has gone over this with me. If I call on the Lord Jesus to save my miserable, wretched soul, acknowledging that I'm nothing but a hell-deserving sinner, and by faith, believing that He will save me by His grace . . . He will do it."

"That's what the repentant thief did, right?"

"Right."

"So what about George Roberts?" Quint asked.

Tears spilled down George's sallow cheeks. Setting his gaze on Quint, he said, "George Roberts will do the same as that malefactor — right now."

Philip and Quint had the joy of leading their father to the Lord. Afterward, they stayed with him, giving him assurance verses until he had absolute peace that all was well with his soul.

"Papa," said Philip, "we have to go now. We haven't been home since we picked Quint up at the train station."

Suddenly, George's eyes widened. "I . . . I hadn't even thought about the fact that you came here all the way from Montana, Quint. I was too frightened after watching Homer die to even think straight." He paused, then said, "You came because the doctors said I'm dying?"

Quint took hold of his father's hand, squeezed firmly, and replied, "You know I won't lie to you. Yes, that's why I came. I wanted to see you one more time before you left this world."

The shadow of a smile crossed George's face. "And to try one more time to get me saved, even as your brother and Elaine keep doing."

"Yes, sir."

Running his weary gaze between them, George said, "You are the best sons a man could ever have. Thanks for not giving up on me."

"We couldn't give up, Papa," said Philip. "We love you too much. We wanted to have you in heaven with the rest of us, including Mama."

More tears welled up in the eyes of the newborn child of God. "Oh yes. My darling

Eva. Just like your pastor said at her funeral — she's in heaven with Jesus. I love my family here, but I can't wait to be with my darling Eva."

"And just think," said Philip, "one day we'll all be together up there. Alex and Gina are both saved. And I have no doubt that Missy will be saved at a very young age like they were."

"Right," said Quint. "Here on earth we have our times of parting and saying good-bye. But in heaven there will be no more parting and no more good-byes."

"Sounds wonderful to me," said George.

The brothers promised their father they would be back the next day. Just as they were leaving, Nurse Stone came in. She was thrilled to learn that her patient had just been saved.

Quint and Philip walked down the hall with a spring in their step, praising the Lord for answered prayer.

When Quint and Philip picked up Elaine and the children, there was joy in everyone's heart when they learned that Grandpa had opened his heart to Jesus. Although little Missy didn't understand what all the excitement was about, she made happy sounds too.

As they headed out of Chicago toward Aurora, Alex said, "Papa, could Gina and I go with you and Mama tomorrow to see Grandpa?"

"Don't you remember, son?" said Elaine. "Both of you asked to go see Grandpa when he first went in the hospital, and we were told that children under the age of eighteen are not allowed to visit patients."

"But since Uncle Quint is a doctor, we thought maybe he could talk to the boss of the hospital and tell him we need to see Grandpa real bad. We want to tell him how glad we are that he got saved."

Missy, who was on Quint's lap, looked up at him and said, "Unca Quint . . . doctah."

Everyone laughed.

"That's right, sweetie," said Gina. "Uncle Quint is a doctor."

Missy snuggled tighter into Quint's arms and giggled. "Unca Quint . . . doctah."

Quint laughed. "Yes, Missy, and because I am, I'm going to have a talk with the chief administrator of the hospital and see if I can persuade him to make an exception for your brother and sister so they can get in to see Grandpa."

"See, Mama?" said Gina. "We'll get to see Grandpa because Uncle Quint knows how to talk to hospital bosses!"

★ ★ ★

The next day, Philip, Elaine, and the children were sitting in the waiting area of the hospital. Looking toward the door of the office where he had seen his uncle enter some ten minutes earlier, Alex said, "I sure hope Uncle Quint can get that chief administrator to let us in and see Grandpa."

"He will," said Gina. "Just wait and see."

Missy looked toward the office door and said, "Wuv Unca Quint."

"We all love Uncle Quint, sweetie," said Elaine.

"I wish he'd move back to Chicago so we could be with him more," Gina said.

Suddenly their attention was drawn to the office door as it swung open. Quint was shaking hands with the chief administrator.

"It's okay," said Gina. "See how friendly they are?"

Quint hurried toward the waiting area, smiling from ear to ear. "I have good news," he said.

Missy raised her arms. "Pick up, Unca Quint."

Quint lifted her up in his arms and said to the others, "Mr. Bowman has granted permission for Alex and Gina to visit Grandpa one at a time with at least one parent. Each visit is to last no more than five minutes."

"See?" said Gina. "I told you he would do it!"

"We had no doubts," said Philip. "Let's do it this way. Elaine and Gina will go in first. Alex and I will go in next, then Uncle Quint will go in alone."

Elaine stood up. "Ready to go, Gina?"

As Elaine led her daughter down the corridor, she felt the girl's steps lag. Stopping, she looked down at her daughter's upturned face and saw the panic in her eyes. "Honey, what's the matter?"

Gina looked at the floor, then brought her gaze back to her mother's. "Mama, I'm scared. I want to see Grandpa very much, but he's going to die, and . . . and I've never been around a dying person before. I —"

"Come here, honey." Elaine pulled her to the side of the corridor and slipped an arm around her. "Remember Philippians 4:13? 'I can do all things through Christ which strengtheneth me.' "

Tears were now coursing down Gina's cheeks.

"It doesn't say I can do some things, honey. It says I can do all things. Jesus will give you the strength to do this if you will let Him."

Gina wiped the tears from her cheeks and gave her mother a firm smile. "I will let

Him. I do want to see Grandpa and tell him how happy I am that he got saved. It's just a little hard. He has always lived with us, and I can't imagine him not being with us anymore."

Elaine held her close and whispered a prayer, asking the Lord to calm her daughter's heart. By the time she closed her prayer, Gina's cheeks were dry, and Elaine knew God's peace was flooding her aching heart.

Gina gave her mother a warm smile and said, "Okay. I'm ready. But will you please hold my hand and not let go?"

"Of course. But more importantly, God is holding your hand, and He won't let go either."

When they stepped inside the room, George lay with his eyes closed. When he heard the soft footsteps, he turned his head to see who had entered the room. His dull eyes brightened.

When Elaine felt Gina stiffen, she put her lips close to her ear, let go of her daughter's hand, and said, "Go on."

Gina hurried to the bed, opening her arms. As she bent down to embrace him, she burst into tears and said, "Oh, Grandpa, I'm so glad you got saved! Now you'll be in heaven with us!"

"Yes, darlin'. Jesus saved this wicked

sinner and I'm going to heaven!"

Elaine wept as she hugged him. "I can't tell you what a blessing it is to know you've opened your heart to Jesus!"

"And what a fool I've been to ridicule all of you for your faith! I would have gone to hell if this precious family of mine hadn't prayed for me and talked to me about Jesus. Now I know I'll see my precious Eva when I die, and the rest of you will join us."

When their time was up, they hugged and kissed him again and left the room.

When Philip and Alex entered the room, George repeated to them what he had said to Elaine and Gina. Tears coursed down his sunken cheeks as he took hold of Philip's hand and said, "Son, I must ask your forgiveness."

"For what?"

"For being such a terrible father."

"What do you mean?"

"You know, for the hard time I gave you and Quint about being Christians. I was so hard on both of you. I'll be going to heaven soon, and I can ask your mother to forgive me then. But I've got to ask you and Quint to forgive me before I go."

A smile curved Philip's lips. "Papa, you're forgiven. But I want to say that it was only in these spiritual matters that you made life miserable for us. In all other ways, you were a good father. I have many wonderful memories of your hard work to make a living for the family, and we had many happy times together."

George turned watery eyes toward his grandson. "Can you forgive me, Alex?"

The boy wrapped his arms around his grandfather's neck. "I forgive you, Grandpa. I love you."

"I love you too, Alex."

Out in the waiting area, little Missy was sitting on Quint's lap. Uncle and niece were sharing hugs and kisses while Elaine and Gina looked on.

Soon Philip and Alex appeared with eyes reddened from weeping. Quint told Missy he was going to go see Grandpa now, and she went to her mother. Meeting Philip and Alex in the lobby, Quint said, "How'd it go?"

"Very good," said the older brother. "He's very sorry for the way he treated Mama and us and asked my forgiveness. He's quite eager to ask your forgiveness too."

Quint grinned. "Well, I'll just go in there and tell him he's forgiven."

On the ride home, the Roberts family

talked about the change in Grandpa.

Alex said, "Grandpa is such a different man. I've never seen him so loving and tender."

"That he is," agreed Elaine. "Having the Lord in his heart has made a profound effect on him. It's so wonderful to see him like this."

"He's a new man, all right," said Philip. "But that's what salvation does for a man — makes him a new creature in Christ."

"And to think how many times I almost gave up on ever seeing him saved," Quint said. "He just seemed like a lost cause. Praise the Lord! Indeed, there is nothing too hard for Him!"

The next day, Quint headed for the hospital alone to see his father, for he was scheduled to leave for Montana the following morning. On his way, he stopped at the Western Union office and sent a wire to Dr. and Mrs. Holmes, joyfully telling them that his father had received the Lord. He asked them to advise the pastor so he could pass the good news on to the church. He would be home in five or six days, depending on the Montana weather.

Quint entered the hospital lobby, then started up the stairs. As he climbed, he was feeling mixed emotions. With his father so close to death, this was going to be the last time he would see him on earth. There was joy in knowing that Papa would be there to meet him in heaven one day, but he felt sadness that when he walked out of the room, it would be the last time they would be together in this life.

Drawing up to the closed door, Quint took a deep breath and whispered, "Help me, Father," then moved inside.

Before he could touch the door, it came open and Nurse Stone appeared. She stopped abruptly when she saw him. "Oh. Dr. Roberts."

Quint looked past her and saw two doctors bending over his father.

"Doctor, your father has taken a serious turn for the worse. No one is allowed in the room."

"Not even another M.D.?"

"Well-l-l . . . let me tell them who you are. I'll be right back."

Leaving the door slightly ajar, she hurried to the bed. Her voice was low and Quint couldn't understand what she was saying. Only seconds passed when she came back and said, "You may come in, Doctor."

Both doctors watched Quint as he moved up to the bed and saw that his father's eyes were closed and he was breathing in short gasps.

The older doctor took hold of Quint's arm and guided him a few steps from the bed. Speaking in a low tone, he introduced himself as Dr. Joseph Claremore. "I'm sorry, but there's nothing else we can do, Dr. Roberts."

"I understand."

"The end can come at any minute. He is barely conscious and failing fast. We'll leave you alone with him if you would like."

"Yes. That's fine, Doctor. Thank you."

Claremore returned to the side of the bed and told both the other doctor and Nurse Stone to come with him and give Dr. Roberts time with his father.

As they were slowly moving toward the door, Nelda paused and said, "Dr. Roberts, I'm sorry there wasn't more we could do, but I'm so happy to know your father got saved."

"Thank the Lord for that," said Quint. "And thank you for taking such good care of him."

Nelda smiled, told him she would be at the nurse's station, and followed the doctors out the door.

Heavy of heart, Quint moved up beside his father and laid a hand on his arm.

George's eyelids fluttered and he looked up at him but couldn't seem to focus.

"Papa, it's Quint."

George swallowed with difficulty and said, "I-I'm about to go, son." His voice was barely audible.

"I know."

"Take hold of my hand, would you?"

Quint's eyes were misty as he took the thin, quivering hand in his own.

"I'm going to see Jesus and your mother very soon."

"Yes, you are."

"Give my love to Philip and his family." Suddenly George stiffened and gasped for breath. He squeezed Quint's hand and said, "I'll meet you in heav—"

Quint held on to the limp, bony hand and said, "Thank You, Lord, for drawing Papa to Yourself before it was too late. And thank You for allowing me these few minutes with him before You took him home."

6

Quint sent a wire to Dr. and Mrs. Obadiah Holmes, advising them of George Roberts's death, and that he would be a couple of days later getting home.

The funeral was held at Philip and Elaine's church in Aurora and conducted by Pastor Ken Shaffer. Quint was a special source of strength to his niece and nephew, both in the church service and the graveside service.

The following day, Philip and his family took Quint to the Chicago railroad station. When they stood beside his train, which was already boarding passengers, Philip held out his hands to Missy, who was in her uncle's arms and said, "Let Papa hold you, honey, while Mama and your brother and sister hug Uncle Quint good-bye."

Missy's face twisted up and tinted slightly. "Want stay with Unca Quint."

The conductor's voice rang through the

depot: "All aboar-r-r-d! All aboar-r-r-d!"

As Philip started to take the reluctant three-year-old away from Quint, the latter said, "This is going to be hard enough, big brother. Let me hold her while I hug the rest of you good-bye with my other arm."

Philip lightly pinched Missy's cheek. "Maybe it's a good thing you don't live here, Quint. You'd have this one spoiled rotten."

Missy clung to her uncle's arm while he folded Alex and Gina in the other one and pulled them close to him.

Gina said, "Uncle Quint, please move back here so we can be with you more."

"Yes, please," Alex said.

"Well, I can't," he said softly. "It's God's will for me to be in Bozeman. I know this beyond a doubt. And besides, Dr. Holmes is depending on me to take over his practice when it's time for him to retire. But tell you what . . . I'll come back and visit again just as soon as I can."

"Promise?" Alex said, sniffling.

"I promise. And maybe someday your parents can bring you to Montana to see me."

Gina turned to her parents. "Will you, Papa, Mama?"

"We'll see," said Philip. "Maybe we can."

"Right," said Elaine. "We'll set that as a goal."

Quint kissed the children's cheeks and said, "We'll look forward to that, won't we?"

The conductor made another call.

Still holding Missy, who was now crying because her siblings were, Quint hugged Elaine, then Philip. He then kissed Missy's cheek and said, "Sweetheart, Uncle Quint has to go now."

Missy blurted, "No!" and encircled his neck with both arms, clinging to him with all her might.

The bell on the engine began to clang.

Philip took hold of Missy's arms and pried them away from Quint's neck. She ejected a loud wail as Quint picked up his luggage. He gave the others a teary smile and headed for the coach. When he reached the metal steps of the platform, he paused and looked back.

"I love you, Uncle Quint!" Alex and Gina said together, tears streaming down their cheeks.

"Wuv Unca Quint!" Missy called.

The engine's whistle ejected a long, loud blast.

Quint climbed aboard. He had to take a seat on the opposite side of the coach and wasn't able to wave to the little family when the train pulled out of the depot.

He eased back in the seat, and as he thought about the children, his mind went to Susan Bedford. They had planned to have at least three children. "Lord," he said under his breath, "it really would be wonderful if You were to bring the right young woman into my life so we could marry and I could become the father of children just like Alex, Gina, and Missy."

Spring of 1876 came to Georgia with warm air and sunshine.

It was a beautiful morning in Atlanta as Annamarie Taylor walked along the street with a light step, reveling in the sunshine that caressed her shoulders. She smiled at the sweet trilling of the birds as they flitted from tree to tree, building their nests to prepare for the additions that would soon come to their families.

"Lord," said Annamarie, "You are so good to bless us with the beauty of nature, with eyes to see Your wonderful handiwork, and with ears to hear the music of it."

Daffodils bobbed their golden heads in the soft breeze and a glorious perfume wafted on the air from the white and lavender hyacinths that lifted their petals to be kissed by the sun.

"Yes, Lord," Annamarie said with a lilt in her voice, "it is indeed a splendid day!"

She had buried her father the previous year, just before Christmas, and missed him very much. She still lived in the house that had been shelled by the Union army back in September of 1864, but it had been completely restored two years after the War was over. She had it fixed up nicely and enjoyed her comfortable home.

As she turned the corner and strolled toward her place of employment, the sign over the door caught her eye: PETERSON'S CLOTHING STORE. Since the fateful day over a decade ago when Annamarie had been told that her fiancé Paul Peterson had died in battle, he had never been far from her thoughts.

Time and God's matchless grace had eased the grief from her heart, but still she thought fondly of Paul as she remembered their love and the plans they had made for a life together.

Maybe someday God, in His wisdom and His perfect time, will bring someone else into my life, she thought. *In the meantime, I'll wrap my life up in serving Him as I wait upon Him.*

Annamarie had a deep desire to be a wife and mother, but since the Lord had not brought the right man into her life, though she had prayed so earnestly for this, she stayed as busy as she could with her job at the store and her Sunday school class. However, she still had time on her hands occasionally. Time to think about what she might be missing in life.

As she neared the door of the clothing store, she gave one last look at the beautiful spring morning, then started to insert the key into the lock. It came open, however, to reveal the smiling face of Harry Peterson.

"Good morning, sweet Annamarie," he said cheerfully. "Another beautiful day."

"That it is." She smiled in return, stepping inside.

Harry closed the door and locked it, then followed her to the counter where Lila was making the cash drawers ready for the day.

Looking up, Lila said, "Well, there's our almost daughter-in-law. You all right this morning, dear?"

"Just fine."

The Petersons had told her on many occasions that they wished they had another son she could marry.

"Honey," said Harry to Lila, "maybe we shouldn't call her our almost daughter-in-law anymore. We may be putting undue pressure on her."

"You mean pressure that I would feel if I were to find myself falling for some man with marriage in mind?" asked Annamarie.

"Well, something like that."

Running her gaze between them, she said, "You're not going to cause me any pressure. You've met the young men at church that I've dated over these years, and I never felt I would hurt you if I fell in love with one of them and married."

"It's hard for me to understand why you haven't found a man to marry yet, Annamarie," said Lila. "Such a lovely, charming young lady ought to have potential husbands beating her door down."

Annamarie smiled. "I've had several young men who wanted to get serious, but I wouldn't let them because in my heart I didn't feel any one of them was God's choice for me. If and when He sends that man into my life, I'll know it."

Harry patted her arm. "That's it, little gal. It's better to wait till the Lord sends the man of His choice than to grab a fellow just because he's available, then end up miserable because you got the wrong man."

"That's for sure," agreed Lila. "Anyway, as long as you're here in Atlanta and need a job, you've got one."

"That means more to me than I could

ever tell you. Well, it's about time to open up. We'd better finish getting these cash drawers in order."

On a Sunday morning in early April, Annamarie was standing at the door of her Sunday school classroom, welcoming her eleven- and twelve-year-old girls as usual with a hug for each one.

When she opened her arms to eleven-year-old Lorna Maxwell, she noticed that the collar on Lorna's worn and threadbare dress had come loose on one side. The girl had worn the same dress to Sunday school for at least the past eight or nine months. Though it had always been clean, Annamarie had watched it deteriorate week by week.

Not wanting to embarrass Lorna, Annamarie said nothing, but a small seed was planted in her mind and she would pursue it further when she had time. She knew the Maxwells were quite poor. Bob Maxwell worked at a local lumber mill and barely made enough to provide food and shelter for his family. Clothing and shoes had to last a long time.

Lorna was the oldest of five children; Betty Maxwell had given birth to number five just two weeks ago. Annamarie had visited in the Maxwell home many times. She had always found the small, cramped house clean, but the family dressed in threadbare clothing and shoes with cardboard inside to cover the holes in the soles.

During class that day, Annamarie gave a lesson from Psalm 23:1: "The LORD is my shepherd; I shall not want." She pointed out that the LORD has many ways to supply the needs of His sheep and asked the girls to give her some examples as to how they had seen Him supply for His own.

When it was almost time to close the lesson, Annamarie pointed out that most of the time, the Lord used other human beings to supply the needs of His sheep, though sometimes He supplied in ways that came directly from His own hand.

Class was closed in prayer, and as the girls passed by their teacher on the way out, Lorna Maxwell was the last to leave.

The sweet girl warmed her teacher with a smile and said, "Thank you for the good lesson, Miss Taylor. It really helped me and encouraged me."

Annamarie hugged her and said, "I'm glad, Lorna. I love you."

"I love you too," said the girl and planted a tender kiss on her teacher's cheek.

On Monday evening, Betty and Lorna

Maxwell were cleaning up the kitchen after supper while Bob sat in the small parlor, holding his new little daughter. The other children played on the floor.

At the sound of a knock at the front door, Bob called out that he would get it and headed for the door with the baby in his arms. He found Annamarie Taylor on the porch, her arms laden with packages.

"Miss Taylor, how nice to see you! Please come in." He called toward the back of the house, "Hey, everybody, it's Miss Annamarie Taylor!"

Lorna appeared first, with her siblings on her heels, and Betty not far behind.

Lorna's eyes widened at what she saw. "Miss Taylor, what's this?"

"Let's go into the parlor, and I'll explain," Annamarie said.

When all the packages had been laid on the tattered couch, Annamarie took a deep breath, ran her gaze across the faces of the family and said, "It is a real blessing to me to be able to help when I see someone has a need. Each of these packages contains clothing for the very special children who live in this house."

Annamarie saw a defensive look cross Bob's face. She hastened to say, "Of course, I sure could use some help around my house from a strong, husky man. I've got a door that needs new hinges, and there's some work needed in the yard that I just can't do."

The defensive look on Bob's face gave way to a broad grin. "Anything I can do for you, Miss Taylor, would be a pleasure. Well, let's see what this dear lady has brought for the Maxwell brood!"

While Bob and Betty watched their children open the packages, they looked on with joy and were deeply touched by Annamarie's kindness and generosity. The four older children showed their appreciation with hugs and kisses. Lorna was especially happy with her new dress.

There were even two packages of baby's clothes, for which Betty thanked Annamarie with tears in her eyes.

That night, Annamarie lay in bed and relived the sweet moment when the Maxwell children opened their packages. Once again she could see the joy in their eyes and the smiles on their little faces. Her heart warmed as she relived the hugs and kisses.

Her throat tightened and she felt the warmth of tears behind her eyes before they began to spill down her cheeks. Her voice quivered as she said, "Lord Jesus, I do so very much wish I could have my own children to shower my love upon. I . . . will soon be thirty-one, Lord. I'm asking You to send the right man into my life to be my husband . . . and to let me have my own children to love."

As she continued to weep and pray about it, doubts assailed her that it would ever happen.

Sitting up suddenly in the bed, she wiped her cheeks with the sheet and said, "Lord, I refuse to let these doubts gain control over me. I can't believe that You want me to be a spinster for the rest of my life. This burning desire to be a wife and mother is here in my heart because You put it there. Okay, so the man I was to marry ten years ago is already in heaven with You. I still know in my heart that You can give me a husband and a family."

She paused, then said, "Dear God, I was reading just the other day in Genesis where You were promising Abraham that Sarah would bear him a son in their old age, and You said to him, 'Is anything too hard for the LORD?' I know there is nothing too hard for You. I'm not going to give in to these doubts that plague me. I'm trusting You to answer my prayers in this matter."

One day the following week, as she walked

to work, Annamarie's mind was on the new girl Harry Peterson had hired. Business had become so good that they needed more help in the store. Though Annamarie had not yet met Bethany Mitchell, the Petersons had told her that Bethany was a Christian and they felt she would be a real asset to them.

As she drew up to the door, Annamarie saw a pretty blond coming from the opposite direction on the sidewalk. The young woman said, "Good morning. You're Annamarie Taylor, aren't you?"

A smile broke across Annamarie's face. "Yes, I am. And you must be Bethany Mitchell."

"I sure am. Mr. and Mrs. Peterson have told me much about you, and I have to say you are every bit as beautiful as they said."

Annamarie blushed. "You're very kind. Actually, it is you who are every bit as beautiful as they said."

Bethany laughed. "Well, at least they made us feel good, didn't they?"

Both were still laughing as they moved inside the store to find the Petersons behind the counter.

Harry smiled. "Well, Lila, it looks like Annamarie and Bethany have met and are already having a good time."

Bethany was given some pointers by

Harry and Lila on store policy, and they told her since she didn't have retail store experience, they would give her plenty of time to learn. They asked Annamarie to take her under her wing.

As the day progressed and the two young women had spare moments to talk, Annamarie learned that Bethany lived with her mother and belonged to a Bible-believing church located just twelve blocks from her own church.

The Petersons encouraged Annamarie and Bethany to go to lunch together so they could get acquainted faster.

While eating at a nearby café, Bethany looked across the table at her new friend and said, "The Petersons told me about your almost becoming their daughter-in-law. I'm so sorry for what happened to their son."

"It was a very difficult experience for us," said Annamarie. "I love them very much and I know they would have been wonderful in-laws. I know, too, that Paul would have been a wonderful husband."

"I'm sure that's true." Bethany paused. "My father was also killed in the Civil War."

"Oh, I'm so sorry. How old were you at the time?"

"I was eight. I'm twenty now. I still miss my papa very much."

120

"I can understand that, believe me."

"Is your father dead, too?"

"Yes. He died last December."

"And your mother?"

"She was killed when Sherman attacked Atlanta. Cannonball hit the house."

"Oh. I'm sorry."

"I'm sure your mother appreciates having you living with her," said Annamarie.

Bethany smiled. "Yes. However, I won't be living with her much longer. I'm engaged to marry John Ballard, a fine Christian young man. John is in the printing business with his father."

"Well, wonderful! I'm glad for you. When is the wedding to take place?"

"We haven't set a date as yet, but we expect to within the next couple of weeks. I told the Petersons that I would work at least six months after John and I marry. I felt I should let them know right up front that I won't always be a career girl. I want to be a housewife and a mother."

Annamarie smiled. "That's very good. I hope it all works out for you." After a pause, she said, "What did you do before you came with the Petersons?"

"I worked in the office of Atlanta Lumber Company. I was a bookkeeper. I lost my job because the company was sold to a new owner. He let me go so he could give his daughter-in-law my job."

"Mmm-hmm. That kind of thing happens now and then."

"It's all right, though. I really like the Petersons, and it's a real joy to be working for Christian people."

Annamarie smiled. "You'll come to love them just like I do. They're precious people."

Two evenings later, Annamarie was invited to supper with Bethany and her mother, Frieda.

During the meal, they talked about Harold Mitchell being killed in the Civil War, then Frieda brought up Paul Peterson, saying that Bethany had told her about his death.

"What about now?" Frieda asked. "Is there a young man in your life?"

"No, Mrs. Mitchell."

"Such a lovely young woman. It surprises me that you aren't already married."

"Well, I've dated several young men in the past, but I haven't yet found the young man the Lord has chosen for me."

Frieda nodded. "You sure wouldn't want to latch on to the wrong one."

"That's the way I look at it. But I will say

that I have my anxious moments about that right one. I'll soon be thirty-one."

Bethany reached across the table and patted her new friend's hand. "I have no doubt the Lord already has that fortunate young man in His hand and is working in his life just like He is working in yours. One of these days He will bring the two of you together."

"I've sure been praying to that end," Annamarie said.

On the following Sunday, the girls in Annamarie's Sunday school class sat spellbound as she taught a lesson on the crucifixion of the Saviour. They were so caught up in the story that they sat on the edges of their seats, mouths hanging open and eyes wide. When Annamarie spoke of the blood flowing from His hands and feet and told of the love Jesus had shown for each and every one of them, the girls were wiping tears from their cheeks.

After class, as the girls walked together toward the main room for the morning preaching service, one of them said, "Miss Taylor sure does love Jesus, doesn't she?"

Another said, "She really does. And sometimes her love for Him just seems to spill over. Today it spilled all over me."

Lorna Maxwell, who was wearing the new dress Annamarie had bought her, said, "And something else that spills over is Miss Taylor's love for the girls in her class."

As the days went by, Annamarie and Bethany became close friends.

Bethany's heart was heavy for Annamarie because little things that came from Annamarie's lips showed that she felt life was passing her by. Though she had her job and her Sunday school class and was busy serving the Lord, she wanted so much to be a wife and mother. Bethany made it a matter of daily prayer and often asked her fiancé, John, to pray with her about it.

One day Bethany came to work humming happily. She was the last one to arrive. Annamarie and the Petersons were behind the counter. All three smiled, knowing without being told what Bethany was so happy about.

"Okay, Miss Hummingbird," Annamarie said, "when is the wedding?"

Her eyes dancing, Bethany replied, "Saturday, May 27! On that day, I will become Mrs. John Ballard!"

Annamarie rushed around the end of the counter and folded her friend in her arms. "Oh, honey, I'm so happy for you!"

After the Petersons had offered their congratulations, Bethany said, "Annamarie, there is something I want very, very, very much."

"Well, you just name it, and if I can produce it, you'll have it."

"I want you to be my maid of honor in the wedding."

"Me? But you have so many friends that go back all the way to your childhood. I —"

"But you're my very best friend, Annamarie. I want you to be my maid of honor. Will you?"

"Of course I will. It will be the greatest honor I could ever have, other than being a child of the King of kings!"

MAIL ORDER BRIDE SERIES · NO. 7 · 1876 · USA · AL & JOANNA LACY

7

The next four weeks were taken up with wedding preparations.

Annamarie Taylor was an excellent seamstress, and she and Bethany spent hours together in the evenings while Annamarie sewed the wedding dress.

John expressed his appreciation to Annamarie, and she told him she was glad he was going to wear a wedding ring, a practice men were just beginning to follow. John said he believed husbands ought to wear a ring to show they are married, as wives had been doing for centuries.

On the night before the wedding, Bethany asked Annamarie to stay all night at the Mitchell house. As soon as supper was over, the two young women went to Annamarie's room where she began to arrange Bethany's hair in front of a large mirror, experimenting to find the perfect style.

After nearly two hours, they finally agreed

on a style. Bethany eyed her friend's reflection in the mirror and said with feigned envy, "If my hair were as luxuriant as yours, Annamarie, this would have been easier."

Annamarie grinned at Bethany's reflection. "You think so, huh?"

"I sure do."

Picking up the hair brush, Annamarie gave her own gleaming tresses a few strokes. The dark curls fell almost to her waist and picked up shining glints cast by the lantern light.

Bethany turned around and set appreciative eyes on her friend. "You are so beautiful, my friend."

Annamarie smiled and dipped her head. "You're very kind, Bethany, but you are the one getting married tomorrow, not me."

"Your day is coming, honey. One of these days the Lord is going to send that special man into your life and he will fall all over himself the first time he lays eyes on you. You will know him when you see him, and you'll fall in love too. And when you marry him, you'll be the most beautiful bride ever."

Annamarie gave her friend a quizzical look. "Do you really think there is such a thing as love at first sight?"

"Oh yes! The first time I laid eyes on John,

I knew he was the one for me, and he felt the same way. I'd say it especially happens to Christians when they meet that one person the Lord has picked out for them."

"That's the way I've always believed too," said Annamarie.

Bethany took another look at her hair in the mirror. "This is the way we'll fix it for the wedding then. Well, I'd best get to bed. Other than the day I got saved, tomorrow will be the biggest day of my life!"

Annamarie stood at the front of the church during the wedding ceremony, holding a bouquet of flowers. John's ring was on her thumb. She glanced at the best man and noticed that he looked almost as nervous as the groom. She smiled to herself and focused her thoughts on the ceremony.

When the pastor led John and Bethany in saying their vows, there was a stirring within Annamarie as she thought of Paul and the dream they had cherished of one day standing before their pastor in a ceremony like this and becoming husband and wife.

In her heart, she said, *Lord, I'm having doubts again. Is it too late for me? Most women who reach my age unmarried stay that way. Can I really find romance and be a wife and mother? Oh, dear God, help me to believe I can.*

Nothing is too hard for You. My life and my future are in Your hands. Please help me to stay out of Your way while You work out Your will for me.

Suddenly Annamarie became aware of dead silence. She lifted her eyes and saw the pastor looking at her, his eyebrows raised, and she realized he was waiting for something. Her face reddened in embarrassment and she looked to Bethany.

"The ring," Bethany whispered.

An O formed on Annamarie's mouth, and she slid the ring from her thumb and laid it in Bethany's palm.

Sorry, she mouthed to the pastor, and the ceremony continued. From that moment on, the maid of honor kept her mind on the present wedding and not on the one she dreamed about in her future.

By late May, spring was in full bloom in Montana.

Dr. Quint Roberts guided the one-horse buggy over the crest of the last hill as he headed west into the valley where Bozeman lay tinted red-gold by the lowering sun. The mountains surrounding the valley were beginning to turn blue as they boldly took their jagged bite out of the flaming sky. A warmth spread over the weary physician, accompanied with a little tingle of gladness. He loved the West: the vast open spaces and the beckoning mountains, the sweet smell of pine mingled with that of the spring grass, and the myriad colorful wildflowers that grew everywhere in abundance.

It had been a full day of house calls within a ten-mile radius of Bozeman — the last one being exactly ten miles eastward, where he had delivered a set of twin boys to a young ranch couple.

Soon Quint was on Main Street, waving back at people who raised hands in greeting. He also loved the western hospitality he had found since coming to Montana.

He hauled up in front of the post office, pulled rein, and set the brake. He spoke to a pair of elderly men sitting on a bench and went inside.

"Howdy, Nate," he said to the man behind the counter. "Any mail for me?"

"Just one plump envelope, Doc." Postmaster Nate Barton took the envelope from a cubbyhole behind him. "It's from your brother."

"Good! That Roberts bunch in Illinois owes me some letters."

Barton chuckled. "Well, I guess they've paid their debt."

"Yeah, and am I glad. I miss them so much."

When he arrived home, Quint hurriedly removed the horse's harness and put him in the small corral, then poured oats in the feed trough, forked him some hay, and checked the water tank before heading for the house.

He went no further than the kitchen table and sat down, then pulled out the envelope and tore it open. Inside were five letters plus several sheets of paper with drawings by Missy.

He read the children's letters first. Alex told about school letting out in a few days and of his plans for the summer. Gina wrote of how glad she was to see him when he came back to see Grandpa before he died, of how much she missed him, and that she was very much looking forward to seeing him whenever the Lord allowed them to be together again.

Missy's letter was penned by Gina, but it thrilled "Unca Quint's" heart just the same. He knew by the wording and older sister Gina's spelling that the message was from the precious little three-year-old.

A lump rose up in Quint's throat. Alex had turned fourteen on March 12. Gina had turned thirteen on May 7, and Missy would be four years old on August 20.

In both Philip's and Elaine's letters, they

told Quint they were putting a little money aside every week so that within a year or so, maybe they could come to Montana to see him.

Elaine told him of things the children had done. Philip wrote that on Saturday, June 10, he and Elaine were going sailing on Lake Michigan with some friends from church.

Quint smiled at the news. Philip and Elaine had carried a heavy load when Papa lived with them. It was good that the two of them could get away and have some fun.

He placed the letters and Missy's drawings back inside the envelope and got up to prepare supper. When he had finished his meal and cleaned up the kitchen, he went to the parlor and eased his tired body into the softness of his favorite overstuffed chair and closed his eyes. His thoughts went to Philip and Elaine's upcoming day on Lake Michigan, and he let himself indulge for a few minutes in a daydream of relaxing on one of Montana's lakes — or relaxing anywhere, for that matter!

Someday, he thought, *maybe I can have a little time for myself. But right now I need to put Dr. Quint Roberts to bed. Who knows when someone will have a medical emergency?*

That thought had no more than passed through his mind when there was a loud pounding on the front door.

Rising wearily from the chair, he smiled to himself and said, "Well, Quint, this is what you're here for."

On Saturday morning, June 10, Drs. Quint Roberts and Obadiah Holmes were treating an elderly man with a broken leg. Other patients were in the waiting room, where nurse-receptionist Frances Myers sat at a desk.

Frances was assuring a mother with a sick baby that one of the doctors would be free to look at the baby very soon when the outside door opened with force and a man wearing a deputy marshal's badge came through the door.

It took Frances a couple of seconds to place the deputy, and then she remembered he was from the mining town of Butte, some eighty miles west of Bozeman.

"Hello, Deputy —"

"Cale Harper, ma'am," he said breathlessly.

"Yes, I remember now. What can I do for you?"

"Ma'am, there's been a cave-in at one of the mines. Men are trapped, but they're digging them out a few at a time. Dr. Chalmers is on the scene but he desperately needs help. Can either Dr. Holmes or Dr. Roberts come?"

Frances rose from her chair. "I'll be right back, Deputy. The doctors are splinting a broken leg."

Seconds later, Frances returned and said to the deputy, "The doctors are almost finished. Dr. Roberts says he will go with you. It so happens that his saddled horse is at the hitching rail outside."

"Good," said Harper. "It will be a real relief to Dr. Chalmers to have help. He has his hands full."

Moments later, Quint was on his horse and galloping toward Butte with the deputy.

In Aurora, Illinois, on that same morning, Philip and Elaine Roberts were at Max and Ada Becker's house next door, giving their children orders to be good and to mind "Grandpa" and "Grandma" Becker.

Ada smiled, pushed a gray lock of hair from her eyes, and said, "These precious children are always good when they stay with us. Right, Max?"

"Oh, most assuredly," said the stoop-shouldered man.

Philip and Elaine hugged their children then headed out the door. The Beckers and the children followed and watched

Philip and Elaine climb into the buggy where Frank and Elsie Higgins waited. The two couples waved jauntily as the buggy pulled away from the front of the house.

Soon Alex and Gina were playing with neighborhood children in the Becker backyard while Max and Ada occupied Missy inside the house.

It was just after three o'clock when Max walked past the parlor window and his attention was drawn to a police wagon just pulling up in front of the house. Ada was coming down the stairs after putting Missy down for a nap and saw her husband staring out the window.

"What are you looking at?" she asked and went to stand beside him.

He pointed with his chin. "That wagon that says Chicago Police Department on its side. It just pulled up."

Ada blinked. "What do you suppose they want?"

"Don't know, dear, but we're about to find out."

Ada stayed a few steps back while her husband opened the door just as the two officers stepped up on the porch. The older of the two was in plain clothes, and the other wore a uniform.

Before Max could speak, the older man said, "Mr. Becker?"

"Yes?"

"Sir, I am Lieutenant Arnold Westberg of the Chicago Police Department, and this is Officer Daryl Johnson." As he spoke, Westberg displayed his badge and identification. "May we step inside please?"

"Of course." Max frowned as he stepped back to allow them entrance. "What's this about, Lieutenant?"

Westberg spotted Ada. "Are you Mrs. Becker?"

"I am," she said, her heart in her throat.

The lieutenant looked around, searching for any other occupants. "Are we alone?"

"Yes," said Max. "We're taking care of some neighbor children. Two are in the backyard and one is upstairs taking a nap. Please. What is this about?"

"May we sit down?"

"Of course. Here in the parlor."

The officers waited until Ada was seated, then sat down facing the silver-haired couple.

"The children you are taking care of are Alex, Gina, and Melissa Roberts, correct?" said Westberg.

Max and Ada nodded silently, eyes wide.

"There has been a boating accident on

Lake Michigan. Philip and Elaine Roberts drowned, along with Frank Higgins."

Ada and Max Becker stared at the lieutenant in horror, trying to find their voices. Ada finally gasped, "Oh-h-h! Oh-h-h! How did it happen? You didn't mention Elsie. What about her?"

"Elsie Higgins is alive and at Cook County Hospital. She is injured, but the doctors say she will recover. Mrs. Higgins told the people who rescued her that a sudden squall came up on the lake and was powerful enough to turn the sailboat over. She was fortunate enough to be able to cling to a piece of the sail till people in another boat could get to her. The other three went down quickly after the boat capsized. It was Mrs. Higgins who told us about the Roberts children being here in your home."

Ada threw a hand to her mouth, a sick sensation sweeping over her. Tears filled her eyes. "Oh my. Oh my, oh my. Whatever will happen to these darling children?"

Officer Johnson spoke up. "Do you folks know if there are any family members who could take the children?"

Max's voice sounded weak as he replied, "Their only relative is a bachelor uncle. He's — he is Philip's younger brother. He's a doctor."

"He lives out west in the wild Montana Territory," Ada said. "Not a very good environment for young children. Missy — I mean, Melissa — is not much more than a baby —" Her words broke off and tears bubbled up in her eyes.

Max patted her shoulder. "God's in control here, dear. Let's not forget that He is always able."

"Yes, yes, of course. You're right, honey." She wiped the tears as they spilled down her wrinkled cheeks.

"Do you know this uncle?" Westberg asked.

"We met him when he was here last November," Max said.

"Do you think he would take the children?"

Max and Ada exchanged glances, then Max said, "I feel quite sure he would. We saw a lot of love between him and those children when he was here."

Westberg nodded. "And what is the doctor's first name?"

"Quint," said Max. "Q-U-I-N-T."

"All right. Then I suggest, Mr. Becker, that you send a wire to this Dr. Quint Roberts, advising him of the deaths of his brother and sister-in-law and asking him if he will take the children into his home."

"But he's a bachelor," said Ada. "I know he loves those children very much, but what kind of a home can he provide for them?"

"Whatever he works out, it'll be better than the alternative, ma'am," said Officer Johnson.

"What do you mean?"

"If the good doctor doesn't take them, they'll be placed in an orphanage or put up for adoption by the state. Either way, they'll be in the hands of strangers."

"That's right," said Lieutenant Westberg. "You should make that fact very clear in your wire to Dr. Roberts."

"Tell you what, gentlemen," said Max, "we belong to the same church Philip and Elaine do — I . . . I mean, did. I believe it would be best if Pastor Shaffer and his wife were the ones to break this awful news to the children. Pastor Shaffer can also be the one to send the wire to Dr. Roberts. I really think it would be better for the children to hear it from the Shaffers, and the wire would carry more weight with Dr. Roberts if it comes from the children's pastor."

"That'll be fine," said Westberg. "I need either you or Pastor Shaffer to let me know as soon as they hear back from Dr. Roberts. This needs to be handled promptly. I'm in the downtown station."

"I'll see that you hear from us as soon as possible, Lieutenant," said Max.

Pastor and Mrs. Ken Shaffer sat in the parlor of the parsonage with Max Becker, aghast at hearing the news. When Cheryl began to cry, her husband grasped her hand and said, "There is no way for us to understand this tragic loss, sweetheart. In His faultless wisdom, the Lord has allowed it to happen." He turned to Max. "What about the children?"

Max relayed his conversation with the police officers concerning Dr. Quint Roberts and the wire that needed to be sent.

The pastor agreed to send the wire and break the news to Alex and Gina.

"Pastor," said Max, "Ada and I have seen Dr. Roberts with the children. All three of them absolutely adore him. It's quite obvious that he feels the same way about them."

"You're right," said Cheryl. "From the little I could observe at church, Uncle Quint and his nieces and nephew have a deep love for each other."

The pastor nodded. "I've got a feeling that whatever it takes to make a home for those precious children, Dr. Roberts will do it."

"Ada is a bit concerned that he lives in the wilds of Montana," said Max. "She doesn't think it would be a very good environment for the children."

"Well, it's not exactly the wilds, Max," Shaffer said. "Bozeman is a decent-sized town, and Dr. Roberts told me about his church. Sounds like a very good one. His pastor, Dale Morgan, used to pastor a church in Crown Point, Indiana. Though I've never met him, I know he did a great job there in Crown Point. And like I said, as far as the home is concerned, I'm sure their uncle will do whatever is necessary to provide a proper home for them."

Cheryl began to cry again. Shaking her head, she said through her tears, "What a terrible tragedy! Only a few months ago those precious children lost their grandfather, and now their parents!"

Max nodded. "Poor little things," he said, his eyes misting.

The pastor rose to his feet. "Well, we mustn't sit around here any longer. We need to go to those precious children, Cheryl. Then we have to go to the hospital and see Elsie."

Cheryl reached for her husband's hand and he helped her up.

"Alex and Gina are going to need all the

strength we can give them," said the preacher. "Let's pause now to ask our heavenly Father's grace and mercy on them."

8

Missy Roberts woke from her nap and rubbed her eyes, then climbed out of bed. She made her way down the hall and slowly descended the stairs, sliding her hand along the banister.

When she entered the parlor and saw "Grandma" Becker sitting alone in her rocking chair, she made a beeline toward the elderly woman.

Ada was staring out the window, but when she heard little feet padding on the floor, she turned and opened her arms. "Come here, sweetie."

Missy climbed up in Ada's lap and laid her head on her breast.

"Did you have a good nap?"

Not yet quite awake, Missy nodded.

Ada held the little body close and sent a prayer heavenward, asking for God's mercy on Missy and her siblings.

Ada saw the neighbor children heading to their own homes but could still hear Alex and Gina's chatter coming from the backyard as they took turns on a rope swing that hung from a sturdy limb on one of the oak trees.

Suddenly her attention was drawn to the street and the approach of her husband and the Shaffers. Missy's head came up when the sound of footsteps sounded on the front porch. "Mama! Papa!" she called.

Ada's heart felt like it would break for the little tyke. "No, honey. It's Pastor and Mrs. Shaffer."

When they came in, Max was quick to take in the scene in the parlor, with Missy planted firmly on Ada's lap.

He ran his eyes toward the sounds of Alex and Gina in the backyard. Ada gave him a sad smile and shook her gray head slightly. Then she greeted the Shaffers and invited them to sit down.

"I'll . . . ah . . . go get Alex and Gina," Max said, and moved toward the parlor door.

As he headed down the hall toward the back of the house, he felt a wave of nausea. "Lord," he breathed, "these poor children are going to need Your help right now. The rest of us are too."

He paused at the screen door. Gina was laughing at Alex, who was standing in front of her as she rode the swing. He moved with precision, dodging her each time she came down and laughing at her every time she narrowly missed him.

Max observed the happy scene. "God help us all," he said, then pushed the screen door open.

Alex noticed him first. "Hello, Grandpa Becker!"

Gina kept a tight grip on the ropes and looked over her shoulder at the elderly man.

Max tried but was unable to force a smile. "I need both of you to come in the house, please."

Alex caught Gina in a backward arc and stopped her, saying, "Grandpa wants us to come in the house."

"All right." She slipped out of the swing. "I wonder what he wants. It isn't quite suppertime yet."

When they drew up to the porch, Gina frowned. "Grandpa, is something wrong?"

"Pastor and Mrs. Shaffer are here. They have something they need to talk to you about."

A quizzical look captured their young faces as they climbed the steps and moved inside the house behind Max. He put an arm around each of their shoulders and walked them down the hall.

"Grandpa, what is it?" Alex said.

Max swallowed hard. "I'll let Pastor and Mrs. Shaffer tell you."

Upon entering the parlor, Alex and Gina looked at the Shaffers sitting side by side on the couch, their faces as gray and solemn as Grandpa Becker's. One glance at Grandma, who was holding Missy, showed them a fourth gloomy face.

Missy was wide awake now and wiggling. She slid from Ada's lap but remained leaning against her legs. Her thumb, which had long ago lost its appeal, once again made its way into her mouth. Her round eyes searched the adult faces around her, then she climbed up into Grandma Becker's lap again, sensing the need for the security that awaited her there.

Alex and Gina eyed each other, then looked back at Pastor and Mrs. Shaffer and finally moved toward them.

Stopping in front of the sofa, Alex said, "Grandpa Becker said you needed to talk to Gina and me, Pastor."

The pastor stood up. "How about both of you coming over here and sitting by Mrs. Shaffer?"

Cheryl scooted to the center of the small couch and Alex and Gina sat on either side of her.

Praying in his heart for wisdom, the

pastor told them of the tragic mishap on Lake Michigan, and that their parents, along with Frank Higgins, had drowned.

The bad news was a powerful jolt to the older children, and their first reaction was to break down and sob uncontrollably.

Cheryl wrapped her arms around Gina and the pastor did the same with Alex as the children broke down and sobbed. Little Missy's face twisted when she saw her sister and brother so broken up, and she began to cry. Ada did what she could to calm the little girl.

After a long time had passed and the sobbing quieted, the pastor spoke in a tender voice and said, "Gina, Alex, Mr. and Mrs. Becker told me you could stay with them as long as needed. You understand, of course, that there will have to be a permanent home found for you?"

Gina sniffed and said, "Our only living relative is Uncle Quint, Pastor Shaffer. He loves us very much. I'm sure he will take us."

Missy was watching and listening with rapt attention.

"Sure, he will," said Alex. "Uncle Quint has told us about his house in Bozeman. It has five bedrooms, so there will be plenty of room for us."

At the second mention of Uncle Quint's name, Missy sat up straight on Ada's lap. The thought of seeing her Uncle Quint brought a dimpling smile to her cheeks. "We go see Unca Quint?" she asked in an excited tone, her tears and thumb forgotten.

Brother and sister looked at her, then at each other, their countenances growing sadder. The sweet little child had no understanding of the magnitude of her innocent question.

The pastor continued speaking. "Mrs. Shaffer and I must go now. I have to send a telegram to your uncle and wait for his reply, then go into Chicago and tell Lieutenant Westberg what your uncle said in his return wire."

"I know Uncle Quint will take us, Pastor," said Gina. "There's no doubt in my mind."

"Or mine," said Alex.

Missy's eyes lit up. "Wanna see Unca Quint!"

When the Shaffers had left, Max put his arms around Alex and Gina and said, "Grandma and I will fix you places to sleep here in our house. And we mean it . . . you children can stay with us till it's time to go live with Uncle Quint."

"I'll get supper going," said Ada. "Alex,

Gina, I'll need you to take care of Missy while I fix the meal."

An hour later they sat down to eat, but supper was a dejected affair. Because her siblings showed no inclination to eat, Missy refrained, thinking it was the right thing to do. Finally, after much persuasion by the Beckers, the children ate a few spoonfuls of hot chicken soup and some cornbread.

When they had eaten as much as it appeared they were going to, Ada said, "How about some chocolate cake? I just made it yesterday."

"Maybe later, Grandma," Gina said. "Thank you, but I just don't feel like eating any more right now."

"Me either, Grandma," Alex said. "Maybe later."

Ada nodded, then looked at Missy, who sat next to big sister, and said, "How about you, sweetheart? Would you like some chocolate cake?"

"Maybe later."

Just before dark, while Max sat on the back porch with Alex and Missy, Ada went with Gina to the Roberts house next door to gather their sleeping clothes and fresh clothing for the next day.

As they stepped into the sparkling clean

kitchen, Gina's line of sight went to her mother's apron hanging on a hook beside the back door. She sucked in a sharp breath and Ada laid a hand on her shoulder as Gina raised the apron to her nose. The lemon verbena scent of her mother still emanated from it. Gina broke into sobs and buried her face in the apron.

Ada wrapped her arms around the distraught girl and uttered soothing words as she caressed Gina's back, trying to bring comfort to her.

Choking off a sob, Gina drew a shuddering breath and her smothered voice asked, "Grandma, why did this horrible thing have to happen? Did we do something wrong?"

"Oh, my sweet child, none of you has done anything to cause this to happen. This is just God's plan for your lives. I know it is very hard for you to understand, but God's way is always perfect. It doesn't seem possible now, but someday you and Alex and Missy will be able to look back on this time of despair and see the Lord's own precious hand in it all. You and your brother and sister are very young, but God in His wisdom will work His plan for you, and the time will come when you will thank Him for His working it out in His perfect way."

Gina dried her eyes and face on her mother's apron and hung it back on the peg, giving it a loving caress. When she turned back to Grandma Becker she was able to give a wan smile. "Thank you, Grandma. I know God is in control. I guess I just needed to hear it from someone else. I'm still very young, but I will do my best to help Alex through this and to help little Missy when she is older and realizes our parents are gone. Right now the most important thing is that Uncle Quint learns from Pastor Shaffer about our loss and that we need a home."

"Yes," said Ada, patting her cheek.

At bedtime, Ada placed the three children in one bedroom. The girls were in the double bed. Alex slept on a comfortable pallet on the floor.

After Max and Ada prayed with the children, they left a lantern burning low in the room and went to their own room.

When Gina pulled her little sister close to her under the light covers, Missy said, "I want Mama."

"Mama's not here, honey," Gina said fighting the lump building in her throat.

"Where is she? Where is Papa?"

"They can't come."

Missy began building toward a cry, demanding her mama and her papa. When her voice grew louder, Alex left his blankets on the floor and sat on the side of the bed, trying to help Gina quiet her. But Missy wailed the louder.

Suddenly, Ada was in the room, saying, "Would you children rather I took Missy with me so you can get to sleep?"

"No, Grandma," said Gina. "She'll quiet down pretty soon. You and Grandpa need your sleep."

Missy looked up at Ada. "I want Mama, Papa."

Ada's face pinched. "May I hold her and talk to her?"

Ada lifted Missy into her arms and sat down on the edge of the bed on the opposite side of Alex. Using a hankie from the pocket of her robe, she dried Missy's cheeks and said, "Honey, listen to Grandma. Your mama and papa can't come and see you. They are living in heaven with Jesus now."

Missy furrowed her brow as she tried to comprehend what Ada meant. She had heard talk about Jesus and heaven as far back as she could remember, and she knew that when she said her prayers, she was talking to someone she couldn't see, but He could hear her from somewhere up in the sky.

"Mama and Papa are in the sky?"

"Yes. Actually, above the sky. In heaven with Jesus."

She thought on it for a few seconds. "Then I will talk to Jesus and ask Him to send them back. I want Mama and Papa to come home."

Gina leaned close to Missy. "Sweetie, please try to understand. When people go to heaven, they . . . they can never come back. Mama and Papa . . . well, they can't . . . they can't come home."

When the realization of Gina's faltering words became clear to Missy, her face flushed and twisted. "No-o-o! I want my mama and papa! Jesus will send them back!"

With that, Missy broke into a loud, tearful wail, shaking her head violently.

Ada stood up with the child in her arms, and above the wailing said to Alex and Gina, "I'll take her down to the parlor and try to rock her to sleep. You two see if you can get to sleep."

When Ada carried Missy into the hall and started toward the stairs, Max stepped out of their bedroom and said, "What are you going to do?"

"I'm going to get her quieted down and see if I can rock her to sleep. Will you come

153

down and light a lantern for me?"

"Of course. How about I rock her to sleep so you can go on back to bed?"

"Well, dear, I mean no offense, but you father-types don't have the touch with upset children that the Lord gave us mothers."

Max shrugged his stooped shoulders. "What can I say?"

Moments later, with the lantern burning low in the parlor, Ada sat down in the old rocking chair with Missy on her lap. She pulled the hysterical child close to her breast and talked to her in a soft tone. Soon the wailing dwindled to a whimpering. Ada began humming a soothing tune, praying in her heart as she rocked and hummed. Ever so slowly, the whimpers lessened to sniffles, and finally Ada felt the tiny body relax against her own.

"Lord," Ada whispered, "You say in Your Word, 'Suffer the little children to come unto me . . .' I lift this little one up to You. She is too young by far to understand what has happened. Please, Lord Jesus, in Your own loving way, give her peace and rest."

Soon the sniffling stopped and a low, steady breathing told Ada that Jesus had given His beloved little Missy sleep.

It was midnight in Butte, Montana, and

the second day Dr. Quint Roberts had been working with Dr. Chalmers in the town hall, which they had made into a makeshift hospital. Some of the injured miners had died and others were in critical condition, while others were stabilized and showing improvement. Still others had been released after careful treatment.

Several women volunteers were helping the doctors.

Neither doctor had slept since their vigil began. Wearily, they worked together at a table where they were doing surgery on a miner whose chest had been penetrated by a splintered wooden beam.

When all the slivers had been removed from the man's chest and the wound was sutured up, Quint sighed, looked at his partner, and said, "Okay. He should be fine now."

Chalmers sleeved perspiration from his brow. "Let's get to the next one."

By four o'clock in the morning, three more miners had died, but the bone-tired doctors felt they had lost their last critical patient. When they had made sure that all their patients were resting comfortably, Dr. Chalmers sighed and said, "I could use some strong coffee. Let's take a break."

Moving to a small table near the kitchen

of the town hall, the weary doctors slumped onto a pair of chairs. Both noted that young Mary Hanson was looking at them from behind the counter at the kitchen window. She pointed to a steaming coffeepot on the stove and they nodded. Mary arrived with two cups and the coffeepot on a wooden tray and set it down on the table. The aroma itself made them feel better and they smiled their thanks.

She smiled back and said, "I think our two doctors are going to have to get some rest."

"Sometime soon," said Chalmers.

"Very soon," said Mary, and walked away carrying the empty tray.

Quint lifted the steaming cup to his lips, blew on the hot brew, and took a sip. "A-h-h-h, that's what I needed." He took another sip, set the cup down, and scrubbed a palm over his face, feeling the stubble of his two-day-old beard.

Chalmers swallowed a mouthful of coffee, gave a lopsided grin, and said, "Yeah. I need a shave too, but I guess right now that's the least of our worries."

Quint nodded. He took another swallow of coffee and said, "Dr. Chalmers, I want you to go lie down on one of those empty cots and get some sleep. I'll keep watch."

Chalmers, who was some ten years older

than Quint, shook his head. "Nope. This is my territory. I will keep watch over the patients and you will get some sleep."

"Well, sir, this may be your territory, but as your guest, I believe I should be treated with courtesy. The most courteous thing you can do for me is to go plant your exhausted carcass on one of those cots and grab some sleep."

Brett Chalmers shook his head, grinning. "Well, Dr. Roberts, you do drive a hard bargain. Okay. I'll sleep for a little while, then it's your turn."

The sun was lifting off the eastern horizon into a clear Montana sky when Dr. Chalmers joined his partner again.

At nine-thirty, the sun was shining down on Butte. There were many wives at the town hall, looking after their own injured husbands.

Quint was asleep on one of the cots when he heard what sounded like a woman's voice calling his name from a great distance. He stirred a bit and the voice suddenly seemed closer. He opened his heavy eyes and saw that Lorene Smalley, one of the volunteers, was standing over him, shaking his shoulder.

Blinking, Quint sat up and said, "Yes,

ma'am? Does Dr. Chalmers need me?"

"No, sir. I'm sorry to bother you, Doctor. I know you're very tired, but there is a young man from Bozeman in the foyer who says he needs to see you. He says it is very important. His name is Lenny Hartman."

A hard lump formed in Quint's throat when he heard Lenny Hartman's name. His mind flashed back to the stormy night in November when Lenny brought him the news that his father was dying.

Rising to his feet, he said, "Thank you, Lorene."

Quint squared his shoulders and walked toward the foyer. He found Lenny pacing nervously, twisting the soft cap in his hands.

"Hello, Lenny. You look upset. What is it?"

"Dr. Roberts, it seems to be my lot to deliver bad news to you."

Taking a yellow envelope from his shirt pocket, Lenny said, "I'm here in place of Chet Utley. I have this telegram for you."

Quint accepted the envelope from Lenny's trembling hand and looked into the young man's troubled eyes as he opened it, then began reading the telegram from Pastor Ken Shaffer. Suddenly his knees buckled and his eyes were glazed with grief and began to mist over with tears.

"I'm so sorry, Dr. Roberts. Chet told me what it was so I would understand the urgency of riding the eighty miles to deliver it to you. He also told me I need to wait for your answer."

His voice hoarse with anguish, Quint said, "Thank you for riding all the way here, Lenny. You wait here. I'll go tell Dr. Chalmers about this and ride back to Bozeman with you."

Quint entered the hall, then paused and drew a deep breath. *Those children need me, and no matter what the obstacles, they're coming to live with me, and that's all there is to it.*

He took off his stained lab coat and lifted his hat from a wall peg, then headed for the cot where Dr. Brett Chalmers was kneeling over a patient.

Chalmers looked up as Quint said, "Doctor, I just received a telegram from the Western Union office in Bozeman. I need to talk to you."

Chalmers told the patient he would be back shortly and walked a few steps away with Quint. "What's wrong, Doctor?"

Quint explained the message of the telegram and said, "I have to get to my nieces and nephew as soon as possible. I hate to leave you at this point, but I have no choice."

"I understand," said Chalmers. "Don't worry about it. We have our patients on their way to recovery, and I can handle it by myself now."

Quint nodded. "All right. Thanks for understanding."

Chalmers looked Quint in the eye and said, "Please accept my most sincere condolences in your shattering loss, my friend."

Quint thanked him, then hurried toward the foyer.

9

Dr. Obadiah and Maggie Holmes sat in stunned silence as Quint Roberts told them of the deaths of his brother and sister-in-law. He explained that he must go to Illinois and get his nephew and nieces and bring them back to Bozeman.

"Quint, I admire you for what you're doing," Holmes said. "I'll handle things here. Just go and get those children."

"I know it puts an extra load on you when I'm not here, Doctor," said Quint, "and I want you to know that I deeply appreciate your understanding in this matter."

"You're going to need a lot of prayer, Quint. Suddenly becoming father to three children isn't going to be easy."

"I know. You and Maggie pray for me, won't you?"

"We sure will," Maggie said.

"We'll not only pray," the doctor said, "but when you get them here, if we can help in any way, we'll do it."

"You're both so kind," said Quint, rising from his chair. "Well, I've got to go to the Wells Fargo office, then go see Pastor and Mrs. Morgan and let them know about this."

Quint bought his ticket to Billings and made a reservation on the train from Billings to Chicago. He then went to the Western Union office and sent a telegram to Pastor Ken Shaffer, telling him when he was scheduled to arrive in Chicago.

When that was done, Quint went to his pastor's home.

Both Dale and Loretta Morgan assured him they would be praying for him and the children, and they would inform the people of the church and ask them to be praying.

It was late in the afternoon the same day when Pastor and Mrs. Ken Shaffer knocked on the door of the Becker home. Ada was there to greet them, a look of expectancy in her eyes. "Please come in. Max is in the backyard with the children. Do you have good news?"

"We sure do!" said the pastor.

"Oh, praise the Lord! Let's go on out to the backyard so you can tell the children."

Max and Alex were standing beside the

oak tree where Gina was gently pushing Missy in the rope swing.

Gina saw them first and said, "Pastor and Mrs. Shaffer are here!"

The four of them headed for the house, with Gina leading her little sister by the hand.

As they drew up to the porch, Ada said, "Pastor Shaffer has something to tell you, children."

When the Roberts children and Max had mounted the porch steps, the preacher said, "I received a telegram from your Uncle Quint a little while ago. He will be here next Thursday to take you to Montana to live with him!"

Gina hugged her brother. "We knew he would take us, didn't we, Alex?"

"We sure did!"

Gina cupped her little sister's face in her hands and said, "Missy, Uncle Quint is coming to get us! We're going to go live with him!"

Seeing the smiles of joy on her siblings' faces, Missy clapped her hands. "Unca Quint! Unca Quint coming to see us! Will he bring Papa and Mama?"

The smile on Gina's lips drained away. She picked Missy up and said, "No, honey. Papa and Mama aren't with Uncle Quint.

They're in heaven with Jesus. But we'll be very happy living with Uncle Quint."

Missy thought on Gina's words. Her little face pinched. "Want Papa and Mama too." Then she began to cry.

Gina carried her down the steps and walked slowly around the backyard, talking to her in soothing tones, doing her best to comfort her baby sister.

Quint watched the lush green landscape go by as the train carried him eastward across the Nebraska plains. It was obvious that Nebraska had experienced abundant spring rains.

Quint's mind was on his new responsibilities for his nieces and nephew. He pondered the situation for a while, then began talking to his heavenly Father in a low tone. "Lord, this is indeed a monumental task I'm about to take upon myself. I'm going to need wisdom, and plenty of it. I know a whole lot more about boys than I do about girls.

"I know I'm going to fall far short on the mothering part. What I really need is a wife who could be a mother to them. You're excellent at providing wives for men who need them, Lord. When You created Adam, You said, 'It is not good that the man should be alone.' So You created Eve and gave her to

Adam to be his wife. And there was Your friend, Abraham. When he needed a wife, You gave him Sarah. They had Isaac, and when he grew into manhood and needed a wife, in such a beautiful way You brought Rebekah into his life.

"I could go on and on, but I need You to do the same for me . . . now more than ever. I've got three precious children about to move into my home. I want things right for them. I need You to send me the wife You have chosen for me."

As Quint was praying, the conductor entered the coach and announced that the train would arrive in Grand Island in ten minutes. The train began to slow down. Soon it was rolling into the depot and chugging to a halt with brakes screeching.

While a few passengers were leaving the coach, Quint stood up to stretch his legs. He noted that the coach was little more than half full.

Moments later, passengers began boarding the train and Quint returned to his seat. Only a few new passengers were filing into the car. The last one caught Quint's eye. She appeared to be in her mid- to late-twenties, was dressed neatly, and wore her dark brown hair in an attractive style under a lovely hat. She was quite pretty, and when their eyes met, she gave him a friendly smile.

The young woman was carrying a large overnight bag. She chose the empty seat directly across the aisle from Quint, then struggled to lift the bag into the overhead rack.

Quint jumped up and said, "May I do that for you, ma'am? It looks pretty heavy."

She smiled at him again. "Oh, would you?"

Quint took the bag and placed it in the rack.

"Thank you, sir," she said, her smile widening. "It's good to know there really are some gentlemen left in this world."

"My pleasure, ma'am."

Soon the train was rolling full speed again. Quint bent over and picked up his small satchel, intending to take out his Bible. He happened to glance across the aisle and saw that the young woman had a Bible in her hands and was reading it. He noted that her left hand bore no ring. Just then she looked up and caught his eye. She smiled at him, then went back to her reading.

Quint stood up and moved across the aisle.

"Pardon me, ma'am . . ."

"Yes, sir?"

"Would it be all right if I sat down here beside you for a moment?"

"Why, of course," she said.

"I noticed that you're reading God's Word," Quint said as he eased down on the seat.

"Yes. I love it."

"Do you know the Author?"

"Yes, I do. His name is Jesus Christ, and I have known Him as my personal Saviour since I was thirteen years old."

"That's wonderful! I've known Him since I was six, and what a wonderful Saviour He is."

This information brought an even warmer smile to her lips. She extended her hand. "Hello, brother in Christ. My name is Gilda Simmons."

He took hold of her hand and said, "And hello to you, sister in Christ. My name is Quint Roberts. I'm a medical doctor, practicing in Bozeman, Montana. Right now, I'm on my way to Chicago on a family matter. Is your home in Grand Island, or are you headed for home now?"

"I . . . ah . . . I'm headed home to Chicago."

Quint was captivated by her silken voice. It was almost as if she were singing as she talked. She had a warm and compelling manner too. A chance meeting? Maybe.

"So you were born in Chicago too? What part?"

"The south side, near Calumet Park."

Quint grinned. "Well, what do you know? I was born in Mount Greenwood."

"Really? We were practically neighbors."

"Sure enough," said Quint, letting his eyes fall on the open Bible in her hands. "I see you're reading in Romans chapter 8."

"Yes. Just letting the Lord remind me that verse 28 is still in here. It's such a comfort."

"Indeed."

"I love the way it starts out," she said, placing a finger on the first line of the verse. " 'And we know that all things work together for good to them that love God, to them who are the called according to his purpose.' It's wonderful to know that God has a purpose in my life. Though all things are not good that come my way, it says that all things work together for good."

"Yes," said Quint. "It's wonderful to have that assurance, isn't it? Although I have to admit that sometimes I lose sight of the truths in this verse."

Gilda nodded. "Don't we all? I came real close to losing my grip on it quite recently. That's why you found me meditating on it."

"Something pretty bad happened, I guess."

Gilda closed her Bible. "Well, let me say that it certainly was unpleasant. I — Oh, you're probably not interested in my situation."

"On the contrary. I'm very interested. Please go on. I'd really like to hear about it."

Gilda picked up her purse from the floor by her feet and slipped the Bible inside. "Dr. Roberts, you no doubt are acquainted with the mail order bride system that has been going on in this country for many years."

"Yes, I am."

"Well, just about a month ago, I answered a mail order bride ad in the *Chicago Tribune*, and it seemed that the Lord had led me to the man I was to marry. His name is Clifford Wilcox. In his ad he said he was a born-again man and offered to pay my way to Grand Island so we could get acquainted and find out if we were meant for each other."

"Mmm-hmm."

"I was really excited, because I was orphaned at ten years of age and had been brought up in the home of an aunt and uncle who were very poor. They also lived in Calumet Park. Clifford Wilcox had inherited his father's plush hotel in downtown Grand Island and was a man of wealth. I told myself if I married him, I would no longer have to live from hand to mouth, if you know what I mean."

"Yes, I do."

"Anyway, the very moment I got off the train in Grand Island and met Clifford, I felt something was not right." She drew a ragged breath. "Dr. Roberts, the man was anything but a gentleman. He didn't even offer to take the heavy bag from me when I stepped off the train. Nor did he help me into the buggy when we were ready to leave the depot."

The doctor was shaking his head and frowning.

"Clifford put me in a room in his hotel and left me there nearly a whole day before he came back. His only comment was that he had a lot of work down in the office that had to be taken care of. When he took me to the hotel restaurant for a meal, he didn't bother to thank the Lord for the food before we started eating. And during the meal, he told me that he had been jilted by a young woman, and I realized as he talked that he was seeking a bride on the rebound."

Quint's brow furrowed. "Not so good, huh?"

"It got worse. When Sunday came, Clifford took me to church, but it was definitely not a Bible-believing, gospel-preaching church. By this time, I was wondering if Clifford had made up the story about being a born-again man. When I tried to talk to him about salvation, I found out he knew absolutely nothing about it. When I asked him why he said in his ad that he was born-again, he said the woman who jilted him made light of born-again people. He decided he wanted a woman who was the opposite of what she was, so he worded the ad as he did, hoping to get a good woman."

"I see."

"Dr. Roberts, Clifford was anything but a Christian or a gentleman. He was crude in his manner and most certainly didn't know how to treat a lady. I knew the whole thing was wrong and told him it wouldn't work. I told him that I wanted to go home. So Clifford drove me to the depot in his buggy, stopped it near the front door, and told me to get out. When I was out of the buggy, he snapped the reins and hurried away."

Quint's heart was racing. "I'm sorry you had to suffer disappointment with Clifford, Miss Simmons. I can see this has been tough on you."

"It has, Doctor. But it's caused me to lay hold of Romans 8:28, and I know the Lord is going to work out His perfect plan for my life."

"He sure will. I don't want to bore you with my story, but I was jilted by the girl I planned to marry when I came home from the Civil War. I served as a doctor in the Union army."

"Your story wouldn't bore me at all," said Gilda, a compassionate look in her eyes. "I'd like to hear it."

Quint told her of his romance with Susan Bedford and how she married another man while he was away in the War. When he finished, the compassionate look returned to Gilda's eyes as she said, "Oh, Dr. Roberts, I'm so sorry you were hurt like that."

"Thank you."

"So, has it turned out all right? I mean, is there someone special in your life now? I assume you're not married as yet."

He shook his head. "Not married, and up to this point there is no one special."

Gilda smiled. "Well, since Romans 8:28 is still in the Bible, I'm sure the Lord will work out His plan for you too."

"Having this conversation with you, ma'am, has encouraged me about it. I . . . ah . . . I was wondering . . . I'll be in Chicago a few days on family business. Would you allow me to come by your uncle's home and see you before I return to Montana?" His heart was racing still.

Gilda's features tinted. She cleared her throat gently. "Well . . . ah . . . Dr. Roberts, I haven't told you the rest of the story."

"Oh?"

"I hate to admit this, but like Susan Bedford jilted you, I did the same thing to the young man I had promised myself to two years ago. His name is Jim Weston. He's a fine Christian man."

Quint could only nod.

"Jim is a construction worker in Chicago. It's good honest work, but he'll never make much money. I got my eyes off the Lord, Doctor, and because of having to live in a poor home since I was ten years old, I had made up my mind that I wanted better things in life than Jim would be able to provide. It was such an awful thing to do to Jim, dumping him and heading for Grand Island."

Quint could only nod again.

Gilda sniffed and said, "When I got to Grand Island and saw Clifford for what he was, I suddenly realized I was in love with Jim Weston." The tears were flowing faster as Gilda sniffed again and said, "I also saw that I had wronged Jim and made a very foolish mistake. First, I asked God to forgive me, then I sent a wire to Jim, asking him to forgive me and told him that I wouldn't be marrying Clifford Wilcox. A wire came back from Jim. He said I was forgiven and that he still wanted to marry me."

"Jim must be some kind of man," Quint said.

"I couldn't have blamed him if he'd told me he never wanted to lay eyes on me again." She drew a shuddering breath. "But, praise the Lord, I'm on my way home now to be reconciled to Jim. I'm ready to marry him and live a life without wealth."

Quint swallowed hard and said, "I'm glad for you. I hope you and Jim will be very happy together."

Gilda thanked him, then said, "Tell me how you ended up in Montana, Doctor. And I'd like to hear about your practice there in Bozeman."

When the train pulled into the railroad terminal at Chicago, Quint took the heavy bag down from the rack for Gilda and offered to carry it off the train for her. She assured him she could handle it, thanked him for his kindness to her, and hurried to get off the train.

Quint let a couple of people go ahead of him, purposely staying in the coach until Gilda had moved out the door. When he got to the door, he saw Gilda standing on the platform in the arms of the man she loved.

Quint chastised himself for being so quick to think that Gilda might be the one for him. He ran his gaze over the crowd and spotted the face of Pastor Ken Shaffer, who was threading his way through the press. Quint extended his hand and Shaffer said, "I'm so sorry about your loss, Dr. Roberts. We all loved Philip and Elaine very much. They were such faithful workers in the church, and both were a special blessing to me personally. I will miss them, and so will our people."

"I'll miss them, too, Pastor. But I can't wish them back. Not after they've looked into the bright face of Jesus. This world would be too dark a place for them now."

"You're right about that. Let me say right now, Doctor, that I'm so glad you're going to take Alex, Gina, and Missy to live with you. It was a real relief to me when I received your reply by wire."

"It was a settled thing for me the instant I received your telegram," Quint said. "I wouldn't let those sweet children live with anybody but me."

"I know they'll get all the love and help they'll need from you. Of course, Missy is a bit confused by it all and is expecting her parents to return to her from heaven, but the full impact of it has hit the other two quite hard. They're very much looking forward to living with you. This tragedy would be much worse if they didn't have their Uncle Quint."

"With the Lord's help, we'll get them through it, Pastor Shaffer. Is the funeral still planned for tomorrow morning?"

"Yes. Ten o'clock."

Quint placed his hand luggage in the back of the buggy while the preacher untied the horse from the hitching post. They climbed onto the seat and headed west for Aurora. They talked for a while, then sat in silence with the steady sound of pounding hooves and rattling wheels in their ears.

Many emotions assailed Quint as the buggy rolled westward. Having arrived home to bury Philip and Elaine brought a fresh ache to his heart. *I know You do all things well, Father,* he said in a silent prayer, *and I'm not questioning Your will at all. I'm only seeking your wisdom and grace to be all the comfort I can to those orphaned children, as well as to be both father and mother to them.*

Quint gained much-needed strength from his silent time with the Lord, and looked forward to seeing his nieces and nephew.

When the buggy pulled up in front of the

Becker house, the door flew open. Alex and Gina bounded across the porch, calling his name. When Quint hugged them, both children broke into tears. He spoke words of comfort, holding them tight.

Pastor Shaffer looked on with pleasure, knowing the orphans would have a good home.

Missy was next out the door. "Unca Quint!" she cried and darted toward him.

Quint scooped her up into his arms. As he hugged her, she said, "Mama and Papa are at your house."

Quint glanced to Alex and Gina. Both of them shrugged as if to say they had tried to make Missy understand but so far had not been able to.

Quint held the little girl close.

Max and Ada appeared on the porch. Tears misted their eyes as they beheld the scene. This was the first actual happy moment they had seen for the children since they received the news that their parents were dead.

At the funeral service the next morning, a deep sadness lay in Alex and Gina's eyes. They sat on each side of their uncle and looked at the pair of closed coffins in front of the pulpit. Max sat next to Alex. Ada had elected to keep Missy at home.

Tears streamed down the children's faces as they clung to their uncle who had an arm around each of them.

Though Quint's own heart was torn, he put aside his own grief, giving Alex and Gina all of his love and support.

The graveside service was a difficult ordeal for the three of them.

On their way back to the house from the cemetery, Quint sat in the backseat between Alex and Gina while Max drove. The children began talking about their parents, bringing to life a myriad of happy memories as they recalled the wonderful years they had with them.

Suddenly, Gina squeezed Quint's arm. Her eyes brimming with tears, she said, "Uncle Quint, thank you for coming to get us. We're looking forward to living under your protection and care. We love you so much."

Alex cleared the lump in his throat and said, "If it weren't for you, we would've had to go to an orphanage or be split up for adoption."

Quint hugged them tight and with a tear-clogged voice said, "I promise you that with God's help I will do my best to give you a good home and make you happy. It'll take some adjusting for all of us, and some time and effort, but I feel blessed to have you and to know that you want to come and live with me."

10

On the day after the funeral, Quint Roberts and Max Becker went to an attorney and set it up so Max would be the agent to sell the house. When it sold, Max would be paid a generous fee for his help and the rest of the money would be sent to Quint, who would put it aside for Alex, Gina, and Missy.

At midmorning the next day, Max and Ada stood on the platform at the Chicago depot and waved good-bye to Quint and the children as the train pulled away. Missy sat with her uncle in seats that faced Alex and Gina's.

As soon as the train was out of the city and the land turned to green pastures, Missy pressed her nose against the glass and said, "Look, Unca Quint! Cows!"

He leaned close beside her and said, "My little Missy likes cows, don't you?"

"Uh-huh."

"Well, you'll like it where we're going

then, because we have lots of cows in Montana."

After a while, Missy grew tired of staring out the window and lay down on the seat beside her uncle. Soon she was asleep.

"I've been thinking about something, kids, and I'd like to see what you think about it," Quint said to his niece and nephew. "I'd like to adopt the three of you. I know I can never take the place of your real father, but I want to be the best father to you that I can. If I adopt you, the law will consider you my children, not just my nieces and nephew."

"Oh yes!" Gina said. "That would be wonderful! We'd love to have you adopt us. Wouldn't we, Alex?"

"We sure would!"

"Okay. When we get home, I'll take you to Judge Gregory, who's a friend of mine. He'll do the legal work to make you my adopted children."

Missy awakened just before noon. Quint asked Gina to take her to the washroom, then they all went to the dining car for lunch.

When they returned to their coach, Missy observed the countryside rushing by for a while, then crawled up onto her uncle's lap and rested her head on his chest. Soon she was asleep again.

Quint pointed out to Alex and Gina that they were crossing the Iowa border, then said, "When we get home, I'm going to put an ad in the local newspaper and see if I can find a woman to hire as a live-in house-keeper. She could wash and iron your clothes and keep house and cook the meals."

"How long do you think it will take to find her, Uncle Quint?" Gina asked.

"Kind of hard to say, honey. We might find someone right away, and again, it might take some time."

Gina nodded. "You know that I worked with Mama in the kitchen a lot, and I can cook. I can also do washing and ironing, and clean house. So, until we can get a house-keeper, I'll do my best to handle these chores. I realize that when school starts, I won't be able to keep up with it, but maybe by that time we'll have our housekeeper."

"I can help Gina with the housecleaning and that kind of stuff, Uncle Quint," said Alex, "but I don't know much about washing and ironing, and I know absolutely nothing about cooking."

Quint laughed. "Well, I appreciate the offer, Alex."

By nightfall, the train was rolling across

Nebraska. At dawn the next morning, they were in Wyoming, heading north out of Cheyenne City.

The Rocky Mountains were a short distance to the west. As the sun peeped over the eastern horizon, it filled the coach with a bright yellow glow. The majestic spires of the Rockies were a golden rose color, and the light of a new day seeped into the lower clefts of the towering rocks and gilded the tips of the pines at the edge of the timberline.

Alex and Gina awakened at the same time. Quint pointed toward the windows on the other side of the coach, and when their eyes beheld the mountains for the first time, they were speechless.

After breakfast, Quint and his brood were back in their coach. All three children stared out the windows with wide eyes. At times they craned their necks to take in the sights and marveled at the vast open spaces.

Suddenly Missy pointed and cried out, "Cows!"

Alex laughed. "Missy, those aren't cows. Those are buffalo. I've seen pictures of them before."

Gina's mouth dropped open. "Oh, Uncle Quint! There are so many of them!"

"That's a pretty big herd, all right. You'll

see lots more of them, I guarantee you."

A few minutes later, Missy pointed out the window again. "Look! Cows!"

Alex laughed. "She's right this time. Look at all the cattle!"

Great herds of cattle grazed lazily on the abundant grass, the pastures stretching as far as the eye could see. Only moments later, they saw more buffalo. And as the train rolled on they saw herds of wild horses.

In late afternoon, Missy climbed onto her uncle's lap once again and laid her head against his chest. She was not yet sure what all was happening to her once well-ordered life. Up until a few days ago, she was a busy, happy little girl, playing daily with her dolls and "helping" Mama with things around the house. Each afternoon she had waited eagerly for her papa to come and spend time with her. Then all of a sudden, her mama and papa were gone. Everyone told her they were in heaven; but all she knew was that heaven was somewhere in the sky. She wanted them to come back.

She lifted her head and looked up into Quint's eyes. "Unca Quint, I want Mama an' Papa to come to your house."

Quint swallowed hard. "Honey, they can't come to my house. They're in heaven with Jesus."

Her little face twisted and tears glistened in her eyes. "Why won't they come back? Don't they wuv us anymore?"

Quint cupped the side of her face. "Of course they still love you, sweetheart, but when people go to be with Jesus, they can't come back here anymore. They're waiting for us to come to be with them in heaven someday."

Missy laid her head on his chest and soon succumbed to the sleep that was tugging at her.

A short time later, the train was nearing Sheridan, Wyoming, when Alex looked out the window and said, "Look!"

Gina leaned close to her brother to see.

"What are those animals, Uncle Quint?" Alex asked.

A small herd of antelope fled from the noise of the engine, bounding agilely over the rolling terrain.

"Those are antelope."

"Are they like deer?" Gina asked.

"They're actually in the bovine family, along with cattle, sheep, and goats."

"They sure can run fast," Alex said. "Look at 'em!"

His excited voice penetrated Missy's ears. She sat up, wiped the sleep from her eyes, and yawned. "What's runnin' fast, Alex?"

Big brother took her onto his lap so she could see the last few antelope before they were out of sight. Pointing, he said, "There, see them? They're called antelope. See how fast they're running?"

"Mmm-hmm." Missy let her eyes take in the vast emptiness with no houses, stores, or streets. "Where did everybody go? Doesn't anybody like to live here?" She lowered her face and looked into Alex's eyes.

Alex looked to his uncle for help.

Leaning close to the little one, Quint said, "Sweetie pie, most people back where you used to live have never come out here to the West. They don't know how great it is. But some people are coming out here to look it over, and lots of them like it so well that they move out here. Someday there'll be lots more people."

The conductor came through the coach, announcing arrival in Sheridan in ten minutes. The passengers were welcome to eat supper at one of the two eating establishments at the Sheridan depot.

During their meal, the children were fascinated by the style of clothing worn by the locals. They had never seen the like before.

It was just after sunrise the next morning when the train pulled into Billings,

Montana. At nine o'clock, the weary travelers boarded the Wells Fargo stage for Bozeman, along with two businessmen from Livingston. In late afternoon, when the stage stopped at Livingston and the two businessmen got off, it was just the doctor and his three children on the stage to Bozeman.

Alex and Gina were enthralled with the beauty of the rugged country between Billings and Bozeman. When the sun was lowering over the mountains to the west, the stagecoach topped the last steep rise before heading down the winding road into the valley surrounded by bold and rugged mountains.

The golden red of the sunset capped the peaks and began receding eastward in the valley, letting the shadows settle into the low spots.

"Oh, Uncle Quint!" Gina said. "It's so beautiful! I love it already."

"Me too!" Alex said.

"Me too!" Missy echoed.

Quint pointed to the collection of houses and commercial buildings in the center of the valley. "Look, kids, there's Bozeman. Our new home!"

"Where's Unca Quint's house?" asked the little one.

"We can't see it yet, honey," said Quint, "but we'll be there in a little while. Then you can see it."

When the stage hauled up to the Fargo office, Quint introduced his nieces and nephew to the agent, who welcomed them to Bozeman. Quint told the agent he would be back shortly for the large trunk that contained the children's clothing.

It was a short walk to Quint's large two-story house. When Quint led them into the front yard of his place, Alex said, "Wow! I thought we had a big house in Aurora, but this one's really big!"

"Big house!" added Missy.

Quint gave them a tour of the ground floor, showing them the parlor with its large fireplace. There was a large formal dining room with a fireplace, a sewing room, and a huge kitchen with walk-in pantry and a storeroom.

Upstairs, Quint showed them his bedroom, then said, "Now, kids, there are four more bedrooms. Each has a fireplace, just like in my room. Two of the rooms have two double beds; the others each have one double bed. I want you to pick the rooms you want."

"Uncle Quint," Gina said, "Missy and I should share a bedroom. She's too little yet to be left alone."

"Of course. Just go ahead and pick the one you want."

While the girls were looking at the rooms with two double beds, Alex quickly chose the room with a window that overlooked the backyard. It was still light enough for him to see the large, sturdy cottonwood tree that stood near his window. He was gazing at it when Quint entered the room and said, "This the one you want?"

"Yes, sir. I like the view from here better than the other room. And . . . ah . . . Uncle Quint . . ."

"Mmm-hmm?"

"Could we have a rope swing put in that tree?"

"Of course. I'll see to it as soon as I can."

"Thanks! That would be great!"

Down the hall, the sisters had decided on the room that overlooked the spacious side lawn and flower garden. It was large and had plenty of closet space. The two white iron beds were covered with colorful quilts, and each had two soft pillows. The windows were hung with ruffled white priscilla curtains, and one of them had a window seat.

Alex went into the girls' room and told them about the big cottonwood tree in the backyard, and that Uncle Quint was going to put a rope swing in it for them.

"Anything else you kids need or want, just tell me," Quint said. "We'll go shopping and get it for you."

Gina rushed to him, wrapped her arms around him, and said, "Uncle Quint, you're so good to us. We love you so much!"

"Tell you what," he said, "I'll take you to one of our cafés for supper, then we'll go get the trunk."

After supper the children rode to the Fargo office with their uncle. When they returned with the trunk, Alex helped him carry it up the stairs and place it in the girls' room. As they began to unpack it, Quint said, "You go ahead and put your things away. I'm going over to Dr. Holmes's house and let him know that I'm back. I know he and Mrs. Holmes will want me to bring you to the office in the morning so they can meet you. Be back in a little while."

Alex gathered all of his clothes in his arms and carried them down the hall.

While the girls were putting their things away, Gina said, "Missy, which bed do you want?"

Missy paused, looked from bed to bed, ran her gaze to the door, then looked all around the room. "Guess I'll take the one close to the door. I'll feel safer that way."

"All right."

When Quint returned home, he found the three Roberts children sitting in the parlor. "Everything put away?" he asked.

"Yes, sir," Alex said. "I put the trunk in my closet, since there's plenty of room in there."

"Good. I was right about Dr. and Mrs. Holmes. They're very eager to meet you. I'll take you in the morning. So what would you like to do now?"

"I think we need to get to bed," said Gina.

"I agree. Your uncle is plenty tired too."

The tired family ascended the stairs, and when they reached the door of Quint's room, he said, "Get ready for bed, and I'll be in shortly to tuck you in."

Ten minutes later, Quint tapped on Alex's door. Quint found him already under the covers, his arms folded over his chest on the outside.

"Anything you need, pal?" Quint asked.

"As Mama used to say: just a hug and I'll be off to dreamland."

Quint leaned down and hugged the boy. "You get off to dreamland now."

"I will. Thank you, Uncle Quint, for taking us in. It would've been awful to go to an orphanage, and even worse to be put up for adoption and maybe the girls and I would be split up."

"I wouldn't have it any other way, Alex. Everything is going to be just fine for all of us." Quint stood up, doused the lantern on the table beside the bed, and headed for the door. "Good night, now. If you need me, you know where my room is."

"G'night," Alex managed before his eyes closed and he gave in to sleep.

When Quint approached the girls' room, the door was standing open. The single lantern on the table between the beds was still burning. By its light Quint saw Gina sitting on the window seat, gazing out the window. Missy was in bed and already asleep. Her rag doll was clasped tightly to her cheek. Her rosy mouth was slightly open, and her breathing was soft and even.

A contentment he could not put into words flooded through him as he gazed down at the precious child.

Moving across the room toward Gina, Quint said, "What are you doing, honey?"

Gina smiled at him, then looked back out the window. "I was just marveling at the beauty of God's star-filled sky," she said in a whisper, as if to speak too loudly would disturb the tranquil scene. "The stars seem so much closer to earth here than back East, and the sky just somehow looks bigger."

Quint sat down beside her and gazed at

the dazzling night sky, then said, "I know what you mean. The vastness of the heavens and the brilliance of the stars really made me fall in love with the West."

Gina kept her eyes on the black velvet canopy alive with countless stars. "Uncle Quint, you're so generous to bring us here and give us a home. We'll try very hard not to interrupt your life more than is necessary. We'll work hard around here and do all we can to take care of ourselves. Taking the three of us into your home is quite a task for someone who has never been married, let alone never had children. I promise we'll be good and try to stay out of your way."

Tears were visible on the girl's cheeks.

Quint slipped an arm around his niece, thinking how mature she was for thirteen. "Gina, honey, you have this all wrong," he said, pressing her head to his shoulder. "You three are doing me a favor by coming to live here. You could never be in the way, and you're not interrupting my life in the least. You are making my empty life one of joy and fulfillment."

Gina gripped his arm and sniffed.

"You and Missy and Alex are not guests here, sweetie. It's your home as much as it's mine. We're a family. And that will even get better when the adoption's done."

"Oh, Uncle Quint, this means so much to Alex and me. Missy doesn't understand, of course, but one day it will mean as much to her. With Mama and Papa gone, we're so glad to be a family with you."

"Not as glad as I am. We'll do our chores together. We'll play together. We'll share one another's heartaches and joys, and most of all, we'll love each other more and more as time passes. God, in His infinite wisdom, has brought us together, and by His grace He will use us for His glory."

Gina tilted her head back so she could look into his eyes. A smile broke through her tears. "Thank you, Uncle Quint."

He shook his head. "No. Thank you, Gina. Thank you for being such a sweet girl. Now you need to get a good night's sleep."

As he spoke, Quint guided her from the window seat with a hand on her shoulder. One last hug and she climbed into bed.

He doused the lantern and said, "If you need me, you know where my room is. Good night, Gina. I love you."

"I love you too," she said softly.

When Quint reached the door, he stepped into the hall and left it ajar, allowing the soft light from the hall lantern to flow in.

As he moved down the hall toward his own room, a satisfied smile crossed his face.

"Thank You, Lord," he said.

After enjoying a delicious breakfast prepared by Gina, the foursome left the house and headed for the doctors' office.

On the way, Quint told them he was going back to work tomorrow, but that he had explained to Dr. Holmes last night that he had to take the children to Judge Gregory Carter's chambers to set up the adoption today, plus put an ad in the newspaper for a housekeeper.

They were just coming to Main Street at the intersection where the doctor's office was located.

"So tomorrow," said Quint, "you three will be at the house alone during the day. When we get home later, I'll take you to meet the neighbors, so in case you ever need help, you will know who to call on. You'll be a good girl, won't you, Missy, and mind Alex and Gina?"

The little one looked up at her uncle and grinned. "I will be good, Unca Quint."

"Of course you will," he said, as if he shouldn't have asked the question. "I can't imagine my little Missy ever being bad."

Alex and Gina looked at each other and rolled their eyes.

When they reached the Holmes building,

Quint guided his little family into the office and waiting room. Several patients were waiting to see Dr. Holmes. Quint knew all of them and introduced his nieces and nephew, explaining that they had come to live with him.

Maggie Holmes came from the examining and surgery room at that moment and moved toward her desk. When she saw Quint, her eyes flicked to the three children. She smiled and said, "Well, hello, Alex, Gina, and Missy! I'm Mrs. Holmes. Welcome to Bozeman."

Synchronized perfectly, the sisters did a curtsy, Alex bowed like a French gentleman, and all three said, "We are glad to meet you, Mrs. Holmes."

Maggie hugged all three to her ample bosom.

"Dr. Holmes wants to meet you too," she said, "and so does our nurse, Mrs. Myers. They're working on a patient in the back room at the moment, but they'll be finished shortly. I'll go back and tell them you're here."

Maggie returned with Dr. Holmes and his nurse. While Maggie was guiding the next patient to the examining room, the three children won over Dr. Obadiah Holmes and Frances Myers in the same manner they had won over Maggie.

Quint then told his partner that he needed to keep moving and would see him tomorrow morning.

Holmes ran his gaze over the packed waiting room and said, "I will be very glad to have you back, I assure you."

The next stop was the *Bozeman Courier*, where the children met editor-in-chief Donald Crenshaw and his two office employees, Jessie Holcomb and Mandy Towner. Quint briefly told what had happened to his brother and sister-in-law and that the children had come to live with him. Now he wanted to put an ad in the paper for a live-in housekeeper.

Mandy Towner worked with Quint on wording the ad, saying it would be in tomorrow's edition. Quint thanked her, and the children followed him out the door.

The Gallatin County courthouse was a block's walk from the newspaper office. The children were all eyes when Quint led them inside. The walls of the foyer held portraits of George Washington, Abraham Lincoln, and the current president of the United States, Ulysses S. Grant.

They approached a closed door with a sign on it that read: Judge Gregory L. Carter.

Quint turned the knob and ushered the

three children in ahead of him. A lady sat at a desk, busily writing something on a file folder. She looked up at the three young faces, then set her eyes on the tall dark-haired man. A smile graced her features as she said, "Good morning, Dr. Roberts. What can I do for you?"

"Good morning, Mrs. Wiley. These are my nephew and nieces, Alex, Gina, and Missy." He explained about the deaths of Philip and Elaine and of his desire to legally adopt their children.

"I think that's wonderful, Doctor," Laura said. "Judge Carter is in court right now, but he should be back in his chambers in an hour or so. Why don't I go ahead and get some information written down? It'll make it faster when you sit down with Judge Carter."

"Fine," said Quint. "Alex, Gina, take Missy to the couch and sit down while I give Mrs. Wiley some information."

When the children had gone across the room, Laura whispered, "Those poor little ones. Losing their parents had to have been terribly hard for them."

"Yes, but they're very special children. They've handled it marvelously."

"I'm so glad they have you to care for them."

Quint smiled. "I think it's the other way, Laura. I'm so glad I have them to care for their lonely ol' bachelor uncle!"

11

Quint Roberts and the children waited almost an hour for Judge Gregory Carter to return. Laura Wiley had provided Missy several pieces of paper and a pencil, and the little one was entertaining the others by drawing pictures of animals.

Finally, they heard a door opening and closing inside the judge's chambers. Laura rose from her desk and knocked on the judge's door.

A muffled voice said, "Yes, Laura?"

"There's someone here to see you, Judge."

The door opened and a stout, silver-haired man of sixty appeared. His eyes took in his visitors and a smile broke across his face. "Well, hello, Doctor. These have to be your nieces and nephew."

Quint rose from the couch. "Yes. How did you know?"

"I happened to meet your pastor at the

general store a couple of days ago and he told me you were back in Illinois to bring your recently orphaned nieces and nephew home with you. What can I do for you?"

"I want to adopt them, sir," Quint said. "Mrs. Wiley took some information from me while we were waiting for you to arrive."

"I have it here, Judge," said Laura, handing him the folder in her hand.

"All right," said Carter, "please come into my chambers — and bring those pretty girls and that handsome boy with you."

When Quint and the children settled in the large, well-furnished office, the judge said, "Now, I want each of you to tell me your name."

The girls looked at each other, then Gina said, "I'm Gina, sir," and curtsied politely.

Carter smiled. "And what's your last name, dear?"

"Oh, Roberts, sir," she said, blushing. "My full name is Gina Marie Roberts."

"Well, you certainly are a fine young lady." He turned to the little one. "And what's your name, honey?"

"Missy." She dipped her head and curtsied nervously.

"It's actually Melissa, sir," Gina said, laying a hand on her little sister's shoulder. "Melissa Sue Roberts."

"That's a pretty name for such a pretty girl," Carter said.

Missy looked up at him. "Thank you, sir."

Carter smiled. "And a polite little girl too." He turned to Alex. "And this boy is a gentleman, Dr. Roberts. He let the girls give their names first. Now, what is your name, son?"

"They call me Alex, sir, but my real name is George Alexander Roberts."

Carter's bushy silver eyebrows arched. "My, that's an impressive name. Let me guess. The 'George' is for George Washington, and the 'Alexander' is for Alexander the Great."

Alex grinned. "No, sir. I was named after my two grandfathers . . . George Roberts and Alexander Dumont."

The judge laughed. "All right, so I guessed wrong. But I imagine since you go by Alex, your sisters would agree that you are their Alexander the Great."

"He's the best brother in the whole world," Gina said.

Missy nodded. "Yes, in the whole world."

Carter smiled at Quint. "Looks to me like you've got some very nice children to adopt, Doctor."

"You're right about that, Judge. My brother and his wife were good parents.

They taught these children well."

"That's quite evident." The judge turned toward his desk. "Well, let's sit down here and talk adoption."

The judge took out the papers his secretary had placed in the folder and read them over. Nodding, he said, "Looks like we have most of the information needed, Doctor. However, I must have proof that their parents are deceased. It isn't that I doubt you, but it's the law that I have written proof."

"Of course." Quint reached into his shirt pocket and took out a white envelope. "The death certificates are in this envelope."

Carter pulled out the certificates and read them. "All right, everything is in order here." Laying the certificates aside, he said, "Doctor, by law I also must ask any child over twelve years old if he or she is in agreement with the adoption. According to the information you gave Laura, Alex is fourteen and Gina is thirteen."

"That's right."

The judge looked at the boy and said, "Alex, do you want your uncle to adopt you?"

"Oh yes, sir. I sure do."

"Me too, Judge Carter," Gina said. "He's already been like a parent to us, and we love him with all our hearts."

"That's right, sir," Alex said. "And Uncle Quint has always shown us that he loves us."

Gina turned to her little sister. "We love Uncle Quint very much, don't we, Missy?"

Missy nodded enthusiastically. "Uh-huh. Wuv Unca Quint!"

The judge smiled. "Well, Doctor, I'd say we can proceed with the adoption. I'll have Laura complete these papers right now. Won't take but a few minutes, since most of it is already done."

Ten minutes later, Carter returned to his office and handed Quint a brown envelope. "These are your legal adoption papers, Dr. Roberts. These children are now yours." Then to the children: "Alex, Gina, Missy, this man is still your uncle, of course, but he is now also your adoptive father."

Gina bounded off her chair and threw her arms around Quint's neck, almost toppling him over. Brother and little sister joined her.

Quint thanked the judge and his secretary and led his three children out of the court-house into the brilliant Montana sunshine. As they started down the boardwalk, Alex exchanged glances with Gina. She nodded, and Alex said, "Ah . . . Uncle Quint . . ."

"Yes?"

"Gina and I just want to tell you that seeing the judge was only a formality as far as we're concerned. We know that our parents wouldn't want anybody but you to adopt us, and in our hearts you were already our adopted father before we entered Judge Carter's chambers."

"Thank you, Alex. That means more than I can tell you."

Gina spoke up. "We understand that you aren't trying to take the place of our parents, but to us you're now our father here on earth and we will obey you, follow you, and look up to you always."

"That's right," said Alex.

"That's right," echoed Missy.

Tears filled Quint's eyes as he looked at the three serious faces. "You already have made me so very proud of you, and I know your mama and papa, looking down from heaven, feel the same way."

When Missy heard the mention of her parents in heaven, a frown puckered her brow. Quint looked down at her and waited for a question, but it didn't come. Soon the frown disappeared. She shrugged her tiny shoulders and smiled up at her beloved Unca Quint.

Without breaking stride, Quint reached down and took her up into his arms.

"Uncle Quint . . ." It was Alex looking up at him. "Since you're our adopted father, could we call you Papa?"

"Of course, but . . . I was thinking . . . since you called your real father Papa, and still do when you speak of him, how about calling me Dad?"

Alex looked at Gina and said, "What do you think?"

"Well, I'd like to call him Daddy." She looked up at Quint as they stepped up on the boardwalk and continued toward home. "Could I call you Daddy?"

"Of course! I'd love it."

"Since I'm a boy, I'll call you Dad," Alex said.

Gina looked at her little sister. "And we girls will call him Daddy. Okay, Missy?"

Missy nodded. "Call Unca Quint Daddy."

Alex and Gina laughed, then Gina said, "And Daddy, when you get married, Missy and I will call our new mother Mommy, and Alex can call her Mom if he wants to."

"So what makes you think I'm going to get married?" Quint said.

Gina's blue eyes twinkled as she looked up at him with a sly smile. "A handsome young doctor like you isn't going to stay single forever. Especially since Alex and I have been praying that the Lord will give you a wife who will be our mother."

"Oh, you have, eh? How long has this been going on?"

"Ever since we learned you were coming to Aurora to bring us to live with you in Bozeman."

"But this wife of mine you've been praying about couldn't be your mother unless I had adopted you."

Gina's face tinted. She glanced at her brother, then said, "Well, you see, Daddy, we also started praying that you would adopt us."

Quint chuckled. "You little scamps!"

Alex spoke up. "We figure since the Lord answered our prayers about your adopting us, He'll also answer our prayers and give you a wife."

Quint messed up Alex's hair, then pinched Gina's ear. "Well, then, you two just keep on praying."

"Oh, we will!" Gina said, giggling.

Quint opened the front door for the children and said, "After lunch, we'll go to the parsonage so you can meet Pastor and Mrs. Morgan."

There was energy in their steps as the new family entered the house. The pain of their recent loss was beginning to ease and a feeling of oneness and unity filled their tender hearts.

Quint found the Morgans at the parsonage and introduced them to the children. The pastor and his wife showed their love to Alex, Gina, and Missy, and the children readily responded.

Loretta Morgan held Missy on her lap while Pastor Dale told Alex and Gina who their Sunday school teachers would be. The two older children volunteered their testimonies, telling the Morgans about the time they came to know the Lord and that they had both been baptized after they were saved.

The pastor smiled at Quint. "I can tell you right now, these two have been taught well. They'll be real assets to our young people's department."

Loretta kissed Missy's cheek and said, "And this little girl will be an asset to our preschool department. We're so glad the Lord has allowed all three of you children to come and live with your uncle."

"Thank you, Mrs. Morgan," Gina said. "Only he's our daddy now too."

Loretta put a hand to her mouth. "Oh yes! Pardon me. I'm so glad the Lord has allowed you to come here and live with your new daddy!"

Alex grinned. "Gina and I told Dad after we left the courthouse today that we're praying the Lord will give him a wife so we'll have a new mother too."

"Wonderful!" said the pastor. "Where are you going to get this wife, Doctor?"

Quint chuckled hollowly. "Well, I'm not sure, Pastor, but the Lord must have her ready to cross my path somewhere along the line. And maybe even soon."

It was a hot, humid night in Atlanta, Georgia. Bob and Betty Maxwell were sitting on the front porch of their humble cottage, watching their four older children chase fireflies in the yard. Betty was holding the baby and commenting on the noisy crickets when she saw a dark figure coming along the street and said something to Bob. The person was too far away yet to be recognized.

In the yard, the children were laughing and having a good time when Lorna's attention was drawn to the approaching figure. She squinted to see if it was someone she knew. Suddenly the cloud that had been obscuring the pale half-moon drifted and let soft beams illuminate the face. "Mother! Daddy!" Lorna called. "Look who's here! It's Miss Taylor!"

"Hello!" called Annamarie as she turned into the yard, her arms loaded with packages.

The Maxwell children gathered close and followed her as she moved up to the porch. Bob jumped up from his chair. "Here, Miss Taylor, let me help you with those."

While Annamarie was being relieved of her load, she said, "Presents for everybody!"

The smaller children squealed with joy.

Tears sprang to Betty's eyes and she moved up to Annamarie with the baby in her arms. "Miss Taylor, this is the third time you have done this kind of thing for us. You really shouldn't."

"That's right," said Bob. "You're just too good to us."

"It's my pleasure. The Lord has blessed me financially so I can share with you, and it makes me happy to do this."

Betty hugged her neck, saying, "And we love you for it."

The children opened their packages first and found new clothing and shoes. There was clothing in the baby's and the parents' packages too.

The entire family thanked Annamarie with grateful hearts.

Two weeks later Annamarie was sitting on the front porch swing of her house, fanning herself while watching the fireflies skitter about the yard. The sound of the nightly cricket concert surrounded her.

Above the pleasant night sounds, Annamarie heard the clip-clop of a horse's hooves, then spotted a buggy with lanterns burning on both sides. She was about to put her attention elsewhere when she saw the buggy angle across the street and stop at the edge of her yard. A man and a woman got out and headed toward the house.

She moved to the steps. The light of the porch lantern showed her faces she did not recognize.

"Miss Annamarie Taylor?" the man said.

"Yes."

"I'm Orville Bradford, and this is my wife, Charlene. We're the directors of Atlanta's City Orphanage, and we would like to talk to you. Would you have a few minutes?"

"Of course. Let's go inside and sit in the parlor."

When the Bradfords were seated, Annamarie said, "What can I do for you?"

"Miss Taylor," said Orville, "we have learned through people in your church about the love you show the girls in your Sunday school class, and also of what you've done for the Maxwell family."

"We think it's wonderful!" Charlene said. "We're looking for a lady of your caliber to help us at the orphanage. It would be on a volunteer basis and we would appreciate whatever amount of time you could give us."

Before Annamarie could speak, Orville said, "Charlene is quite overworked and can't spend the time with the children that she would like. They need a mother figure, and I can't give them that."

Annamarie laughed. "I guess you can't, Mr. Bradford. Though I'm not married and have never been a mother, my heart has always been tender toward children and I might add, especially toward orphans. I'll do what I can to help."

"We know you're employed at Peterson's Clothing Store, Miss Taylor," Charlene said, "and we're aware that you must have time to prepare your lessons for the Sunday school class and time for your other church activities, but we will gladly accept whatever time you can give us."

Annamarie thought on it a moment. In her heart she was thanking God for this opportunity, not only to fill some empty, lonely hours but to have a part in the lives of the orphans. She said, "I could come to the orphanage Tuesday and Friday evenings, and Saturday mornings. I visit for my Sunday school class on Monday and Thursday evenings, and Saturday afternoons. On Wednesday evenings, I'm always in the midweek service at my church."

The Bradfords exchanged pleased looks. "We had no idea you could give us this much time," Orville said. "When could you start?"

Annamarie looked at the ceiling thoughtfully. "Well, how about tomorrow. Say from eight o'clock till noon?"

"That would be marvelous!" Charlene said. "Orville will come and pick you up."

"Would 7:45 be satisfactory?" Orville asked.

"Oh, that won't be necessary. At least in good weather. I walk to work, and the orphanage is closer than the store."

"I'd sure be glad to provide you a ride."

"Only if it's raining in the morning, Mr. Bradford. And at this point, it doesn't look like that's a possibility."

By noon the next day, the children of City Orphanage had stolen Annamarie Taylor's heart.

Gina and Alex were doing their best to keep the house clean, even getting some "help" daily from their little sister. Gina had taught her brother how to help her with the wash and how to hang it on the clothesline in the backyard. But the house was large and the laundry for four people sometimes seemed monumental.

Gina cooked simple meals that were filling and satisfying, but her cooking knowledge and skills were quite limited, which meant that the Roberts family ate the same few things repeatedly.

One warm summer evening, after they sat down to the table, Quint called on Alex to pray. When the amen was said, and Gina was loading Missy's plate for her, Quint noted how very tired Gina looked.

She's working too hard. She's only a young girl and I've let her take on the responsibility of this whole family. I've got to make a concentrated effort to find a housekeeper.

No sooner had these thoughts entered Quint's mind when Alex said, "Dad, are you going to keep advertising in the paper for a housekeeper? It's been over a month since you started putting the ad in every edition."

"Yes. I can't give up. School will be starting in seven weeks and both of you will have to get enrolled. The Lord has just got to give us a housekeeper by then."

"Daddy," said Gina, "if the Lord shouldn't choose to send us a housekeeper by the time school starts, Alex can go ahead and enroll in school and I'll stay home and take care of Missy."

Quint shook his head, "Honey, it isn't right that you have to stay out of school. You need your education, and I don't want you to get behind. The Lord will certainly provide us a housekeeper soon."

"Well, maybe the Lord wants you to look for a wife and not a housekeeper," Gina said.

He grinned at her. "I don't know where to look. Certainly, every Christian young woman in Bozeman is either already married or engaged to be married."

Alex raised his eyebrows. "How about that young widow in the church? You know, Stella Adamson. Maybe you should get to know her better."

Quint swallowed the sip of coffee in his mouth and shook his head. "No, no. The lady isn't my type, Alex. She just wouldn't do."

"What about Mrs. Donegan's niece?" Gina said. "The one from Billings that was at church with her last Sunday. She's a very nice Christian lady, and very pretty. And I think she's only a few years older than you. She's never been married, according to what one of the girls in my class told me."

Quint chuckled. "Gina Marie Roberts, Dora Schelling is fourteen years older than I am. She's been here before. I'm looking for a mother for *you,* not for me!"

Alex laughed, then Missy joined in with a giggle.

Gina shrugged. "Well, one thing you can say for Miss Schelling: She holds her age well. I thought sure she was younger than that."

That night at bedtime, the family knelt beside Missy's bed and prayed together. The custom was that Missy would pray first, with a little help from big sister; then Gina prayed next followed by Alex. Quint always prayed last.

When Alex was almost finished praying, he said, "And Lord, please send some new Christian young lady to Bozeman who is beautiful and smart and is looking for a handsome Christian doctor for a husband who is soon going to have his own practice."

At that instant, Gina came out with a loud "Amen!"

After Quint had closed off the prayer time, he said, "Alex, my boy, you really put some strong restrictions on this woman you want the Lord to send for me to marry. Do you really think He's going to just float down out of the clouds a beautiful young Christian woman who's smart and looking for a doctor for a husband?"

"Not exactly, but there's a verse in the Old Testament that Pastor Shaffer preached on one time. It was where God told Abraham and Sarah that even though they were real old, He was going to give them a baby. Remember that?"

"Yes. It's in Genesis chapter 18."

"And remember that Sarah laughed when God said this, thinking she was too old to have a baby and there was nothing God could do to change that. And God said to Abraham that Sarah shouldn't have laughed. Then He said, 'Is anything too hard for the LORD?' "

Quint grinned. "I sure do remember. God showed Abraham and Sarah that He could do what He said. He gave them Isaac in their old age."

"Then since nothing's too hard for the Lord, can't He answer my prayer and send a beautiful Christian young lady who's smart and wants to marry a handsome Christian doctor?"

Gina set steady eyes on Quint. "Well, can't He, Daddy?"

"Of course God can do that. There's nothing too hard for Him. But Alex . . ."

"Yes, sir?"

"Why did you ask the Lord for her to be smart?"

"Simple. You're plenty smart, and it wouldn't make a good marriage if she wasn't on your intelligence level."

Missy giggled. "Unca Quint Daddy is smart! Uh-huh!"

Quint laughed, then looked at Alex again. "You also asked the Lord to send a beautiful lady into my life. I like the idea, but why is it necessary that she be beautiful?"

Alex sent a glance to Gina, then looked back at Quint. "Well, as long as I'm praying and asking the Lord to send you a wife, I figure it wouldn't hurt anything if she prettied the place up when she moved in!"

Quint laughed heartily.

"Big brother, you're a genius!" Gina said.

Alex shrugged. "I can't help it. I was born that way!"

12

Maggie Holmes was at her desk in the combined office–waiting room when the outside door opened and a short, portly woman in her late fifties came in. The three patients who were waiting to see Dr. Holmes turned their attention on the newcomer.

"Hello," said Maggie in a friendly tone. "Let me get your name on the list here. I'm Dr. Holmes's wife, Maggie. It shouldn't be too long a wait. If you're in pain I'll do what I can to —"

"No, no," said the woman, whose hair was mostly silver. "I'm not here because I'm hurting or ill. I need to see Dr. Quint Roberts on a matter of business."

"Oh. Well, Dr. Roberts is out doing house calls right now, but I'm expecting him back soon. Would you like to wait?"

"Yes. It's best that I do. I'm from Butte, and I need to see him before I head back home."

"Certainly. Just take a seat over here."

"I will in a moment. I have some people outside who drove me here in their buggy. I need to let them know the situation."

The portly woman was gone less than five minutes then returned and took a seat.

Patients came and went for over half an hour before Dr. Roberts came in, carrying his black medical bag.

"Doctor," Maggie said, "the lady by the window is wanting to see you on a business matter."

Quint turned and stepped to the woman, who rose to her feet. "I'm Dr. Roberts, ma'am," he said.

"My name is Mabel Ritter, Doctor. I'd like to talk to you about the live-in housekeeper's job you've been listing in the classified section of the *Courier*. That is, if it's still open."

"It sure is, ma'am. Let's step into my private office so we can talk." As they moved toward the hallway, Quint said, "Maggie, this shouldn't take long. Tell Dr. Holmes I'll be able to help him in a little while."

"Will do," said Maggie with a smile.

"I don't believe I've ever seen you before, ma'am," Quint said. "You must not live in Bozeman."

"No, Doctor. I live in Butte. Been there eleven years now."

Quint opened the door to his office and ushered the woman in ahead of him. He gestured for her to sit down on a padded wooden chair in front of the desk.

"I assume it's Mrs. Ritter," he said.

"Yes. I was widowed five years ago. Since then I've been working as a cook at the Gold Nugget Café in Butte. However, the owner of the café decided a month ago to leave Butte and go elsewhere. He tried to sell the café but had no offers on it. So last week he closed it down and left town. I live in a boardinghouse in Butte but can no longer afford to pay the rent. I've noticed your ad in the *Courier* several times over the past few weeks and thought I'd come and see if the job was still open."

"Since you've been cooking in the café, I certainly don't need to wonder about how you'll do in the kitchen," Quint said, smiling.

"I wouldn't think so," she said, matching his smile.

"And you saw in the ad that I'm single and have three adopted children in my home: a fourteen-year-old boy and two girls, thirteen and three. The youngest will be four on August 20."

"Yes, I knew that. What are their names?"

"The boy is Alex. The oldest girl is Gina, and the little girl is Melissa. We call her Missy."

"How long have you had them?"

"Since mid-June."

"I'm amazed, Doctor, that as a single man you'd be allowed to adopt even one child, let alone three."

"That's because I'm their uncle, Mrs. Ritter. My brother and his wife drowned in a boating mishap on Lake Michigan. I am the only living relative the children have. So these precious young ones are orphans with me as their father figure. But they're in need of a mother figure too. Would this be any kind of a problem for you?"

"I don't believe so, Doctor. I was never able to have any children of my own, but I had three brothers and four sisters while growing up, and only three were older than me. So I know all about children."

"That would give you some experience, all right."

Quint laid out exactly what her job would entail, explaining that in addition to all the housework, washing, ironing, and cooking, she would have Missy at home to look after by herself when Alex and Gina were in school, which would start the second week of September.

"I understand, Doctor," Mabel said, "and I assure you that I can handle it."

Quint nodded. "Alex and Gina are hard workers, Mrs. Ritter. They'll be willing to help you around the house when you need them. When school starts, they'll no doubt have homework, but they'll still have time to do things for you, so if you take the job, please feel free to call on them for help."

Mabel nodded.

"Now, a couple of other things . . ."

Quint explained that he and the older children were born-again Christians and involved in their church. It would not be mandatory that she go to church with them, but she would be welcome to do so.

Mabel indicated she would love to attend church with them.

Next, Quint brought up her salary and made his offer. Mabel was quite pleased at the amount and told him it was very generous.

"Just so you'll know about the accommodations, ma'am, the house has five bedrooms, all upstairs. Three, of course, are occupied. One of the other two has two double beds, and the other has one. The rooms are both quite large, I might add."

"I would no doubt choose the room with just the one bed, Doctor. That way, if you had guests, they'd have two beds if needed."

"I appreciate your attitude, Mrs. Ritter. Any questions for me?"

"None that I can think of right off. I'll have some as time goes on, I'm sure."

"Well, please don't hesitate to ask. The job is yours if you want it."

A smile spread over Mabel's round face. "I want it, Doctor!"

"Good. How soon can you start?"

"Right now, if you want. Some friends brought me here from Butte and I have an overnight satchel with me. They've already said they'd bring my other belongings tomorrow if you hired me and wanted me to go to work right away."

Quint went outside with Mabel and told the man and woman who had brought her how to find his house when they came back the next day with her other belongings. Mabel took her overnight bag from the buggy and her friends drove away.

When they went back into the office, the young doctor found the waiting room full. He asked Mabel if she would mind waiting for a couple of hours while he helped Dr. Holmes. Mabel told him to go do his work, she would gladly wait.

Two hours later, Quint carried Mabel's overnight satchel as they walked toward the neighborhood where his house was located. Quint explained to her that the children were handling the deaths of their parents quite well, but still had crying spells at times and sometimes had bad dreams. Missy, especially, cried for her mother.

Mabel told him she understood and would try to be a help to them.

Upon entering the house they could hear happy sounds coming from the backyard. Missy was in the rope swing with Gina, and both girls were giggling as their brother pushed them higher.

Suddenly Missy's eyes went to the porch and she cried, "Unca Quint Daddy is home!"

When the other two looked that direction, Quint called, "Alex, Gina, Missy, there's someone here I want you to meet. The Lord has answered our prayers!"

Alex stopped the swing and the girls hopped out. All three ran to the porch and bounded up the stairs, looking back and forth between their adoptive father and the round-faced woman.

"Children," Quint said, "I want you to meet Mabel Ritter. She's our new live-in housekeeper."

Mabel smiled and said, "And I already

know your names. You're Alex, you're Gina, and you are Missy."

Gina and Missy curtsied, telling Mabel they were very happy to meet her. Alex did his French gentleman's bow, saying the same.

"And I'm very happy to meet all three of you," Mabel said.

Gina moved toward Mabel, opening her arms to embrace her. But Mabel frowned and took a half-step back. Gina bit down on her lower lip but said nothing.

"Well, kids," Quint said, "let's take Mrs. Ritter upstairs and let her see her room. I told her what was available, and she wants the room with the one bed."

Gina stepped up and offered her hand. "You'll like the room, Mrs. Ritter. Come on."

Mabel took the hand hesitantly, then smiled and said, "Dr. Roberts, I would be more comfortable if you and the children would call me by my first name rather than Mrs. Ritter."

"Fine. Mabel it is. Since she has requested this, children, you can call her by that name too."

Seeing that Mabel had taken Gina's hand, Missy offered her own hand, and Mabel took it without hesitation. They led her

226

through the door and toward the staircase with Alex and Quint following.

When they entered the room, Mabel was astonished at how large and lovely it was. "Doctor, this will do nicely. It's beautiful."

"I'm glad you like it," said Quint, placing her overnight bag on the bed. "Well, kids, we'd better give Mabel some time to herself so she can get settled in her room."

Mabel moved to the bed and laid her hand on the overnight bag. "I'll come downstairs as soon as I unpack my bag, Doctor. Maybe Gina will show me around in the kitchen so I can get acquainted with it."

"I'll be glad to help you cook the meals, ma'am," said Gina.

"That will be fine," said Mabel.

"Is there anything else we can do for you right now?" Quint asked.

"Not that I can think of, Doctor."

"All right. See you in a little while."

Mabel watched the door close behind them and chuckled to herself. In a whisper, she said, "You did all right for yourself, ol' girl. There'll be a lot of work here, but as the doctor said, the older two will help. And just look at this room! Sure makes that boarding-house room look shabby. You've never had anything as nice as this, or even close. Yep, Mabel, you landed a good one, you did!"

★ ★ ★

At supper that evening, Mabel proved herself to be an excellent cook, and the family was lavish with their praise. Mabel smiled and told them that part of it was because she had Gina's help.

After supper, Quint and Alex took Missy out to the swing while Gina stayed to help Mabel do the dishes and clean up the kitchen. While they worked together, Gina told Mabel about their home in Aurora, Illinois, and the details of her parents' death. She told her about the love Quint had shown them and how very much she and her siblings loved him.

When Gina asked questions about Mabel's life in Butte, she received only brief answers.

At bedtime, when Quint was with the children in the girl's room for prayer, Gina said, "Daddy, did I do wrong by trying to hug Mabel this afternoon?"

"Absolutely not, honey. You're an affectionate person and you were trying to make Mabel feel welcome. I'm sure she'll warm up to all three of you once she's settled in and gets to know you."

"I wonder if she's very affectionate to her grandchildren," Alex said.

"She doesn't have any," Quint said. "She

said she was never able to have any children."

"Oh."

"I don't know much about Mabel's background, of course," Quint said, "but maybe she's had some things happen that make it hard for her to show or accept affection. Let's give her some time and be real nice to her, okay?"

Three heads nodded.

Gina said timidly, "Daddy, now that we have a housekeeper, does this mean you won't be looking for a wife?"

Quint grinned at her. "Sweetie, I'm still wide open for the Lord to send me a beautiful, smart young lady to be my wife. We'll just have to leave that in His hands."

Gina nodded. "I don't mean to sound as if I'm not thankful we now have a housekeeper. Mabel seems nice enough, I guess, and she is a good cook. But I don't think she's mother material. I'm going to keep asking the Lord for a wife for you and a mother for us."

As the days passed, Mabel warmed up some to the children but in no way was eager to show affection or receive it. Seeing this, Quint assured them in private that in time it would get better.

Missy turned four on August 20 and was given a birthday party, with some of her friends from her Sunday school class in attendance, along with her Sunday school teacher. Mabel and Gina made her a chocolate birthday cake, which was Missy's favorite.

As August turned into September, there was little improvement in Mabel's attitude toward the children, though Quint found her an excellent cook and housekeeper.

He took Alex and Gina to the school during the first week of September and enrolled them. The next week school began, and both Alex and Gina loved it. They found that a number of the children in the school were members of their church.

At the close of the third day of school, Alex and Gina were walking home, and as they neared the house, they saw Mabel in the backyard beating on rugs she had draped over the clothesline.

When they stepped through the front door, they could hear Missy wailing upstairs.

"She sounds frightened," Alex said.

They left their schoolbooks on the bottom step and bounded up the stairs and into the girls' room. It was unoccupied. They could still hear their little sister wailing at the top of her lungs somewhere nearby.

"Sounds like she's in the spare bedroom," Alex said, and dashed back into the hall.

Gina was on his heels as he plunged into the spare bedroom. But again there was no sign of Missy. The screams were louder now and both of them looked toward the closet. A straight-backed wooden chair was braced under the doorknob.

Alex grabbed the chair, tossed it aside, and yanked the door open.

Missy was sitting on the floor, her eyes wild with terror and her pale face wet with tears. She sobbed Alex's name and reached for him, wailing, "I want Mama! I want Mama-a-a!"

Gina caressed her little sister's head, saying, "Sweetheart, Mama can't come to you. Alex and I will take care of you."

Missy's sobbing began to subside as Alex held her and Gina continued to speak to her in soothing tones. She was about to ask Missy why Mabel had locked her in the closet when they heard footsteps in the hall and suddenly Mabel appeared at the door, a scowl on her brow and her mouth turned down.

Missy saw her and ejected a shrill scream.

Gina patted her hand. "It's all right, honey. It's all right."

The woman stepped into the room and was about to speak when Alex said, "Mabel, why did you lock Missy in the closet?"

Mabel put her hands on her hips. "When she woke up from her nap she was crying for her mother. No matter what I did she wouldn't shut up. When I was scolding her, she ran from me . . . I mean, all the way down the hall and into this room. So to teach her to mind, I put her in the closet."

Missy was still watching Mabel warily and sobbing. Alex turned anger-filled eyes on Mabel and bit his tongue to keep from lashing out at her.

When Gina saw her brother's anger, she said above Missy's sobbing, "Alex, give her to me. I'll take her to our room and quiet her down."

Alex stroked the little one's wet face and said, "It'll be all right, honey."

Gina moved out of the room with Missy in her arms. Alex's eyes locked with Mabel's. She stood motionless, unblinking. He held her gaze silently for a few seconds, then wheeled about and hurried from the room.

Mabel snorted and stepped into the hall to watch Alex until he entered his own room, then went back downstairs.

When Alex had calmed down some, he moved down the hall to the girls' room and eased up to the door. He could hear Gina's voice but nothing from Missy. Tapping lightly, he said just loud enough to be heard, "It's Alex. Can I come in?"

"Sure," came Gina's reply.

The sisters were sitting on Missy's bed, and by now the little one had stopped crying. "Are you all right, honey?" Alex said.

Missy nodded and managed a weak smile.

To Gina, Alex said, "I'm not sure what to do about this."

"Me, either. I don't want to upset things for Daddy. It has helped him so much, having a housekeeper, but I can't stand to see Missy treated like that."

"It isn't right," Alex said. "Missy still has a hard time without Mama and Papa. She shouldn't have to be locked up in a closet because she's too little to understand everything that's happened."

"You're right. But maybe Mabel won't do that again, Alex. I really don't want to upset Daddy. How about we keep it to ourselves this time. If it happens again, we'll tell him."

"Okay, sis. We'll let it go this time but never again."

Gina looked into Missy's eyes. "Do you understand, honey? We won't tell Daddy that Mabel locked you in the closet."

Missy nodded. "We won't tell Unca Quint Daddy."

Gina Roberts felt as though she were magically hovering over the threatening gray waters of Lake Michigan. She saw the heaving sailboat and her parents and Frank and Elsie Higgins struggling to lower the sails lest the boat capsize — but the wind was so strong and the boat was bouncing so hard they were unable to accomplish their task.

She raised her eyes to the howling gray sky and looked out across the lake, her heart pounding with terror. The whole surface of Lake Michigan had been set in violent motion.

Suddenly, Gina saw an enormous wave coming at the boat.

"Mama, Papa, no!" she cried as the massive wave struck and turned the boat over.

She saw all four people fall into the choppy water. Her mother was screaming as she went under the surface, and her father tried to get to her. But part of the frame that held the sail struck him on the head.

Gina could hear herself screaming, then abruptly a shrill voice penetrated her nightmare, saying, "Wake up! Gina, wake up!"

As she began to awaken, she felt strong

hands gripping her shoulders and shaking her hard as the grating voice came again: "Come on, Gina! Wake up and shut up before you —"

"Mabel!" Quint's voice came from the open door, "Don't talk to her like that! Can't you see she's having a nightmare?"

Mabel let go of Gina's shoulders and turned to look at Quint. "I was simply trying to keep her from waking everybody in the house, Doctor."

"Mabel, you need to be gentle with her." Quint sat down on the edge of the bed and looked into Gina's mournful eyes. Her entire body was shaking. "Sweetheart, are you all right?"

"I was having a bad dream about Mama and Papa drowning."

Quint took hold of Gina's hands and looked at Mabel. "You go on back to bed. I'll stay with her."

Mabel glanced at the other bed. Amazingly, though Missy had stirred some, she was still asleep. There was no sound from Alex's room.

"All right, Doctor," Mabel said a bit sheepishly and moved into the hall. The swishing sound of her robe could be heard as she went to her own room.

Gina sat up and Quint folded her in his

arms. "Think you can get back to sleep?" he asked.

"If you'll hold me for a few minutes. The dream was really awful, Daddy."

"I'm sure it was. As time goes on you'll quit having these nightmares, I'm sure."

Gina was already getting drowsy. Quint held her a few more minutes, then kissed her cheek and tucked her back under the covers.

"I love you, Daddy," she mumbled, and was soon back to sleep.

13

The next morning, Missy was still asleep when Gina and Alex met in the hall to go downstairs for breakfast. As they started toward the staircase, Alex said, "I heard voices in the middle of the night. Do you know what was going on?"

Gina touched his arm, stopping him. In a low voice, she told Alex about the nightmare and how Mabel was treating her unkindly when Daddy came in.

"What did he say?"

"He told her not to talk to me like that, and I could tell he was pretty upset with her. She knew it too. She didn't stay long, but Daddy stayed with me till I was ready to go back to sleep."

"Well, maybe it'll get better now that Dad saw a little for himself."

"I sure hope so."

They descended the stairs and headed down the hall toward the kitchen. They heard Quint say from the kitchen, "There was no reason for you to talk to Gina like that, Mabel. Those poor kids have suffered some deep emotional wounds in the loss of their parents. Both Gina and Alex have tried to be brave through it all, and I expect you to show them some compassion and understanding."

Brother and sister stopped and looked at each other.

"Shall we go in?" Gina whispered.

"We'll be late for school if we wait very long. Let's talk kind of loud so they'll hear us coming."

Before they reached the door, they heard Mabel say something, but she cut it short when she heard them approaching.

Breakfast was uneventful, and when the meal was over, Alex and Gina excused themselves to go upstairs to get their homework. Quint came up the stairs soon after and motioned for Alex and Gina to follow him into his room.

When the door was shut, he said, "Gina, I want you to know how sorry I am that Mabel treated you so unkindly last night. I talked to her about it before you and Alex came down to breakfast. I assume you told Alex what she did?"

"Alex heard the voices last night and

238

asked me about it this morning."

"And I didn't like what Gina told me," Alex said. "Why is Mabel so mean? Why can't she treat us decently?"

Quint's eyebrows arched. "Us? You mean she's been mean to you too?"

Alex and Gina looked at each other.

"Have you two been keeping something from me?" Quint asked.

Gina cleared her throat. "Well, ah —"

"Come on. Out with it."

Alex took a quick breath. "Well, Dad, when I said us, I meant Gina and Missy."

"Are you telling me that Mabel has been mean to Missy?"

Alex bit his lip. "Yes."

"Tell me about it."

Quint was appalled when he learned that Mabel had locked Missy in the closet. His first thought was to fire her immediately, but he decided to talk to her first.

"I'm going to have a talk with Mabel tonight after you and Missy are in bed," Quint said. "I want to keep her if I can, but only if this kind of behavior stops immediately. If she admits she was wrong in the way she treated Missy and you, Gina, and promises that it will never happen again, I'll let her stay on. Otherwise, I'll have to let her go. I hope she'll have the right attitude. This family needs her services." He paused, then added, "Sound okay to you?"

"Sure, Dad," Alex said.

"Yes," Gina said with tears misting her eyes. "If we can get this problem taken care of, I would like to see her stay."

"Sis, I've been thinking . . ." Alex said, as he and Gina walked to school.

"About what?"

"This talk Dad is gonna have with Mabel tonight."

"What about it?"

"Well, I hope Mabel won't deny what she did to Missy or try to water it down so it doesn't look as bad as it really was."

"I hope she doesn't either. But if she does, I'm sure Daddy will still believe us."

"Oh, I don't doubt that, but I sure would like to be a fly on the wall when Dad talks to her tonight. I'd like to hear what she says."

Gina was quiet for a few seconds, then said, "How about two flies on the wall?"

"What do you mean?"

"Daddy will probably talk to her in the parlor. How about we slip out of our rooms and listen secretly?"

Alex grinned. "Good idea, sis."

That night, Alex and Gina left their

beds and met in the hall.

"Missy's asleep, isn't she?" Alex whispered.

"Yes. As usual, she was asleep within a minute after you and Daddy left the room."

They tiptoed along the hall and hunkered down at the top of the stairs. From that spot, they could hear every word that was spoken, since the parlor door was just below them and across the downstairs hall. The door had been left open.

Quint sat on a wooden chair in front of Mabel, who was on the couch. Her face was a bit pale as Quint said in a calm and soft voice, "Mabel, I want to talk to you about a couple of things, including the incident in the girls' room last night, which we talked about briefly before breakfast. Gina didn't need scolding, even though she was about to wake up the entire household. She needed love and understanding."

"But Doctor, I didn't know what she was dreaming about."

"I realize that, but if she was crying out in her sleep enough to awaken you, it had to be apparent that it was a nightmare. She needed love and tenderness, Mabel, not to be treated the way I saw you treating her."

Mabel's round features took on a stony look. "I was just trying to keep her from

241

waking up everybody else. You said you wanted to talk about a couple of things. What was the other one?"

"Your treatment of Missy."

"So Alex and Gina told you."

"Not as tattletales. It came up inadvertently. When I pressed them for details, they told me about you locking her in the closet. Mabel, I know you're not their mother, but if you'd try, you could be a little bit like a mother to these kids."

"I didn't hire on as a mother. I hired on as a housekeeper. If you want a mother for the children, Dr. Roberts, you should get married."

"I've thought about that very thing, but there are no marriageable young women in Bozeman."

"What? In a town this size? I can't believe that. There have to be some eligible young women here."

"In my mind, Mabel, eligibility goes beyond a woman being young and unmarried."

"Well then, why don't you put some ads in Eastern newspapers and get yourself a mail order bride? Plenty of other men here in the West are doing it."

"Christian women probably don't even read the mail order bride ads."

"Why not? Christian women need husbands as well as women who aren't Christians. You might just be surprised what would happen if you put some ads in those big newspapers back East."

Quint took a deep breath and let it out slowly.

Mabel stood up and said, "And you'd better put those ads in quickly, Doctor, because I'm quitting. I can see now that I'm just not compatible with the children."

Quint rose to his feet. "I'd like for you to stay and work on being compatible with them. You're excellent as a cook and housekeeper. If you could just learn to show some motherly compassion and understanding, I'm sure they'd respond, and —"

"It simply isn't in me, Doctor. It's best that I go back to Butte. My friends told me if this job didn't work out, they'd take care of me. So you have my resignation as of this moment."

Quint sighed. "Would you stay until I can get someone else?"

"That might take a long time. I'll stay a week, and that's all. Good night. I'm going to bed."

She started toward the parlor door, then stopped and turned around. Her mouth was pulled into a thin line as she said, "One week from today I am no longer here, Doctor." With that, she stomped out of the room.

At the top of the stairs, Alex and Gina made a dash on tiptoes down the hall. As they neared the girls' room, Alex whispered, "We'll talk about this later."

"Yes," she said, stopping at her door. "Good night."

When both were in their rooms with the doors shut, they heard Mabel's short, stiff footsteps moving down the hall, a brief silence, then her door slammed.

The next morning, Alex heard a light tap on his door and Quint calling his name in a hushed voice. When he opened the door, he saw Gina standing beside Quint.

"Daddy wants to talk to us together, Alex," Gina said.

Alex nodded and stepped back to let them enter.

Quint closed the door and said, "I wanted both of you to hear this from me before Mabel tells you. I told you I was going to have a talk with her last night. Well, Mabel feels that she is not the person to take care of my three children, so she's quitting in a week."

Eyes wide, Alex asked, "What are you gonna do?"

"All I can do is run an ad in the *Courier* and try to find another housekeeper. Until I can get one, maybe I can find a woman in the neighborhood who would take care of Missy on school days until you two get home in the afternoons."

"If you can't," Gina said, "I'll see if my teacher will let me do my schoolwork at home so I can be here to look after Missy."

"It wouldn't work, honey," Quint said, shaking his head. "You need to be there in the classroom. I'll come up with someone."

"But I'll go back to doing the housework and cooking until we can get another house-keeper."

"And I'll help her all I can," Alex said.

"I appreciate both of you for having such a good attitude," Quint said, hugging them. "Dr. Holmes is not feeling well and won't be at the office today. I might be late getting home this evening. Alex, will you run an errand for me on the way home from school?"

"Sure, Dad."

Quint took a slip of paper from his shirt pocket and handed it to Alex. "This is the new ad I want to put in the *Courier*. Would you take it to Mr. Crenshaw so he can start running it in the paper tomorrow?"

"Gina and I will stop there on the way home from school."

"All right. Will you also go by the post office and pick up the mail?"

"Sure will."

"Daddy, what will you do if no one responds to the ad?" Gina said. "Missy, especially, needs a woman to be a mother to her when I'm not here. I realize I'm too young to be much of a mother to her but I try. We couldn't ask for a better father than you, but Alex and I need someone to be a mother to us too."

Quint's eyes misted. He patted her arm and said, "I'm sure the ad will get a response, honey. And before I hire the next housekeeper, I'll make sure she loves children."

"To be honest about it, I was hoping Mabel would quit," Alex said as he and his sister walked to school. "She's just not a kind person, and I didn't want little Missy to suffer any more of her abuse."

Gina nodded. "I was hoping Daddy could bring about a change in her, but I guess there's really nothing he could do. I think we should keep a close eye on Missy till Mabel is gone."

"We will, but she's still alone with Mabel

all day when we're in school. I wish that could be different, but since it's only a week, maybe Missy can get through it without any major problems."

"I hope so. I know Mabel's leaving will work a hardship on all of us, but I'm sure we'd rather pitch in and work than to have her still around."

There was silence between them for a moment, then Gina said, "Alex, I've been thinking about something else that was said when Mabel and Daddy were talking last night."

"You mean what Mabel said about Dad getting himself a mail order bride?"

"Yes."

"I thought about that before I went to sleep last night. Dad didn't show any interest at all. From what he said, he doesn't think Christian women read the mail order bride ads."

"Uh-huh. But I have to agree with Mabel. Christian women need husbands too."

"That's for sure. But from what Dad said last night, I'm sure he'll never advertise for one."

Sadness showed in Gina's eyes. "You're right. He won't."

When school let out that afternoon, Alex

and Gina headed down Main Street toward the newspaper office.

"Alex," Gina said, "something came to my mind today during quiet study time while I was doing my geography lesson."

"What was that?"

"I was thinking about what Daddy said last night, that Christian women probably don't read the mail order bride ads."

"Mmm-hmm."

"My geography lesson was on Arizona Territory, and that made me think of Cleora Matison. Remember?"

"Sure, I remember," Alex said. "About six months after she answered that ad and went to Arizona, she brought her husband to Aurora to meet her family."

"And do you remember how happy Cleora and her husband were?"

"I remember Cleora's parents talking to Papa and Mama about how happy they were that the Lord had led so wonderfully in their daughter's life."

They entered the *Courier* office and were greeted by Jessie Holcomb. "Hello, Gina, Alex. Something I can do for you?"

"Yes, ma'am," Alex said. "I need to see Mr. Crenshaw. Dad wants to put an advertisement in the paper."

Jessie glanced behind her, noting that

Donald Crenshaw was alone at his desk, working on an article to be published in the next edition.

"Mr. Crenshaw," she called.

The editor-in-chief looked up. "Yes?"

"Alex Roberts needs to see you."

A smile spread over the man's face. "Certainly. Come on over, Alex. How are you, Gina?"

"Just fine, sir."

While Alex was at Donald Crenshaw's desk, Gina excused herself to Jessie and began strolling around the large office. Near the front entrance she saw a stack of brightly colored brochures with the bold heading: HORTON PUBLISHING COMPANY. She picked one up and began to read. A small seed of an idea made its way into her mind. She pondered it a moment, then shook her head and quickly dismissed it. She found the contents quite interesting, however, and continued reading.

Alex stepped up beside her and said, "Okay, sis. All done. Let's head for the post office."

Gina held up the brochure and said, "Mrs. Holcomb, these brochures are free for the taking, aren't they?"

"Sure are, honey."

When they were on the boardwalk, Alex

said, "What's that brochure about?"

"See the name on it?"

"Horton Publishing Company. Who are they?"

"The company who owns the *Bozeman Courier.*"

"I thought Mr. Crenshaw owned it."

"It says in here that he's editor-in-chief, but that's all. Horton Publishing Company is based in New York City, and they own a bunch of newspapers around the United States. This brochure gives the name and address for each one, along with the names of their top executives. There are fourteen of them, mostly in major cities back East, see: Boston, Portland, Atlanta, New Orleans. The rest are in Ohio, New Jersey, Delaware, and Pennsylvania. And two more newspapers will be starting soon, one in San Francisco and the other in Portland, Oregon."

"Sounds like the Horton company is doing pretty good," Alex said. "This seems to really interest you. What are you getting at?"

"Oh, nothing," Gina replied. "I just thought it was interesting."

They drew up in front of the post office, and Gina said, "I'll wait out here for you."

Alex disappeared into the post office, and Gina opened the brochure and ran her eyes down the columns of newspaper names and addresses one more time.

The week passed, and Mabel Ritter left Bozeman as planned. There had been no response to Dr. Quint Roberts's ads in the *Courier*, though they were in every edition of the paper.

When it grew apparent that Dr. Obadiah Holmes's health was getting worse and he would no longer be able to see patients, he made the decision to stay at home and have his wife, Maggie, take care of him. Although Maggie had worked only part-time, she had done all the clerical work so that nurse Frances Myers could devote her skills to helping the doctors. With Bozeman's growth in population, the patient list was enlarging, and it was no longer possible for Frances to help out with paperwork.

Althea Martin, wife of Eldon Martin, the town's hostler, was hired to handle the office full-time, relieving Maggie to stay home and care for her husband. Maggie, in turn, offered to keep Missy on school days until Alex and Gina came by to get her after school. Greatly relieved at Maggie's offer, Quint took her up on it. Missy loved the Holmeses, and was quite happy with the arrangement.

Every day after school, Alex and Gina

stopped by the post office to pick up the mail, then went by the Holmes house to pick up their little sister and take her home. Some evenings Gina prepared supper, and other times, Quint took them to one of the cafés. Gina prepared breakfast each morning and did the washing, ironing, and housecleaning, along with her schoolwork. Alex pitched in with cleaning the house and hanging up the wash, and Missy "helped" Gina in the kitchen.

One evening after a hard day at the office and a couple of house calls at distant ranches, Quint was enjoying fried chicken with his family. He smacked his lips and said, "Gina, you sure picked up some good pointers from Mabel — but I have to say that you make fried chicken even better than she does."

Gina blushed. "You're kind, Daddy."

"Kindness has nothing to do with it, sweetie. It's just the plain truth."

Alex and Missy spoke their agreement.

Quint ran his gaze over the faces of his adopted children and said, "Kids, I'm so sorry there's such a load on you right now. I'm sure one of these days the Lord will send us a housekeeper."

Gina giggled. "Or even better, Daddy . . . maybe He'll send you a wife!"

14

The weather turned cold the last week of September, and with the cold came multiplied sicknesses, including influenza. Quint Roberts stayed very busy caring for patients in the office, plus making house calls, which sometimes kept him out late at night.

On the nights when Quint arrived home late, the children were sometimes already in bed, but Gina always saved him a plate of food and kept it in the warming oven on the stove.

On the evenings he was able to come home at the normal time, Quint prayed with the children as usual. Alex and Gina never failed to tell the Lord they needed someone to be a mother to them.

This touched Quint's heart every time and put a knot in his stomach.

On Tuesday, October 3, heavy clouds began forming in midafternoon. They blew in from the west and by the time Dr. Roberts was working with Nurse Myers on what was to be the last patient of the day, the sky was spitting snow.

It had been a long and stressful day, with the office constantly full of patients. Both doctor and nurse were exhausted.

With the waiting room finally unoccupied, Althea Martin told Frances Myers she would do the cleaning by herself and told Frances to go home. The weary nurse thanked her and went to say good-bye to the doctor. When she stepped into Quint's private office, he was going over a patient's record at his desk.

"Althea says she'll do the cleaning by herself, Doctor," Frances said. "See you in the morning."

He looked up with tired eyes. "You've done enough for this day, dear lady. Go home and rest your weary bones."

She managed a smile. "I'll just do that. Good night, Doctor."

"See you in the morning, Frances. If it should be snowing hard by then, I'll stop by and pick you up in my buggy."

"All right. If Walt was home, he'd bring me, but he doesn't get back from Billings till Friday."

"Hey, I'm just glad that husband of yours has a job again."

Twenty minutes later, Althea entered the doctor's private office and said, "The cleaning's all done, Dr. Roberts. I'll be going now."

"I want you to know how much I appreciate your doing it by yourself, Althea. Frances had a rough day."

"So did you. Are you going home pretty soon?"

"Soon."

Althea had been gone only a minute or two when Quint heard a tremulous male voice call, "Dr. Roberts . . . you here?"

Quint rose from the desk and moved toward the hall, calling back, "Coming!" When he reached the waiting room, he said, "Oh, hello, Jimmy. You look worried. What's wrong?"

"It's Pa, Doctor," said Jimmy Stillman, his eyes widening. "You've got to come home with me. He nearly cut off his right hand. He's bleedin' somethin' awful!"

"Okay. Try to calm yourself. I'll have to stock up my medical bag, but it'll only take a minute."

Jimmy stayed in the waiting area while Quint went to the back room. He returned shortly, bag in hand, and donned his hat and shrugged into his coat. "Okay, let's go."

Snow was falling lightly as Quint jumped

into his buggy and followed the frightened young man out of town.

It was nearly midnight when Quint arrived back in town. It had stopped snowing but there was a dusting of white on the ground.

Quint was almost asleep on the buggy seat, but the horse knew the way home and nickered softly when he drew up to the small barn and corral. Quint stepped down from the buggy and patted the horse on the neck. "Well, Ranger, I'm glad you stayed alert, anyway."

Quint unhitched the harness from the single tree and led the horse inside the barn. He gave him grain and hay and pumped fresh water into the tank.

He took his medical bag from the buggy, crossed the backyard, and stumbled up the steps and entered the kitchen, where a single lantern illuminated the warm room. He hung his coat and hat on a peg by the door and splashed cold water on his face at the washstand.

Then he opened the door of the warming oven and sniffed the delicious odor of fried chicken. He wolfed down the hot meal, silently thanked Gina for her hard work and thoughtfulness, and dragged himself upstairs. After looking in on the children, who were sleeping soundly, he made his way to his room. A minute later he doused the lantern and crawled into bed.

As his heavy eyelids closed, he said, "Thank You, Lord, for keeping my young ones safe and well this day. Please send us a housekeeper . . . or send me a wife. Give me the strength I'll need tomorrow."

It seemed that Quint's amen was barely off his lips when the neighbor's rooster crowed, pulling him from a sound sleep. He sat up in bed and yawned, stretched his arms and rubbed his eyelids. Light from the rising sun was brightening the room.

After a time of prayer, Quint opened his Bible to the place he had left off the morning before, Jeremiah 33. Quint's eyes misted when he came to the Lord's covenant with David: "If ye can break my covenant of the day, and my covenant of the night, and that there should not be day and night in their season; then may also my covenant be broken with David my servant."

"Thank You, Lord," Quint said, "that You always keep Your promises. And this promise back here in verse 3 . . . You know how many times I have laid claim to it, especially since the children came to live with me. 'Call unto me, and I will answer thee, and shew thee great and mighty things, which thou knowest not.' You have already come through so many times for me when I have claimed this promise, for which I give You my deepest praise."

Quint turned to Psalm 68:19 and said, "And this verse, dear God. What precious words. 'Blessed be the Lord, who daily loadeth us with benefits, even the God of our salvation. Selah.' How can I thank You? You not only supply our needs but You also load us with so many blessings. Father, use the abilities You have given me to mend the sick and broken bodies I will encounter today as a physician, and use me to help those who may be broken in spirit, and as a testimony to those who know You not.

"And again, Lord . . . my children need a mother and their dad needs a wife. Show us great and mighty things, and load us with that benefit, will You? Soon? For our good and Your glory. Thank You for always keeping Your promises."

With faith aflame in his soul and a fresh supply of spiritual strength for the day, Dr. Quint Roberts dressed, then went to awaken the children with a song of praise in his heart.

A week passed, and still there was no response to the ad in the *Courier*.

At bedtime that night, when Missy heard Gina pray about the three of them needing someone to be a mother to them, she began to cry, asking for her mother. Quint and Alex looked on as Gina took Missy in her arms, explaining one more time that Mama couldn't come back from heaven, but adding that she would try harder to take Mama's place for her.

The incident gripped Quint's heart. Later, when he was in his own bed, he said, "Lord, I beg You, if You're not ready to send me a wife, please send us a kind, loving housekeeper very, very soon. The ads in the paper have done nothing. My precious children need a mother figure in their lives. I cannot doubt that You have a plan of some kind for us. In whatever way You have planned to bring it about, please do it soon. I know Your Word says if we wait upon You, we will renew our strength and mount up with wings as eagles. You also say that the effectual fervent prayer of a righteous man avails much. I'm willing to keep waiting, but while I'm doing that, I'm going to keep praying for the housekeeper we need."

When Quint rolled over to go to sleep, his

mind went to his own need and desire for a wife. He reminded the Lord that there just wasn't anybody in Bozeman to pick from. Tears warmed his eyes as he said, "Lord, as Alex and Gina have said, even better than a housekeeper would be a mate for me and a mother for them. If You have that in mind, You'll have to bring her into this town and put a sign on her saying, 'There she is, Quint. I chose her for you.'"

As he was slipping into slumber, Quint wondered just where God would bring the woman from.

The next day, as Alex and Gina left the white clapboard schoolhouse, the afternoon sun greeted them from a crisp, cerulean sky. The leaves on the huge cottonwood trees had turned a bright yellow and were dancing in the gentle breeze. A light dusting of snow had fallen on the surrounding mountains the night before and the white-barked aspens with their brilliant gold leaves stood out in contrast against the deep green of the pine trees.

On the way home, Alex and Gina stopped at the post office to pick up the mail, then headed for the Holmes house to get Missy.

Alex was kicking leaves from the board-walk and noticed the pensive mood of his sister. "What're you thinking about?"

"Oh, our whole situation."

"You mean the fact that Dad's ads in the paper aren't producing us a housekeeper?"

"Mmm-hmm. I've been thinking that we should bring up the mail order bride idea to Daddy. Nothing else is working. Maybe with a little persuasion from us, he'd give it a try."

Alex sighed. "I don't know, sis. I'm afraid it would probably upset him. You know, after what we heard him say to Mabel about it."

"You really think so?"

"Yeah. His mind's made up about that subject."

It was Gina's turn to sigh. "I suppose you're right. We'd better leave well enough alone."

During supper that evening, Quint said, "Kids, you know that Dr. Holmes's health isn't showing much improvement."

A sad look came over Gina's tender eyes. "I feel so bad, Daddy. Dr. Holmes is such a sweet man."

"Is he going to retire now?" Alex asked.

"He has retired officially as of today," Quint said. "Our attorney has the papers completed. I've bought Dr. Holmes's interest in the practice and am now sole owner. I figure if Bozeman and the surrounding areas keep growing as they have been, within a short time I'll have to bring in another doctor to help me."

"You just about need one right now, don't you?" Gina said.

"Just about. For sure I'm going to be quite busy, even as I have been since Dr. Holmes hasn't been able to work."

"Daddy," Gina said, "are you going to keep on putting those ads in the paper? Nothing's coming of them."

"Have to, honey. I thought the Lord would've sent us a housekeeper by now, but He hasn't. All I can do is keep running the ad."

"Maybe the Lord isn't letting anybody respond to the ad because He's going to send you a wife," Gina said.

"I'd be very happy if He did that, Gina, but so far, no prospects have moved into Bozeman. We must keep on praying and trust the Lord to send the woman He wants, whether it be a housekeeper or a wife for me and a mother for you."

"I don't understand why God isn't answering our prayers," Alex said.

"Well, son, God always —"

"More milk, please." Missy lifted her cup

to Gina with a milk mustache on her upper lip.

Gina took the cup and said, "Missy, use your napkin and wipe the milk off your mouth. Go ahead, Daddy, you were saying that God always does something."

"I was going to say that God always answers our prayers. But He doesn't always say yes. Sometimes it's no . . . and most of the time it's wait. I believe His answer to us right now is wait. He does this for many reasons. One reason is to keep us close to Him. If He answered yes every time, we just might not seek His face like we have been these many weeks."

"That makes sense, Daddy."

"But you believe the Lord is saying for us to wait, not that He's saying, 'No, I don't want a woman in the Roberts house'?" Alex asked.

"Yes, Alex. But whatever His answer, it's the right thing and He'll give us the grace to deal with it. So we'll just keep praying and waiting. And in God's perfect time, He'll show us His will in the matter. Let's just be sure that in our hearts our motives are right and leave it all in His capable hands."

"We sure don't want to get ahead of God or get in His way," Gina said. "If we keep on praying, He will bless us."

"I feel very sure that the Lord is going to send us either a housekeeper or a wife and mother. And in my private prayers, I've told Him to send her in whatever way He chooses."

Gina sent a furtive glance to her brother. Their eyes met, but Alex wasn't sure what signal she was trying to send him.

At that instant, Missy's cup slipped from her hands, spilling milk in all directions. Milk went over the table's edge and began dripping on the floor. Gina dashed to the cupboard for a cloth and hurried back to mop it up.

Missy's face clouded up and her lower lip began to quiver as she looked at her father.

"It's all right, sweetheart," said Quint, rising from his chair to pick her up. "You didn't do it on purpose. It's all right."

The next morning as Alex and Gina were walking to school after leaving Missy off at the Holmes's house, Gina said, "Did you pick up on Daddy's words at the table last night?"

"You mean when he said 'send the woman in whatever way He chooses'?"

"Mmm-hmm." Gina took hold of Alex's arm, stopped him, and looked him square in the eye. "What if the Lord chooses to pass by the live-in housekeeper and send us a real mother? And what if the Lord has chosen to send us a mother by mail order bride?"

"Dad won't advertise for a mail order bride. You heard what he told Mabel."

"But what if we do it for him?"

Alex looked at her as if she had lost her mind. "Do it for him? What do you mean?"

"Just think about it."

"I am, and it scares me."

"Alex, listen. Remember the brochure I got at the newspaper office? It has the names and addresses of the other newspapers owned by the Horton Publishing Company."

"I'm aware of that."

"It's like the Lord placed that brochure in my hands for a purpose, Alex. It's perfect. I'm just sure the Lord is in this. He wants us to advertise in those newspapers for a mail order bride for Daddy."

Alex's face took on a sickly pallor. "Gina Marie Roberts, something's come loose inside your head. We could really get ourselves in deep trouble with Dad by doing such a thing."

"My head is perfectly sound, George Alexander Roberts. And I don't think we'd be in trouble with Daddy when he realized it was the Lord who laid it on our hearts to put the ads in the newspapers."

"Wait a minute! Where do you get that 'we' stuff? The Lord hasn't laid it on my heart to do any such thing!"

"Not yet, but He will. You want a mother for Missy, don't you?"

"Well, yes, but —"

"And for me?"

"Of course, but —"

"And how about a mother for yourself?"

"Well, sure, but —"

"And how about a wife for Daddy? When the Lord created Adam, he said it wasn't good that he should be alone."

"I know, but —"

"But what?"

"Well, what if we would get her here and Dad didn't realize it was the Lord who laid it on our — I mean *your* heart to put the ads in the newspapers? I've never seen him mad, but that might do it."

Gina set her jaw. "Alex, didn't Daddy tell us he prays that the Lord will send the woman in whatever way He chooses?"

"Well, yes, but —"

"I'm just sure this is the way the Lord has chosen."

"You are, sis, but I'm not."

"Okay, Mr. Stubborn Mule, what better plan do you have?"

"Well, none, but —"

"Alex, listen to me. What if I'm right? What if the Lord has chosen to speak to my heart about this and I don't obey Him? What if this is the one and only chance Daddy has for a wife and we for a mother? Do you want it to pass by us once and for all, forever?"

Alex swallowed hard. "Well, no."

Tears welled up in Gina's eyes. "Will you just ask the Lord to show you if I'm right?"

Alex blinked and looked at the ground. "Okay."

"Does it seem so far from being right?"

"Well-l-l . . . you've made some good points."

Gina smiled. "So I could be right, then, couldn't I?"

Alex brought his eyes up to meet hers. "You . . . ah . . . could be. But if we do this, we'd better go real slow and careful like. We'd better make dead sure it's the Lord who's telling us to do such a thing."

"Us?"

Alex's pale face went red. "Well-l-l . . . I want to do what's right. Just so I know it's the Lord leading." He took a sharp breath. "And right now, what's right is for us to run or we'll be late to school!"

They arrived at the schoolhouse, out of

breath, just before the teacher standing on the porch rang the bell.

At various times throughout the day, Alex thought about his sister's scheme. How could they advertise in those Eastern newspapers with no money? And if somehow that problem were solved, how would they deal with the letters that came in response to the ads? The women who wrote would expect a reply. How would he and Gina handle that problem?

And if they figured out a way to make it look like Dad's handwriting, what would they say? How would they pick the right woman? And if somehow they did that, and she wanted to come, then what? Where would they get the money to pay for her to come to Bozeman? Or would they tell Dad about it and hand him the letter from the woman he and Gina thought was the right one and let Dad take it from there? Or would they just hand him a stack of letters one day and let him choose which one he wanted?

Alex ran these questions through his mind again and again, and his stomach went sour. He told himself he would try to convince Gina that this was not the way to go. They should let Dad handle his own romance, courtship, and marriage.

15

When Alex and Gina Roberts left school for the day, they chatted for a few minutes with some of their fellow students, then headed toward the post office.

When no one else was around to hear, Alex said, "Sis, I really gave this mail order bride idea of yours some thought today and I think we should scrap it."

"But we both know Daddy won't put ads in the Eastern papers. I know the Lord has put it on my heart and you admitted I have some good points on the subject. You said I could be right, didn't you?"

"Well, yeah, but after thinking it over, I'm not too sure. I think we're meddling where we have no business."

"How about if we're supposed to do it and we don't? Maybe the Lord will say, 'Okay, Alex and Gina didn't listen to Me. Now they and their little sister will never have a mother.' What about that?"

"Okay, but what about this? We don't have much money. Sure, Dad gives us our allowance and we've put a little aside, but do we have enough money to advertise in more than a couple of papers? Or do we even have enough to advertise in any at all? We don't know what it costs."

"There has to be a way, Alex," Gina said with confidence.

"Okay, let's say we find that way. How are we gonna deal with the letters that come back in response to the ads? Those women have to have an answer as if it came from Dad. How will we handle that problem?"

"Well, I —"

"And if we solve that problem, we've got plenty more. How are we gonna make it look like Dad's handwriting when we answer back? And even if we figure that out, what are we gonna say? How will we pick the right one?"

"We'll have to pray about it, Alex. And —"

"Let's say we feel we have the right one and she says she'll come. If I understand the mail order bride system correctly, the prospective groom pays the prospective bride's way from wherever she is to wherever he is. How are we gonna do that?"

"I don't know yet," Gina said, taking a deep breath and letting it out slowly. "If the

Lord is leading us, He will make a way. Maybe . . . maybe at that point we'd tell Daddy what we've done, give the lady's letter to him, and let him take it from there."

"Sis, these 'maybes' scare me."

"Alex, I'm so sure the Lord has spoken to my heart about this. Let's take it a step at a time. Your first question was about the cost of putting the ads in the newspapers. Let's go by the newspaper office right now and ask how much it costs to put ads in the other papers owned by the Horton Company."

Alex sighed. "Oh, all right."

When brother and sister entered the *Bozeman Courier* office, they found only Mandy Towner. She left her desk and met them at the counter. "Hello, Gina, Alex. What can I do for you?"

"Ma'am," said Alex, "we want to find out what it costs to run classified ads in the other newspapers the Horton Company owns. Could you help us?"

"Why, yes," said Mandy, moving back to her desk. She opened a drawer, took out a card with printing on both sides, and returned to the counter. "This lists the different types of ads, then gives the basic cost per word. The cost varies, depending on whether you want some of the words in bold print or italics. If you run the ad for more than a week, it costs less after that. You know, like your father is doing here with that ad for a housekeeper. The prices vary some among the newspapers, depending on their location in the country. Those in the North are higher in price than those in the South, for instance."

"Thank you, ma'am," Alex said as she placed the card in his hand.

"You're very welcome," Mandy said with a smile.

When brother and sister were once again on the boardwalk, Alex said, "I hope Mrs. Towner isn't suspicious of us."

"She didn't seem to be. In her eyes we're just children."

They moved slowly down the street and did some figuring from the information on the card. When they estimated about how many words would have to be in the ad and how many editions they would want to run it in each paper, they were surprised at how expensive it would be.

"Well, that settles it," Alex said. "We don't have the kind of money it'll take to do this, especially if we put ads in several papers. Those in the South would cost a little less, but still, Gina, we don't have enough money."

Gina studied the figures on the paper and said, "How much allowance money have you put aside?"

"Four dollars."

"I have six, so between us we have ten." She used Alex's pencil to do some more figuring. "If we put an ad in only one newspaper, we could run it for a week with the money we have and still have enough left over for the postage we'll need."

Alex rubbed his temple. "Gina, even if this should work and we get letters from women interested in marrying Dad — what then?"

"We'll pick out the one we feel is right, then you'll write the letter to give the handwriting the masculine look."

"But my handwriting isn't very good."

Gina laughed. "Have you forgotten that Daddy's a medical doctor? They never have good handwriting!"

Alex chuckled nervously. "How are we gonna pick the right woman?"

"The Lord will show us."

"Okay, if we get one that wants to come and be Dad's bride, then what do we do? Would we confess what we'd done and show Dad the letter of the one we'd picked? Or would we show him all the letters? Or if somehow the woman we picked could come at her own expense, when would we tell Dad that she was coming?"

"Alex, we'll have to take these problems as they come. We can't cross a bridge till we get to it. The Lord will help us because this is what He wants us to do."

Alex sighed. "Maybe we should just let Dad handle getting himself a wife."

"Daddy will never pursue a mail order bride. But if we can get her here, and she's the one the Lord has chosen for him, he'll fall in love with her and she'll fall in love with him."

Alex touched Gina's arm and stopped her. "Sis, have you thought about the fact that by pretending to be Dad we're being deceptive?"

Gina's eyes filled with tears. "We're just trying to help Daddy, Alex. He wants a wife so very much. And Missy needs a mother in the worst way. And —" She sniffed and brushed the tears from her cheeks. "And so do I. Wouldn't it be wonderful to have a mother again?"

Alex took a deep breath. "All right, sis. Let's do it."

A smile of relief curved Gina's lips. "The first thing we have to do is to pick the newspaper we want to put the ad in. The way we can know if the Lord is guiding us is if we both agree on which newspaper without reservation."

"Okay."

"All right. Let's do it this way. Let's pray and ask the Lord to guide us, then we'll each write down the newspaper we think it is on a separate piece of paper. If we don't put down the same one, we'll eliminate the ones we have already used and write down another one. When we both have written the same newspaper, that will be the one we send the ad to."

"Makes sense to me," Alex said.

Emotion ran high as they prayed right there on the street for guidance. Then Gina took a slip of paper from her notebook and tore it in half. Turning their backs to each other, they each wrote down a newspaper from the list in the brochure.

In just a couple of seconds Gina said over her shoulder, "Got it written down, Alex?"

"Yep."

"Okay, let's compare."

When they placed the slips of paper side by side, Gina let out a squeal and said, "Alex! We did it! We chose the same newspaper the very first time!"

That evening, the Roberts family was just

finishing supper when there was a knock at the front door.

"I'll get it," said Alex, shoving his chair back and dashing toward the hall.

"Probably somebody needing our doctor daddy, Missy," said Gina, using a napkin to wipe her little sister's mouth.

"Dad!" came Alex's voice from the front of the house. "You're needed out here!"

Quint told the girls to stay and finish their meal, then headed for the front of the house. The girls could hear a deep male voice in conversation with Quint, but they couldn't make out what was being said.

Moments later, Alex returned to the kitchen. "That was Mr. Eglund from the hardware store. His youngest son just fell down the stairs at their house and broke his arm. Dad's riding in their buggy with them to the office so he can set the bone and make a cast. He said he won't be back for a couple hours or so."

Quint rode in the buggy with Ralph Eglund and his son. It was a brisk fall evening, and Quint turned his collar up against the chill wind. *I wonder what's going on with Alex and Gina,* he thought. *They seemed nervous at supper, and more quiet than usual. Didn't eat much, either.*

The buggy pulled up in front of the doctor's office, and Quint's mind shifted to the problem at hand.

Alex and Gina started doing the dishes and cleaning up the kitchen with help from their little sister, who was wiping off the table with a wet cloth while humming a tune she'd made up.

Making sure to keep her voice low enough so Missy couldn't hear, Gina said to Alex, "Since Daddy'll be gone for a couple of hours, now would be a good time for us to write the ad so we can get it in the mail tomorrow."

"All right, but what about you-know-who?"

Gina glanced at Missy. "How about we get her to playing with her dolls in our room, then we'll go to your room and write the ad?"

"Sounds good if we can keep her from getting curious."

"I can handle it."

"As soon as we get through here, I'll head on up to my room. Be sure to bring your money. I have paper and envelopes in my desk."

A quarter hour later, Gina slipped into Alex's room and said, "She's braiding the hair on that new doll Daddy gave her. It'll keep her occupied till we're done."

Alex sat down at his desk and Gina pulled up a chair beside him. Working together, they composed the ad, but it didn't sound quite right. They tried twice more but still were not satisfied with it.

"Tell you what, Alex, we're going at this wrong. We need to think like a grown-up, like Daddy would think."

"You're right. We've lived with him long enough to know how he thinks. Let's just really put our minds to it."

After two more attempts, they felt they had it. They read the ad and reread it and at last were satisfied. Alex addressed the envelope and Gina placed the money inside with the letter. She sealed it and let out a huge sigh.

Alex matched the sigh and said, "I'm exhausted. Since Dad's not home yet, I'm going to bed."

"Okay, see you in the morning."

As she closed the door behind her and headed down the hall toward her own room, Gina looked at the envelope and a happy smile graced her face.

On Saturday morning, October 14, Annamarie Taylor arrived at Atlanta's City

Orphanage and entered the office. Orville and Charlene Bradford were talking to a well-dressed young man who smiled at her as she came through the door.

"Good morning, Annamarie," Orville said. "Allow me to introduce you to Scott Denison. He's a reporter from the *Atlanta Herald Tribune.*"

The lovely brunette and the bright-faced reporter exchanged greetings, then he said, "Miss Taylor, Mr. and Mrs. Bradford have been telling people all over the city about the difference you've made here at the orphanage since you started working as a volunteer. I understand you've won the hearts of all the children and many have asked you to adopt them."

Annamarie's features tinted. "Well, I don't know that I've made that much of a difference."

"Oh yes, you have," Charlene said. "This is a changed place since you came with us."

"And because of that, Miss Taylor," Denison said, "I want to do an interview for my paper. Will you allow me to do that?"

Annamarie smiled and said, "Well, ah . . . yes, of course."

"Wonderful! I thought you would. In fact, I was so sure that I've got a photographer from the *Tribune* office on his way over here right now."

"A photographer! Oh, really now, Mr. Denison, you're not serious!"

"I sure am, ma'am. He'll be here by the time we've finished the interview."

"We'll make the rounds with the children, Annamarie," Orville said. "You go ahead and give Scott his interview. And Scott, if I understood, you want to get several shots of Annamarie with the children?"

"That's right. We're going to get several, and I also want to get one of Miss Taylor by herself."

Annamarie rolled her eyes. "Oh no."

Denison laughed. "Oh yes!"

The photographer arrived a few minutes before the interview was finished. He took several photographs of Annamarie with some of the children gathered around her. The last photograph was a close-up of a smiling Annamarie.

At three o'clock the following Monday afternoon, Annamarie was working behind the counter at Peterson's Clothing Store, waiting on a customer, when she saw Scott Denison come in. Lila Peterson stood next to her and was busy with the cash drawer.

Lila whispered from the side of her

mouth, "Just as Harry and I told you, honey. Here he is. And he's got the afternoon edition of the *Tribune* in his hand."

"Hello, Mrs. Peterson," Denison said and stepped up to the counter.

"Nice to see you, Scott," Lila said. "I suppose you want to see Annamarie?"

Denison grinned. "Guess she told you about the interview we did and the pictures we took on Saturday."

"Yes, and Harry and I think she deserves some recognition for what she's doing at the orphanage."

"She sure does, and the *Tribune* is seeing to it that she gets it."

As soon as Annamarie's customer walked away, she set her eyes on the reporter. "Hello, Mr. Denison. Do you want to see me?"

"Yes, ma'am." He lifted the folded newspaper. "I wanted to give you the afternoon edition hot off the press. It'll be on sale in about an hour."

At that moment, Harry Peterson came from the office at the back of the store.

"Hello, Harry," Denison said. "I was just about to give Miss Taylor her personal copy of the afternoon edition."

Harry moved up beside his wife. "Well, let's take a look at it."

Denison handed the newspaper to Annamarie. When she unfolded it, the front page came into full view.

"Well, will you look at that!" Harry exclaimed.

A gasp escaped Lila's lips.

Annamarie was startled to see the large close-up photograph of herself in the lower right-hand corner of the front page. Bold headlines lauded her as a woman who loved children and was making a difference in the joy and happiness of the children in Atlanta's City Orphanage. Small print beneath the photograph told the reader to find the full story on page 3.

"Here, Annamarie," said Harry, taking the paper from her trembling hands, "let me hold it for you."

The top half of page 3 had several photographs of Annamarie with different orphans gathered around her, plus a full article about her life, including the heartache she had suffered in the loss of her parents and the Civil War death of the man she was to marry.

The article told that in addition to working a full-time job at Peterson's Clothing Store in downtown Atlanta, Annamarie was a Sunday school teacher and devoted three sessions a week at the orphanage. Glowing words followed, which depicted Annamarie as a loving, unselfish young woman, who in spite of her heartaches and life's difficulties was able to rise above them and show her love to others.

When the last word had been read, Lila said, "You did a marvelous job on this, Scott."

"You sure did," Harry said. "It's about time this girl got some recognition for all her untiring effort at the church and the orphanage."

Annamarie's face tinted a deeper hue as she said, "Mr. Denison, I'm afraid you've flattered me here."

"Not at all. In no way have I judged you too favorably. You're a remarkable young lady."

"How well we know," Lila said. "We'll always wish we could've had her for our daughter-in-law, as she and Paul had planned."

"I do want to thank you, Mr. Denison," Annamarie said. "You did a beautiful job on the article."

Denison shook his head. "The thanks belongs to you, Miss Taylor."

When Annamarie entered her house that evening, only silence greeted her. She took off her coat and hat and hung them up in the foyer closet then turned and ran her gaze over the room and the staircase that mounted to the second floor.

"It's a cozy home, Annamarie," she said to herself. "But it needs voices and laughter and the sounds of an active family. The only sounds in this house are my movements and me talking out loud to myself, like right now." A smile parted her lips. "Oh well, guess I'd better quit daydreaming and prepare my dinner."

She grabbed an apron off the back of a chair at the kitchen table. While the meal was cooking, Annamarie set one plate on the flowered cloth covering the pine table, along with one knife, one fork, one spoon, and one cup and saucer.

"This is pitiful," she said to herself. "I have so much love in my heart to share with a husband and children. I'm blessed to be strong and healthy. Surely God has a plan for me where I can be used of Him to be a help mate for my husband and a mother who can raise precious children to know and serve Him."

When her simple meal was on the table, she bowed her head and thanked the Lord for His provision and asked Him to help her to be content in whatever state she found herself.

After the kitchen was cleaned up, Annamarie went to the parlor, where she had left the newspaper. Sitting down in her favorite rocker, she picked up the paper and looked at her picture on the front page. Studying it, she was glad that so far her thirty-one years had not brought any wrinkles. Maybe some prominent laugh lines at her mouth, but no more.

She turned back to page 3 and reread the article. It most certainly depicted the love she had for children.

Tears filled her eyes as she looked at the six photographs of herself with different orphan children gathered around her in each one. Her gaze settled on the one she liked best. There were six children, ranging from four to twelve years of age, flanking her on both sides as she sat on a wooden chair. A sweet little four-year-old girl sat on her lap.

While the tears spilled down her cheeks unhindered, Annamarie said in a choked voice, "Dear God in heaven, please let me marry and have children of my own."

After a while, Annamarie casually scanned the paper, slowly turning the pages. Soon she was at the classified section. She was about to turn the page and move on when her eyes fell on a black-bordered section labeled: Mail Order Brides.

16

Annamarie had noticed the mail order bride section in newspapers many times before but had never given it a second thought. She took a moment to let her eyes run down the section, noting that men of various walks of life out West were seeking brides — ranchers, farmers, lawmen, bankers, merchants, miners, and —

Smiling to herself, she said, "And even a physician. Hmm. Bozeman, Montana."

She started to turn the page when her eye caught the word "born-again." She slowly read from the beginning of the ad. Dr. Quint Roberts, who had his own medical practice in Bozeman, Montana, was prayerfully seeking a bride. He was thirty-four years old and had never been married.

Roberts had recently adopted his brother's three children, whose parents had been killed. In addition to seeking a bride, he was also seeking a mother for the children. The ad went on to say that Dr. Roberts was a born-again Christian and was seeking a born-again bride. A testimony of the applicant's salvation experience must be included with the reply.

Annamarie's heart pounded with excitement and her mouth went dry. This doctor was obviously a born-again man — the only kind she would ever marry. And the three orphans he had adopted needed a mother. Orphans!

Was this the Lord's answer to the end of her life as a spinster? Would He finally let her be a wife and mother?

Is anything too hard for the Lord? If God is in it, He will give the young doctor and me a genuine love for each other. I must act quickly!

Annamarie went to her small round-topped desk and laid the folded newspaper on it. She lit the wick of the finely etched glass lamp on the desk and raised it to get maximum light, then took out paper, pen, and envelope from the shallow drawer and opened the inkwell.

She closed her eyes and said, "Dear Lord Jesus, this ad is something I never dreamed of seeing. A born-again man wanting a born-again mail order bride. He seems like a very special man, Lord. And there's something pulling at my heart. If this is You leading, then please guide my every step. You said it in Your Word: 'The steps of a good man are ordered by the Lord: and he delighteth in his way. Though he fall, he shall not be utterly cast down: for the Lord upholdeth him with his hand.'

"I ask You not to even let me stumble, Lord, let alone fall. You know my heart and how I have prayed for so long that You would bring the right man into my life." Tears surfaced, and as Annamarie wiped them from her eyes, she said, "Lord Jesus, please guide and direct me. I only want Your will in my life."

She prayed until peace flooded her soul, then she dipped the pen in the inkwell. She dated the letter October 16, 1876, and wrote, "Dear Dr. Roberts . . ."

Annamarie began by telling about her parents and the joy she had growing up in a Christian home. She told him she was once promised to a Confederate soldier, who was killed in the Civil War. She had started praying that the Lord would allow her to marry a good Christian man, but until now, He had not brought that man into her life. She told Dr. Roberts of her love for children, and her special love for orphans. She told him that if he felt she should come to Bozeman, he need not send travel money.

She would cover the expenses, and if he wished, he could reimburse her. She then wrote a detailed account of receiving the Lord Jesus Christ as her Saviour.

"Dr. Roberts, I am thrilled at the opportunity to be considered as your prospective bride and the adoptive mother of Alex, Gina, and Melissa. I know the Lord will guide you in your decision about me. You no doubt will receive many letters and will need to seek God's leading. However, I await your reply with great anticipation.

"Sincerely yours, Annamarie Taylor."

When she was done with the letter, which covered three pages, she took a pair of scissors out of the desk drawer and clipped her picture from the front page, and the article and pictures from page 3.

She folded them neatly, placed them in the envelope with the letter, and sealed it.

On Tuesday, October 24, Alex and Gina Roberts left the school in the afternoon and headed for the post office. When Alex asked the postal clerk for Dr. Roberts's mail, the clerk reached into a cubbyhole and pulled out a single envelope. As he handed it to Alex, he smiled and said, "Not much mail today, son. Just this one letter."

Alex thanked him. As he and Gina headed

for the door, Alex looked at the envelope.

"Oh, boy!" he whispered. "It's from a lady in Atlanta! The first letter!"

Outside, Gina gestured toward the wooden bench in front of the building. "Let's sit down and read it."

They hurried to the bench and sat down, laying their schoolbooks aside. Gina looked at the upper left-hand corner and said, "Her name is Miss Annamarie Taylor. I like her name. Annamarie. Pretty, isn't it?"

"Sure is." Alex's hand shook as he took out the multipaged letter. Newspaper clippings slipped from the pages and floated downward. Gina quickly retrieved them and held them so Alex could see too. When Gina noted the name "Annamarie Taylor" beneath the large close-up photograph, she exclaimed, "Alex, she's beautiful!"

"Wow! She sure is!"

"Look at this picture," Gina said. "Miss Taylor has a little girl about Missy's age sitting on her lap."

"She loves children, you can see that for sure."

Alex read the letter aloud, stopping now and then to comment on something Miss Taylor had said. When he finished reading the letter, he looked at his sister and said, "This is some kind of lady, Gina. I feel like I know her already. She has such a warm personality."

"And such a sweet spirit about her. You can tell she loves the Lord."

"Yes. The way she forms her words makes me think of Mama. Did you notice that?"

"I didn't, but now that you mention it, I see what you mean. Well, should I read the article to you now?"

"Go ahead."

Alex let his eyes scan the pictures on the page while Gina read the article to him. When she finished, she said, "She really loves children, doesn't she, Alex? I'll bet she's a marvelous Sunday school teacher."

"The thing that really stands out to me is the love she has for our kind of children . . . orphans."

Gina nodded. "What more could we ask for, Alex? Miss Taylor would be the perfect wife for Daddy and the perfect mother for us and Missy."

Alex looked back at the pages of the letter in his hand. "Sis, I . . . I —"

"What?"

"Well, I don't think we need to wait for any more letters. You used the word yourself. 'Perfect.' She's the perfect wife for Dad. She's the perfect mother for us and Missy. She has to be the one the Lord has chosen.

And it sounds like she really wants to be dad's wife and our mother. Not only that," he said, his eyes sparkling, "but she's very good-looking! That's not the most important thing, but it sure doesn't hurt!"

Gina giggled. "That's the male in my brother talking."

Alex laughed and shrugged his shoulders. "And think of this, sis — the lady is even willing to pay her way to get here. She has to be the Lord's choice for us! He's already answered our prayers about the travel money!"

Gina was so excited she could hardly sit still. Happiness danced in her eyes as she said, "It couldn't be so absolutely perfect if it wasn't of the Lord, Alex. I know she's the one!"

Alex rose to his feet. "We'd better get going. Mrs. Holmes will be worrying about us."

Gina folded the newspaper clippings and handed them to Alex to place back in the envelope.

While they hurried down the boardwalk, Alex said, "I'd love to tell Missy about this letter from Miss Taylor. It would make her so happy. But we dare not breathe a word of it to her. Sure as anything she'd spill the beans to Dad."

"Yeah, she's just too young to keep a secret like this."

"We need to write the letter to Miss Taylor as soon as we get home," Alex said.

"Yes — before Daddy gets home. We've got to get it in the mail tomorrow on the way to school." Gina snapped her fingers. "Alex, I just thought of something!"

"What?"

"Remember when Daddy took over Dr. Holmes's practice, and Donald Crenshaw wrote the story in the *Courier*?"

"What about it?"

"He took that photograph of Daddy standing in front of the office door and used it on the front page of the paper with the article."

Alex's eyes lit up. "Yeah! Do you want to send that page to Miss Taylor?"

"She needs to see how handsome Daddy is, and it will help her if she can read about him taking over the practice."

Alex stopped.

Gina took two steps, then backed up. "What?"

"Dad treasures that article. What if he decides to look at it or show it to somebody who hasn't seen it?"

"Don't you remember? Mr. Crenshaw gave Daddy three copies of that day's paper.

He put his copy in his desk, but the other two are in the bottom drawer of the china closet in the dining room. He never looks in there. He won't know we used one copy to send to Miss Taylor. Oh, Alex, I'm so happy! Daddy's lonely life is going to get better and we're going to have a mother who loves us like Mama did!"

Brother and sister chattered happily as they turned the corner and hastened down the side street that led to the Holmes residence.

Gina stopped suddenly and put her hand out to stop Alex. When he halted and looked at her with a slight frown, she said, "We'd better get ourselves under control or Mrs. Holmes is going to ask us what we're so excited about."

A wide grin spread over Alex's face. "You're right. Let's just take a few deep breaths and calm ourselves."

When Alex and Gina arrived home with Missy, they took her to the girls' room and with little effort got her occupied with her dolls.

While Alex hurried to his room to get the writing materials ready, Gina dashed downstairs to the dining room, took one of the extra editions of the *Courier* in hand, and ran all the way to her brother's room. Breathing hard, she pulled up a chair and sat beside Alex at his small desk.

"Okay," she said, "let's talk about what we want Daddy to say to her."

After some discussion, Alex took pen in hand, dipped it in the inkwell, and did his best to make his handwriting look like that of a mature man. They talked over each line as he wrote and Gina kept a close check on his spelling and grammar.

Suddenly Gina said, "Stop for a minute, Alex. There's something else we need to put in here that we haven't discussed. Remember Cleora Matison telling Papa and Mama that when she wrote to the man she ended up marrying, he told her they would marry only after they both had opportunity to get well acquainted and fall in love? They wouldn't make a move toward the marriage altar until they both were in full agreement that the Lord had brought them together."

"Yeah, I remember that. Cleora told Mama and Papa how much it meant to her that her potential groom had said that. And I remember the man said in the letter that until the wedding he would see that she had a nice place to stay. I think it was a hotel."

"Right."

"I know Dad would do the same, Gina."

"Of course. I'm glad I remembered those details."

"Me too. I'm sure it will make Miss Taylor feel good about coming."

"But it does present a problem."

"You mean because Dad isn't gonna know that she's coming, so he won't have some nice place for her to stay?"

"That's right."

"Well, we need to consider that when we decide to spring this whole thing on him."

"We've got to keep praying about that. We'll have to time it just right. The Lord will help us," Gina said, rubbing her temple.

"He certainly is working everything else out, sis." Alex took a deep breath, poised the pen for use, and said, "Let's get it in the letter. We've got to word it just right."

"Okay. Let's go slow."

They discussed each word before it was penned. When they had that part just right, Annamarie was told that her willingness to go ahead and cover the travel expenses was deeply appreciated because it meant she could come sooner. She would be reimbursed upon her arrival.

Gina stopped Alex again, "She needs to know that the railroad only goes to Billings, and that she will need to book herself on the stage from Billings to Bozeman."

"She'd find that out at the railroad station in Atlanta, sis, but you're right. We — I mean, Dad needs to tell her about it so she'll know before she goes to the railroad station to buy the tickets."

"Mmm-hmm. Go ahead and write that in."

When it was done, Gina said, "All right. Have Dad tell her that he wants her to come as soon as possible . . . that he'll be waiting with great anticipation to hear back from her."

Alex wrote that in, then said, "Anything else?"

Gina read the last few lines, then shook her head. "That'll do it."

"How shall I close it off? 'Your loving future husband'?"

Gina slapped him playfully on the shoulder. "No, silly. You keep it very warm and simple like Miss Taylor did. Close it off with 'Sincerely yours' and sign it."

" 'Dr. Quint Roberts'?"

"Honestly, George Alexander," she said, slapping his shoulder again, "sometimes I wonder about you. That's too formal. Just sign it 'Quint Roberts.' "

When the ink was blotted, Gina enclosed the letter and the newspaper clipping in the envelope. Just as she was sealing it, they heard the patter of Missy's feet coming down the hall.

"Whew!" Alex said. "Just in time!"

17

Late in the afternoon on Wednesday, November 1, Annamarie Taylor sat at her small desk in the parlor and read the letter for the third time. It had been in her mailbox when she got home from work.

Tears ran down her cheeks as she said, "Oh, dear Lord, thank You. Thank You for answering my prayers. I know in my heart that You have chosen Quint Roberts and me for each other. I have no doubt that when we've had a little time to get acquainted, we will fall in love. It's all in Your wonderful plan."

She picked up the newspaper clipping once more and studied it. She was impressed with Dr. Quint Roberts. He had a kind-looking face and was also quite handsome. Smiling, she said, "Quint, you certainly didn't have to be handsome for me to be interested in you, but it doesn't hurt anything that you are!"

The clock on the mantel began to chime. *Six o'clock. The ticket office at the railroad station stays open all night.*

"First things first," she said aloud as she laid the newspaper clipping down and headed for the hall closet. Donning her hat and coat, she rushed out the door.

Upon returning home from the railroad station, Annamarie ate a quick supper, then returned to her desk in the parlor. She looked her tickets over and told herself she was being fair to both the Petersons and the Bradfords by giving them more than two weeks' notice of her plans to leave Atlanta for Bozeman. She would see about selling her house later if she and Quint decided to marry.

Taking paper, envelope, and pen out of the drawer, she began writing her reply to the man who had invited her to Bozeman as his prospective mail order bride. She told him of the absolute peace she had about coming and how thrilled she was that he felt led of the Lord to ask her to come. She assured him that she agreed with the way they would approach the situation when she arrived, and she would have it no other way. She was also very much looking forward to meeting Alex, Gina, and Melissa.

Annamarie gave him the details of her

travel plans. She would leave Atlanta on Wednesday morning, November 22, for Chicago. There she would board another train and head west. She was scheduled to arrive in Bozeman at approximately 2:30 in the afternoon on Sunday, November 26.

She closed off by telling the doctor she thought he was quite handsome, judging by the picture in the *Bozeman Courier.* This time she left off her last name and signed the letter: "Sincerely yours . . . Annamarie."

On Wednesday, November 8, Alex Roberts walked alone toward the post office after school. Missy had a slight cold and Gina had stayed home to take care of her rather than take her out into the frigid November air — doctor's orders.

As he made his way down Main Street, Alex's mind went back to the conversation he and Gina had had at exactly the same time yesterday . . .

"Have you thought about it, big brother?"

"Thought about what, little sister?" Alex watched a cowboy ride by on a beautiful white gelding.

"It was two weeks ago today that Miss Taylor's letter came. And not one other letter has come from a prospective bride.

Wouldn't you say that was a powerful indication that God has chosen Miss Taylor for Daddy's bride and our mother?"

"Can't argue with that. And now that you mention it, the fact that no other letters have come will make it easier on us when it comes time to tell Dad what we've done."

"A whole lot easier!" Gina said. "He'll be able to see God's hand in it, plain and clear."

Alex moved out of the cold into the warmth of the post office and waited for a man and woman to finish their business at the counter, then he stepped up and said, "Hello, Mr. Hickman."

Delbert Hickman grinned at the boy. He turned to empty the contents from the cubbyhole marked "Roberts," and said, "There's quite a bit of mail today, Alex."

When Hickman turned around there were several letters in his hands. Alex's eyes widened and he swallowed hard.

"Thank you, Mr. Hickman," Alex said with a forced smile and took the bundle in hand.

He moved to a table near the door, laid the envelopes on top, and began sorting through them. The first two were business letters for Dr. Quint Roberts. The third made his mouth fall open. It was from Miss Annamarie Taylor!

By the time Alex had sorted through the rest of the envelopes and found them all business letters for his father, he heaved a sigh of relief. Unable to wait until he got home, he tore open the envelope and read Annamarie's letter. As he came to the last line, he was so excited he let out a "Yahoo-o-o!"

He instantly noticed an elderly woman turn and eye him questioningly, as did Delbert Hickman. Alex pressed a wide smile on his lips and said, "Uh . . . some real good news in this letter right here, Mr. Hickman."

The postal clerk smiled and nodded, then went back to his customer.

Alex ran home and bolted through the front door. He stopped in the foyer. "Gina! Gina! You upstairs or downstairs?"

"In the kitchen!"

Alex rushed into the kitchen and found Gina scrubbing clothes on a washboard in a tub of hot, soapy water. Missy was seated at the table, drawing animal pictures. So intent was he on giving Gina the good news that he waved the letter and said, "Gina! Look what came in the mail! It's from Miss T—"

When he saw Gina's eyes widen and flash to Missy, he gulped. Clearing his throat,

Alex smiled at Missy and said, "Honey, I need to talk to Gina alone. Would you go upstairs to your room and play for a while?"

Missy's brows knitted together and her mouth formed into a pout. "How come you can't talk to me, too?"

Alex looked to Gina for help.

Gina was drying her hands on a towel as she said, "Missy, you know when sometimes you and I talk about girl things when Alex isn't around?"

"Uh-huh."

"Why do we do that?"

" 'Cause he's a boy and he wouldn't understand. That's what you always say."

"Right. Well, this time, Alex and I need to talk teenage talk. You wouldn't understand because you're only four. So how about going upstairs to our room and playing with your dolls?"

"Okay," said the little girl, smiling amiably and sliding off the chair. "When can I come back?"

"Alex will stop by and let you know."

Missy nodded and ran out of the room.

Alex wiped a palm across his brow. "I'm sorry, sis. It's just that I'm so excited about this letter. You'll make a good mother someday. You really know how to handle kids."

Gina smiled her thanks then looked at the envelope in his hand. "Tell me! Tell me!"

"How about I just read it to you?"

"All right, but at least tell me. She's coming, isn't she?"

"Yes! Listen . . ."

When Alex finished, Gina jumped up and down, clapping her hands. "Oh, Alex, November 26! That's only two weeks from next Sunday!"

"Yes! Eighteen days from now, the lady who's gonna be our mother will be here!"

Suddenly, Gina's hand went to her mouth. "Now we have to decide when and how to tell Daddy."

"Yeah. We . . . uh . . . do have to work on that, don't we?"

For a long moment, brother and sister quietly stared at each other. Finally, Gina patted Alex on the shoulder and said, "Big brother, we'll get through this. The Lord has planned every detail. He'll help us. He won't fail us now."

Gina went back to her washing, and the two of them discussed when to tell their father what they had done. When they had covered every option they could think of, they still could not decide. They agreed it was best to put much prayer to it before they came to a final decision.

On Wednesday, November 22, Annamarie Taylor stood beside the train she was about to board at Atlanta's railroad station. She held hands with Harry and Lila Peterson. All three wept as Annamarie said, "I love you both very much. Thank you for being so good to me all these years."

"And thank you for being such a faithful and excellent employee, Annamarie," Harry said, "as well as such a dear friend. We'll miss you terribly."

Lila embraced her. "We want you to be happy, honey, because we love you as if you were our own child. And . . . and I'll always wish that you could've been our daughter-in-law."

"Dr. Quint Roberts has no idea what a treasure he's getting," Harry said.

Annamarie smiled but could think of nothing to say in return.

Lila held her at arm's length and said, "We'll be praying for you and trusting that it will all work out. Please write to us and let us know, won't you?"

"I will," said Annamarie, blinking at her tears.

The conductor called for all passengers to board. Embracing Lila one more time, then Harry, Annamarie picked up her overnight bag and said, "I love you both." With that, she turned away and boarded the train.

She found a seat next to a window on the platform side and as the train began to roll she waved to the Petersons.

When the train left Atlanta behind, Annamarie found herself sitting alone. She eased back on the seat and closed her eyes, reliving her last moments with the girls in her Sunday school class. Fresh tears surfaced. Her thoughts then went to her last moments with the children at the orphanage on Saturday. By this time, the tears were trickling down her cheeks.

These past few days have been emotional ones, Annamarie thought. *I've had so many painful good-byes in my life. But I must not look back, I must look forward to my new life. What sweet peace I have!*

"Lord," she whispered, "this is the first day of my new life. I will not look back, for this is the day which the Lord hath made. I have no doubt whatsoever that You're leading Quint and me together. How wonderful it will be to be married to such a fine Christian man! And the marvelous bonus in it all, Lord, is that I'll be mother to three children. Orphans, of all things! Precious God in heaven, You've been so good to me! Yes, this is the day You have made."

Annamarie's mind went back to the passage she had read in her Bible that morning upon rising from bed. How suitable it had been. Deuteronomy 4:39 and 40. Having committed verse 39 to memory, she repeated it to herself: "Know therefore this day, and consider it in thine heart, that the Lord, he is God in heaven above, and upon the earth beneath: there is none else."

With her eyes still closed and the rhythmic clicking of the wheels in her ears, she said, "Yes, Lord! This day!"

She tried to bring the exact words of verse 40 to mind but they wouldn't come. She reached in her purse and took out her small Bible, opened to the passage, and read it in a whisper to herself: " 'Thou shalt keep therefore his statutes, and his commandments, which I command thee this day, that it may go well with thee, and with thy children after thee, and that thou mayest prolong thy days upon the earth, which the LORD thy God giveth thee, for ever.' "

Annamarie returned the Bible to her purse, eased back in the seat again, and closed her eyes. "O Lord," she said in a whisper, "what sweet peace You give when I yield my will to You."

The train arrived in Chicago on time and

Annamarie soon was on the Seattle-bound train that would take her all the way to Billings, Montana, before it veered northwest.

Until the train stopped at Chadron, Nebraska, Annamarie had been alone on the seat. An elderly woman got on and sat down beside her. She returned Annamarie's greeting, but soon showed that she was not interested in conversation.

When the train entered Wyoming Territory at dusk, the woman was sleeping. Annamarie had her eyes closed and was thinking once again about the passage in Deuteronomy 4:39 and 40. Working at memorizing verse 40, she thought about the words "that it may go well with thee, and with thy children after thee."

Suddenly Annamarie sat up and clapped a hand to her face. "Yes! Yes, thy children after thee!"

The elderly woman's head jerked at Annamarie's movement. She opened her eyes and looked at her with eyebrows raised in question. Annamarie smiled at her weakly, then the woman settled back down and closed her eyes.

A faint smile remained on Annamarie's lips as her thoughts went on. *Quint and I can have children of our own! My mind has been so wrapped up at becoming an adoptive mother to*

Alex, Gina, and Melissa that I haven't thought about that! Certainly we will be happy with our ready-made brood and wouldn't trade them for anything . . . but I hope the Lord will bless us with little ones of our own. I want our home to ring with the voices and laughter of little children.

"Lord," she said in a low whisper, "I know each little child is a gift from You, and I pray that the three we already have and any others You might see fit to give us will serve and glorify You. What an awesome responsibility! But I know You will enable Quint and me to raise them in Your nurture and admonition."

Annamarie pictured in her mind what the first moment would be like on Sunday afternoon when she stepped off the stage. A smile curved her lips as she saw the tall, handsome young physician moving toward her. Beside him were three children. Their faces were only a blur, for she had no idea what they looked like. But she could see their warm smiles, and in her imagination they darted ahead of Quint, arms open, and all three embraced her at the same time, with little Melissa squeezed in the middle.

When Annamarie had kissed their foreheads and told them what beautiful children they were, they stepped back and she saw

Quint towering over her, his face a bit flushed . . . unsure just how to approach her. Suddenly she had the same problem. Should she offer her hand? Should she smile and say, "Hello, Quint," and let him dictate what would happen next?

Her reverie was interrupted when the train abruptly cut speed. She sat up, looking around. The woman next to her was asleep, but most of the other passengers were sitting up straight, talking to each other about the train slowing down and wondering why. The next stop would be at Sheridan, but they weren't due to arrive there for another two hours.

When the train came to a stop, some of the men left the coach at both ends to see if they could find out what was happening. Other passengers pressed their faces to the windows but could only see the darkness of nightfall over the vast, open land.

Only a few minutes had passed when the men started filing back into the coach. One man said, "It's all right, folks! Nothing serious. There's just a huge herd of buffalo on the tracks. The crew is waving lanterns at them to scatter them. The conductor said we'll be on our way shortly."

Annamarie heard a woman a few seats behind her say, "Well, Nora, you just got your first taste of how things are here in the Wild West. Lots of wild animals roam these plains — not only buffalo, but horses, cattle, antelope, moose, coyotes, and wolves. Not to mention the cougars and bears in the mountains."

"Oh, I think it's exciting!" came Nora's reply.

Soon the train was on the move, and once again Annamarie eased back in the seat and closed her eyes. Her thoughts went to the upcoming Sunday afternoon once more and her heart fluttered as she contemplated her first meeting with Quint and those precious children.

Opening her eyes again, she looked out the window. Sparks from the engine were floating by, but beyond them she saw a black velvet sky with twinkling stars forming a dazzling coronet around the full moon. Her eyes were drawn to the rugged, snow-covered peaks of the Rocky Mountains bathed in the silver moonlight. She found the display of God's handiwork to be un-speakably awesome.

On Thursday evening, November 23, Dr. Quint Roberts and his children were eating supper together in the Big Sky Café. Quint took pleasure in the happy chatter between

Alex and Gina and noticed how quickly Missy joined in.

When the meal was almost over, a joyous Alex grinned at his oldest sister and said, "Hey, Gina . . ."

"Mmm-hmm?"

"Do you know the difference between a donkey and a postage stamp?"

Gina snorted playfully. "Is this another one of your dumb jokes?"

"Just answer the question, sis."

"No, Alex, I don't know the difference between a donkey and a postage stamp."

Alex chuckled. "I'd sure hate to send you to the post office for a stamp!"

Gina shook her head while Quint laughed and Missy joined in.

Unable to hold it in any longer, Gina burst into laughter and said, "That's a good one, Alex. Where'd you hear it?"

"Nowhere. I just made it up."

"C'mon, now, you didn't either. Who told it to you?"

"Ranger."

Missy shook her head. "Alex, Unca Quint Daddy's horse didn't tell you that! He can't talk!"

Quint laughed. "Well, even if you're not going to tell us where you got it, Alex, it's a good one."

Quint finished the last morsel of food on his plate, took his final sip of coffee, and said, "Alex, Gina, I want to ask you something. I've noticed that for the past several days you two have been happier than I've seen you since your parents' tragedy. The happiest you've been since you came to Bozeman. I'd like to know what has brought on this pleasant change."

"Why don't you tell him, Alex?" Gina said.

The boy's mouth sagged as he gave her a look.

Gina afforded him a sly smile.

Alex's mind was racing for what to say as he cleared his throat and finally said, "Well, Dad, it's really quite simple. You know we've been praying that the Lord would put that advertisement in the *Courier* in front of some nice lady who loves children and will want to be our live-in housekeeper, right?"

Quint nodded.

"Well, Gina and I have prayed extra hard when we've been together on the nights you've been late coming home. You know, after Missy has gone to bed. Well, even though nothing's happened so far, the Lord has given us a special peace in our hearts that everything's going to be all right. We really believe the Lord's going to send us a very special lady real soon. And since we have such peace about it, it makes us happy."

Quint chuckled, shaking his head. "I'll say this, kids, your faith is stronger than mine. I've just about given up. I sure hope you're right. I so desperately want a lady who loves children and will be a mother figure to you."

Missy's face lit up. "Is Mama coming to see us? And Papa?"

Quint reached over, sat her on his lap and wrapped his arms around her. Kissing her forehead, then holding her close, he said, "Sweetheart, Mama and Papa are in heaven with Jesus. Remember? And we've explained to you that they can't come and see you. But I'm your daddy, and I love you very much. And one of these days, Jesus is going to send a new mommy for you and Gina and Alex."

The two older children exchanged glances. There was both elation and apprehension in those glances.

18

In Atlanta, late in the afternoon on Saturday, November 25, Harry and Lila Peterson stepped out of their store after a busy day, ready to enjoy the evening and to be in the house of God on Sunday.

Lila let her gaze stray over the busy street while Harry was locking the door. Suddenly she saw a sight that made her gasp. Harry turned to see what had captured her attention and found her frozen in place, her eyes fixed on something across the street.

He touched her arm and tried to follow her line of sight. "Lila, what is it? You look like you've seen a ghost. I don't see —"

Suddenly he felt as if a razor were poised a hair's breadth from his rapidly beating heart. After a few seconds he was able to get a breath, but his voice was a tremulous whisper as he squeezed Lila's arm and said, "It — it can't be!"

Lila whispered, "It is, Harry, it's him! It's

Paul! I know my own son when I see him!"

Paul Peterson, having aged more than the fifteen years since he had left home to fight in the Civil War, was angling across the busy street, threading his way between buggies, wagons, and carriages.

When he reached the boardwalk he was weeping. "Mama! Papa! Do you know me?"

"Paul!" Lila wailed as he wrapped both of them in his arms.

"Son," Harry said through tears, "we thought you were dead! All this time we thought you were in heaven!"

For a few minutes, the Peterson family stood holding each other and weeping so hard for joy they could say no more.

When the emotion of the moment had subsided, Harry said, "We can hardly wait to hear all about what happened to you, Paul, but let's go home to do it."

"It's quite a story, Papa. Unbelievable, really."

"I already don't believe it, son," Lila said, wiping tears. "This is like a dream!"

When the Petersons arrived home with their son, nobody wanted to eat. They sat down in the parlor and clung to each other for a long moment, then Lila said, "All right, dear, tell us what happened."

Paul took a deep breath. "Mama, Papa,

I've had amnesia, so some of what I have to tell you is from what others have told me."

"Amnesia!" Lila said. "How — when —"

"I'll get to it, Mama. It all started on May 11, 1864. Our unit was fighting the Yankees on the banks of the Shenandoah River just outside the town of Front Royal. We were battling it out with rifles with the Yankees across the river. Our lieutenant had just sent a messenger to Colonel Seymour, asking for cannons, when the Yankees wheeled a half-dozen cannons up directly across from us and cut loose.

"The battle got bloody in a hurry. They had us pinned down, so we couldn't retreat to safety. I was crawling on my belly, trying to locate a few of my men who were no longer firing. All of a sudden I came upon a close friend, Jamey Pitts. The fellows in our unit said we strongly resembled each other. Not so much in the face, but we were exactly the same height and weight, and they said we even walked alike."

Harry and Lila were hanging on every word.

"Anyway, I found Jamey all shot up, but he was still alive and conscious. Shrapnel had ripped into his upper body, leaving what was left of his shirt a bloody mess. He was cold and in a lot of pain, so I tore away what was left of his shirt, tossed it into the river, and put my shirt on him. Of course it had the sergeant's stripes on the sleeves. I told Jamey to stay there and lie flat and I'd be back to get him later.

"I kept on crawling along the riverbank, looking for my other men. Cannonballs were hitting all around. I was probably seventy-five or eighty feet from Jamey when I happened to look back. I saw him, dazed and confused, on his feet. My reflexes went to work and I found myself running toward him to get him out of the line of fire.

"Suddenly a cannonball struck right at his feet and blew him fifteen or twenty feet from the bank. That's all I remember, for a Yankee bullet grazed my head. I woke up from a coma about a month later in a Union hospital in Baltimore. At least that's what they told me when my memory came back just a few days ago."

"You had no memory until just a few days ago?" Harry asked.

"Yes, Papa. They took me to Richmond, where I was able to talk to a couple of men who had been in my unit. They were shocked to see me alive. When we compared notes, so to speak, it turned out that the cannonball that struck Jamey disfigured his face, but he was wearing my shirt, which was still identifiable. So the Confederate army authorities thought it was me, and declared me dead. They presumed that Jamey had been captured and declared it so."

Harry shook his head in wonderment. "So the Yankees in Maryland have had you in your state of amnesia all this time?"

"Well, not really Yankees, Papa. The War's been over for a long time. It was just Americans taking care of an American who didn't know who he was or where he'd come from. They had no way of identifying me."

Lila wiped tears. "I just can't believe it. All these years my boy has been alive and I thought he was dead. I . . . I just can't believe it!"

"All this time to get your memory back," said Harry, still shaking his head. "It was nice of them to take you to Richmond."

"Yes, Papa. When I had talked to my two friends, the Baltimore medical authorities put me on a train to Atlanta and here I am."

Harry looked at Lila. "A dream come true, isn't it?"

Tears spilled down the happy mother's cheeks.

Paul cleared his throat gently. "I . . . I want to get caught up on what's been happening in your lives. And I want to hear about the church, and all. There are lots of people I want to know about . . . but there's one person in particular."

Lila set tender eyes on her son and said, "Annamarie."

"Yes. I've never gotten her out of my heart. I mean, when my memory came back, my mind was slow to come totally clear. The attendants in the nursing home where they kept me said I kept calling for a girl named Annamarie. It kills me to say this, but I suppose she's married and has seven or eight kids by now."

Harry scrubbed a palm over his face.

Lila sighed. "No. As a matter of fact, Annamarie has never married, Paul."

His face lit up. "Really? Does she still live around here?"

Lila raised a palm toward him. "When the news came to us that you'd been killed, Annamarie took it very hard. She grieved over your death for a long time. As the years passed, she had many would-be suitors, but none seemed to her to be the man the Lord had chosen for her to marry."

"Yes?" Paul said.

"Well, to put it plain and simple, son, Annamarie is on her way at this very moment to become the mail order bride of a Dr. Quint Roberts in Bozeman, Montana. She'll arrive in Bozeman tomorrow, in fact."

Paul's face lost color. "You mean I came within just a few days of finding her here?"

"That's right. She left last Wednesday."

His features twisted in pain. "I assume this Dr. — what's his name?"

"Quint Roberts."

"I assume this Dr. Quint Roberts is a Christian."

"Real fine one, from what Annamarie told us," Harry said.

"Good. Then he'll listen to reason."

Harry's brow furrowed deeply. "What are you talking about?"

"Annamarie and this doctor have never met, have they?"

"No," Lila said. "Only through the mail."

"Then she can't love him like she loved — *loves* me. She doesn't even know him!"

"But son," Harry said, "you can't do anything about it now. Like your mother just told you . . . Annamarie will arrive in Bozeman tomorrow."

"Yes, but isn't it true that they won't get married right away? Won't they give it some time so they can make sure they're really meant for each other?"

"From what Annamarie told us," Lila said, "Dr. Roberts is putting her up — I think in a hotel or a boardinghouse — until they have a chance to get acquainted and make sure the Lord has chosen them for each other."

Paul slapped a knee. "See? If she left here Wednesday and arrives in Bozeman tomorrow, it takes something like five days to make the trip. I'll take a train tomorrow and be there by Thursday. Certainly they'll take more time than five days to get acquainted. I can make it! I can get there in time to let Annamarie know I'm still alive and still in love with her . . . and that I still want to marry her!"

On Saturday morning, November 25, Dr. Quint Roberts ate breakfast with his little family, then drove away in his buggy with house calls to make before going to the office for appointments.

Little Missy was still asleep.

Gina was in a frenzy. She wanted everything to be spotless and perfect in the house for Miss Taylor's arrival the next day. The kitchen had to be clean before they tackled the rest of the house. Alex was doing his best to help, but both of them were so excited and nervous that they kept dropping and spilling things, making more of a mess to clean up.

While cleaning up flour that had been spilled on the cupboard and on the floor, Gina sighed and said to Alex, who was mopping the floor by the stove, "Maybe we'd better stop long enough to make our plans while Missy's still asleep. If she were to hear us talking about it, it could all be over before we're ready to tell Daddy."

Alex leaned the mop against the wall and Gina dropped the rag she was using into the pan of soapy water on the stove. They both sagged onto chairs at the table, and Gina dropped her head into her hands. "Oh, Alex, what if Daddy is so angry he sends us back to Illinois?"

Alex shook his head. "He'd never do that, no matter what we did. You know Dad better than that. You're just on edge."

Gina raised her head. "I'm sorry. You're right. I am on edge. Daddy would never do that. We belong to him legally, and just like Jesus has adopted us into His family, Daddy has done the same thing."

"Right. Now, let's talk."

Gina nodded. "Do you still think we should tell Daddy this evening about Miss Taylor?"

"No. I thought about it last night before going to sleep and prayed for guidance from the Lord. I think it'd be best to wait until to-morrow. After church in the morning. Since Miss Taylor is coming in on the 2:30 stage, we could tell him right after Sunday dinner.

We're usually done by 1:30."

"Okay. That way, he won't have much time to lecture us for what we've done. We'll need to be at the Wells Fargo station before 2:30 in case the stage comes in early, which it does sometimes."

"Yeah, especially when the weather's good like it's been for the past few days."

Apprehension showed in Gina's face. "Oh, Alex, I'm still afraid Daddy will be angry with us."

"Well, he'll definitely be shocked, and it may make him a bit displeased with us, but when he sees that the Lord has led us to do this, he'll be glad we did it."

They returned to their work, and soon Missy was up, needing attention. During the rest of the day, when they were out of Missy's presence, Alex and Gina talked more about Miss Taylor's arrival, still nervous about the initial blow when they would tell Quint she would be on tomorrow's afternoon stage.

Neither Alex nor Gina slept well that night.

At breakfast the next morning, Quint waited for the happy chatter and laughter he was getting used to. But it didn't come. He suddenly noticed that Gina's hand was trembling.

"Gina . . ." he said softly.

"Yes, Daddy?"

"Your hand is shaking, honey. Are you all right?"

"Oh, ah . . . it's nothing, Daddy. I'm fine."

"Then why are you shaking?"

"I . . . well, I just woke up feeling a little shaky this morning."

"I see. Has it got anything to do with what's also got your brother acting strange? The last couple of weeks you two have been so happy and carefree. Lots of laughter and joking. This morning you're both acting like you're about to attend the funeral of your best friend."

Alex sighed, looked at Gina, and said, "We might as well tell him now."

"Tell me what?"

Gina's eyes were wide and her face lost its color. "You . . . ah . . . go ahead, Alex."

Alex cleared his throat. "Dad, remember you noticed how happy we seemed and asked us about it?"

"Of course."

"And you remember that we told you we'd been praying for the Lord to send a lady who could be a mother to us, and we had peace about it? And because we had such peace that He was going to do it, it made us very happy. Remember?"

"Yes. I remember well."

"Well, Dad . . ." Alex's voice was strained. "Gina and I did more than pray."

Quint laid his fork down, folded his arms across his chest, and ran his gaze between the two. "So what did you do?"

With Gina's help, Alex confessed what they had done, giving Quint every detail, bringing him up to the minute, telling him that Miss Taylor was going to arrive on the afternoon stage that very day at 2:30.

Quint stared at them silently.

Gina jumped up from her chair, and said, "Daddy, I'll get Miss Taylor's letters and the newspaper clippings we told you about."

Alex sat and stared at his plate while she was gone.

Missy looked at Quint and said, "Are you mad at Alex and Gina, Unca Quint Daddy? They did something bad, didn't they?"

Quint reached over and lovingly pinched her cheek but did not reply.

Gina returned with the letters and the newspaper clippings. Quint moved his plate, took them from her hand, and laid them on the table.

"That's the first one, Daddy," Gina said, pointing to the proper envelope. "The clippings go with it."

Quint nodded solemnly, read the first

letter, then picked up the clippings and set his eyes on the close-up photograph of Annamarie. After studying the photograph for a moment, he then read the second letter.

By this time, Alex and Gina were standing side by side next to Missy's chair. The little one knew that something of import was in the air but did not understand what it was.

In his heart, Quint was asking the Lord to give him wisdom. He was perturbed at Alex and Gina for going behind his back and misleading this fine young woman who was on her way to Bozeman, expecting to become his bride. Yet, as he looked into their pinched faces and saw the apprehension in their eyes, his heart went out to them.

While a puzzled Missy looked on, Quint spoke to Alex and Gina in a firm tone. "Kids, I'm not going to scold you because I know how very much you miss your mother and need her. But I still have to point out that you deceived Miss Taylor. You were dishonest with her to make her think she was in contact with me. She's on her way to Bozeman right now, thinking I've invited her to come here with the prospect of becoming my wife. Now I must meet her at the Wells Fargo station and tell her the shocking truth."

Gina burst into tears and covered her face. "I'm so sorry, Daddy! It's all my fault. It was my idea. I convinced Alex that we should put the ad in a newspaper back East and try to get a Christian woman to come."

Alex began to cry. "No, it was my fault! I'm the oldest, and I should've told Gina that we wouldn't do it. But . . . but Dad, Gina and I just did what we thought the Lord would have us do, since it didn't look like He was going to send a housekeeper through the ads in the *Courier*." The boy took a shuddering breath. "And besides, we knew you were lonely and needed a wife."

Quint's insides were churning.

Alex took another shuddering breath while tears shone on his face and said, "Please forgive us, Dad. We're sorry we deceived Miss Taylor. Please don't be mad at us. Please!"

Gina looked at her father through a mist of tears. "Yes, Daddy, we're sorry. Please forgive us. Please don't be angry at us!"

Missy looked on, and because her siblings were crying, she began to cry. She slipped off her chair, sidled up close to her sister, and clutched Gina's skirt in a tight fist.

Quint moved to Alex and Gina, wrapped his arms around them, and said above their sobbing, "Kids, listen to me. I'm not angry with you. I do wish you had talked to me about it before you put that ad in the Atlanta paper, but what's done is done. Come on, now. Stop crying."

As the weeping subsided and Alex and Gina clung to Quint, Alex said, "Do you forgive us, Dad?"

"Yes, I forgive you."

Gina sniffed. "Do you still love us?"

Quint looked down into her reddened eyes. "Yes, sweetheart, I still love you both. Nothing could ever change that. When God's children do wrong, He doesn't stop loving us. And when we ask Him to forgive us, He always does. I'll never stop loving you . . . and I have forgiven you."

Sniffling, the little one said, "Do you still love me, Unca Quint Daddy?"

Quint bent down, took her into his arms, and kissed her cheek. "Honey, I could never stop loving you, either, but you haven't done anything wrong."

Quint then hugged Alex and Gina with his free arm, kissed the tops of their heads, and said, "This isn't the end of the world. It'll be all right. I'll simply meet Miss Taylor at the stage station, explain the situation, reimburse her for her travel expenses, and send her back to Atlanta."

Gina sniffed and said, "Daddy, could I suggest something?"

"What's that, honey?"

"Well, when you tell Miss Taylor what Alex and I did, maybe she would stay on as your live-in housekeeper and still be like a mother to us."

Quint shook his head. "I seriously doubt that she'd want to do that. After all, she's in for a mighty big shock."

Gina picked up the clipping with the close-up photograph of Annamarie, held it before him, and said, "Don't you think Miss Taylor is pretty, Daddy?"

"Yes. She's a beautiful woman."

"And just think, Daddy, she's a genuine Christian too. And . . . and she's been a Sunday school teacher for years. She loves children. And she especially loves orphans. Daddy, if you could talk her into staying as our live-in housekeeper, I'm sure she would love Missy and Alex and me and want to be like a mother to us. And Pastor Morgan has been trying to get more people in the church to become Sunday school teachers. I'm sure he'd love to have someone with her experience."

Quint lovingly cupped Gina's chin in his hand, looked into her eyes and said, "I will make Miss Taylor the offer, but I really doubt in view of the circumstances that she'll take me up on it."

"She will if God wants her to," Alex said.

Quint playfully cuffed the boy's chin. "Guess I can't argue with that. Hey, we'd better get moving or we'll be late for Sunday school!"

Both Alex and Gina heard little of what was being taught in their separate classes, for they were praying in their hearts that the Lord would work in Miss Taylor's heart so that she would want to stay and be their live-in housekeeper.

In the morning service, while the congregation was on its feet singing a rousing gospel song, Gina prayed softly, "Please, Lord, speak to Miss Taylor's heart. You could've kept Alex and me from sending that ad to the Atlanta paper, but You didn't. We were wrong to deceive Miss Taylor, and both of us have asked You to forgive us for that. And we know You've forgiven us. But Lord, we need her. We need her very, very much."

The song ended and the congregation sat down as Pastor Dale Morgan moved up to the pulpit and began making announcements.

Soon the pump organ was playing while

the ushers passed the plates for the offering.

Gina whispered, "Lord, a few minutes ago I said that Miss Taylor couldn't be more perfect for our housekeeper, but she also couldn't be more perfect for Daddy's wife and our mother. You could work in both of their hearts and —"

The congregation was called to its feet again, and Gina rose with them. While the song was being sung, Gina whispered once more, "Dear Lord, please speak to Daddy before he meets Miss Taylor and put it into his heart to consider her for his wife. She's already willing to be his wife, or she wouldn't be coming. Please, Lord. I'm begging You."

The song was over and when the people were seated, Pastor Morgan walked to the pulpit. "Turn with me in your Bibles, please, to the twenty-fourth chapter of the book of Genesis. Genesis, chapter 24. As most of you know, this chapter reveals God's hand in the lives of Isaac and Rebekah, showing how He chose them for each other and brought them together. I'm going to refresh the story for your minds by telling you what's in the first part of the chapter, then we'll begin reading in verse 50 and go all the way to the end of the chapter."

As the pastor preached his sermon, he

kept coming back to verse 66, and the words suddenly stuck in Quint Roberts's mind: "And the servant told Isaac all things that he had done."

Quint thought of Alex and Gina who had set it up for Annamarie Taylor to come and be his bride — and they had told him all the things they had done.

Moments later, the pastor read verse 67 again: "And Isaac brought her into his mother Sarah's tent, and took Rebekah, and she became his wife; and he loved her: and Isaac was comforted after his mother's death."

While the pastor preached on, Quint's forehead broke out in a cold sweat. Was God trying to get his attention? Isaac had never met Rebekah, but when they did meet, it was love at first sight. Because Rebekah loved Isaac, she was willing to become his bride. And because Isaac loved Rebekah, he took her for his wife. And Rebekah was the source of comfort in Isaac's heart after his mother's death.

Then this thought gripped Quint's mind: Isaac and Rebekah fell in love because God Himself had chosen them for each other . . . and He had used the servant to bring them together.

In his heart, Quint said, *Lord, are You trying to tell me something?*

19

Dawn's early light was seeping through the window at the Big Horn Hotel in Billings when Annamarie Taylor awakened in the big feather bed. It struck her immediately that this was the day — Sunday, November 26, 1876.

Her mouth went dry and there was a twisting in her stomach. She sat up in the big feather bed and said aloud, "Dear Lord, in just a few hours I'll meet Quint and the children."

Deuteronomy 4:39 came to mind. Pressing fingertips to her temples, she recited, "Know therefore this day, and consider it in thine heart, that the Lord he is God in heaven above, and upon the earth beneath: there is none else."

She threw back the covers, put on her robe, and walked to the window. What she could see of Billings's main street was still in gray shadows and there was no one about.

She let her gaze travel to the Wells Fargo station a half-block away, where she would soon board the stage for the last leg of her journey. "Lord, I'm just a little scared right now. Help me to lay hold on Your words. This day, as with all days, You are God in heaven above and upon the earth. There is no other true and living God but You . . . and I am one of Your children. On this day, which You have made, I need Your strength. I'm going to need a special measure of it when I step off that stage in Bozeman. Help me, dear Father. Help me."

A flood of golden sunshine from a cool Montana sky brightened the street as Annamarie stepped out of the hotel, overnight bag in hand. She had learned from the desk clerk that the weather of late had been dry and unusually warm for late November. The air was brisk, but its cool breath felt good as she started down the street toward the Wells Fargo office.

She had taken great care with her grooming and wanted to make the best first impression when she stepped off the stage in Bozeman. Her glossy black hair was swept high on her head and a dark green felt hat with a bronze-colored feather was nestled among the curls. Her traveling suit was also dark green. Black rickrack trimmed the hem of the skirt and the lapels of the jacket. Jet bead buttons fastened the jacket that ended at her slender waist. A softly draped white blouse hugged her graceful neck and reflected the glow on her face.

As she drew near the Fargo station, she saw the crew loading luggage and recognized her own two trunks as they were hoisted onto the rack atop the stagecoach.

"Lord Jesus," she said to herself, "we're together in this. No matter what the outcome of this adventure, I know You're with me. You will never leave me nor forsake me. Oh, I'm so grateful that I know You as my Saviour and that You are in control of my life."

Inside the Fargo office, Annamarie was greeted by the agent and introduced to her fellow passengers. Silver-haired Manfred Stokes was going to Butte, as were the young married couple, Clyde and Rita Everly. Annamarie would be the only passenger getting off at Bozeman.

Soon the agent ushered them out to the stage. The driver, a middle-aged man with slightly stooped shoulders, introduced himself as Mitch Bannister. The shotgunner, who was in his early twenties, greeted the passengers and said his name was Buck

Patton. He told them he would be on watch at all times, though no stagecoach had experienced any robberies or Indian attacks in several months.

"I'm glad to hear that," Clyde Everly said, "seeing as how it was exactly five months ago yesterday that the big battle took place at the Little Big Horn River right here in Montana. I would expect that the Sioux and the Cheyenne might be wanting to shed more white man's blood."

Annamarie felt a chill. She had given no thought at all to the possibility of danger from Indians. Or robbers, for that matter.

When the passengers were aboard, Mitch Bannister told them that since it was unusually warm they could ride with the leather curtains pulled back.

The stage pulled out of Billings and headed west. After a few minutes, Annamarie ran her gaze over the faces of the young couple and said, "How long have you been married?"

"It'll be six months on December 10," Rita said. "I was a June bride."

Clyde grinned as he waggled his head and said, "I guess that made me a June groom."

"And how about you, Miss Taylor?" Rita said. "Tell us about yourself."

Annamarie smiled shyly as all eyes were

on her. "Well, I'm from Atlanta, Georgia, and I'm on my way to Bozeman to become a mail order bride."

"A mail order bride!" Rita said, popping her hands together. "Oh, how exciting! Who are you going to marry?"

"If it goes as planned, I'll be marrying Dr. Quint Roberts. He has his own practice there in Bozeman."

"Dr. Roberts!" Manfred Stokes said. "I know him. He came to Butte to help our town doctor when we had a mine cave-in. Fine doctor, I'll say that."

"I'm glad to hear you feel that way about him, Mr. Stokes."

"I assume, Miss Taylor, that you have never met Dr. Roberts in person, only by correspondence?" Rita said.

"That's correct."

Rita shuddered slightly. "Being a mail order bride sounds romantic, but it would never work for me. If I were you, Miss Taylor, I'd be terribly ill at ease. I mean, to travel so far from home and marry a man I've never met." Rubbing her arms, she said, "Br-r-r-r! I couldn't do it!"

"Well, I said if it goes as planned I'll be marrying Dr. Roberts. You see, he's going to provide me a place to stay until we have time to become acquainted and find out if we're meant for each other. If so, then we'll marry."

Rita frowned. "Oh. I didn't know it was done that way. I thought the woman got off the stage and rushed off to a preacher or a judge for the wedding ceremony."

"I've heard of cases where they did exactly that," Annamarie said, "but Dr. Roberts and I are born-again Christians and we will do it properly. We want to be sure the Lord is leading us."

The mention of the Lord and the use of "born-again Christians" brought a coolness over the conversation.

Clyde Everly broke the awkward silence and said, "Ah . . . Miss Taylor . . . I've heard the term 'born again' before. It seems that someone told me it says in the Bible that if a person doesn't get born again, he can't go to heaven. Is this true?"

"Jesus said, 'Except a man be born again, he cannot see the kingdom of God.' "

"Why do I have to be born again?"

"Because you were born wrong the first time."

"I was?"

"All of us were. You may recall that after God created Adam and put him in the Garden of Eden, he pointed out the tree of the knowledge of good and evil and told

Adam not to eat from it. He warned him that 'in the day that thou eatest thereof thou shalt surely die.' When Adam and Eve took of the forbidden fruit, did God bury them that day?"

"No," Clyde said. "If I remember correctly, they lived long lives."

"So what could God have meant when He said, 'In the day that thou eatest thereof thou shalt surely die' except that they would die spiritually that very day? They were cast out of the garden and cut off from God. Later, they died physically because of their sin.

"The Bible goes on to say that Adam begat his children in his own image, which would mean that they came into the world dead spiritually like their parents . . . separated from God. This is why we must be born again to go to heaven. God won't let anything dead into heaven. That's why I said we were born wrong the first time.

"According to Scripture, when we repent and receive the Lord Jesus Christ into our heart, we are born of the Spirit. We are made children of God. Only God's children can go to heaven when they die physically. What you need to do then, is —"

"Thank you for the explanation, Miss Taylor," Clyde said. "We . . . well, Rita and I were brought up to believe differently. I just thought I'd ask about being born again since you brought it up."

Rita pressed a smile. "Yes, thank you. I . . . I hope it works out for you and the doctor."

Annamarie smiled in return and said, "Thank you, Mrs. Everly." She glanced at Stokes and saw that he had tipped his hat over his face and slumped down on the seat. Whether he was really asleep or not, she couldn't tell.

The Everlys huddled close and talked to each other in low tones.

Annamarie's thoughts went back to Quint Roberts and his adopted children and that she was drawing ever closer to them as the stagecoach rolled westward. She was feeling butterflies in her stomach with every mile that brought her closer to Bozeman.

Soon the Everlys settled back on their seat and closed their eyes. By this time, Manfred Stokes was snoring.

Annamarie let her gaze stray out the window. All she could see was rolling land covered with tawny grass that had been bitten by autumn's frost. She pushed her head out the window far enough to see what lay ahead to the west. The wind chilled her face, but she held the position long enough to take in the breathtaking sight of rugged mountains against a clear Montana sky.

She withdrew back inside the coach and laid her head against the seat. All was quiet around her as the others slept. The steady pounding of the horses' hooves and the rhythmic sway of the stage soon had Annamarie drowsy. She was almost asleep when she felt the coach tilt upward and heard the driver's whip crack as he pressed the six-up team to keep up their speed, even though they were now climbing.

Looking out the window, Annamarie saw the horses straining against the harness, heads down as they pulled the weight up the steep road. Once again, she laid her head back and closed her eyes. She tried to imagine that moment when she would step from the coach and she and Quint would first set eyes on each other.

Soon the Everlys awakened and began to talk about the beauty of the mountains that now surrounded them. They did not engage in conversation with Annamarie. She figured they feared she might start in on the new birth again. Manfred Stokes also awakened. He looked out the window for a few moments and saw where they were, then told them they would really get a feast for their eyes when the stage started down the other side of the pass.

It wasn't long till they reached the top of the pass and the driver pulled the stage off to the side of the road, drawing it to a halt.

"Just be a few minutes, folks," Mitch Bannister called down from the box. "Gotta let the horses catch their breath."

"This is really something to see," Annamarie said. "Georgia has some mountains, but nothing like these."

"Ah, this is beautiful country, ma'am," Stokes said. "That's one reason I live here. The other reason is I'm making a good living with my silver mine. I love it."

Annamarie smiled at him. "I'm glad for you, Mr. Stokes."

"I hope you'll love it here too, ma'am. I wish you a very happy life in Bozeman."

"Thank you, sir. I really believe the Lord has that in store for me."

Some ten minutes had passed when the driver popped the reins and put the team in motion. The crest of the pass was surrounded by tall rocks and for a few minutes the stage weaved among them, then suddenly the vast valley spread out before them.

Annamarie let her eyes drink in the beauty of the valley, bowl-shaped and held in the grasp of the surrounding mountains.

"Bozeman straight ahead, Miss Taylor!" Buck Patton shouted from up top.

"Yes!" she called to him. "It's beautiful!"

Her butterflies seemed to double in number and enlarge in size. She silently thanked the Lord that though she was nervous, she knew He was going to give her a happy new life in this breathtaking valley.

Although Gina had prepared a tasty meal, none of the Roberts family had much of an appetite and only picked at their food. To top it all off, Missy was a bit fussy and felt feverish to the touch.

"I hope you're not coming down with another cold, sweetheart," Quint said as he placed a palm on her forehead. "Gina, I want you to put her down for a nap right after dinner. I'll check on her when I get back."

"Can I go to the stage station with you, Dad?" Alex asked.

"No, son. It's best that you stay here too."

"But we were hoping that you'd change your mind and let us go meet Miss Taylor with you. I realize with Missy feeling poorly you couldn't take her and Gina, but —"

"I believe it's best that I handle this difficult problem alone, Alex."

"We just thought that if we were with you at the stage station," Gina said, "it'd help Miss Taylor to accept your offer of becoming your live-in housekeeper. It still might help, even if just Alex was with you."

"I understand your thinking," Quint said. "Yours and Alex's. But like I said, this is a difficult problem. It's got to be handled properly and I think I should do it alone." Quint rose from his chair. "It's twenty minutes till two o'clock. Since the stage could get in early I'll go ahead and harness Ranger to the buggy and head for the Fargo office." He paused. "And Gina . . ."

"Yes, Daddy?"

"Even though none of us had much appetite, that was a delicious meal. Someday you're going to make some very fortunate man a good wife."

Gina's pretty features tinted.

"Gina cooks almos' as good as Mama," Missy said.

Gina chuckled. "I know why all of you are talking like this. If Miss Taylor doesn't take Daddy up on his offer, you're stuck with me. You want me to feel good about cooking if I still have to do it."

Quint was at the kitchen door, taking his jacket off its peg. "That's not it at all, little lady. You're just becoming an excellent cook, and I want you to know I appreciate it."

Gina smiled sheepishly. "Thank you, Daddy."

Alex and Gina scooted their chairs back and stood up. Missy slid off her chair.

An anxious look captured Gina's face. "You are going to make Miss Taylor the offer to stay on as housekeeper, aren't you, Daddy?"

Quint grinned as he moved to Gina and put his arms around her. "I told you I would. But again, I have no way of knowing what her attitude might be when I tell her the truth about the letters. She may be so upset that she'll just want to head back to Atlanta."

Alex spoke up. "She can't go back right away, Dad, since the stage goes on to Butte and stays there through the night. We'll at least have her until noon tomorrow when the stage comes back through. Maybe by that time she won't want to leave."

Quint said nothing.

"You are gonna let us meet her, aren't you, Dad?" Alex said. "Even if she says she wants to go back, you wouldn't just put her up in the hotel and let her get on the stage tomorrow without seeing us, would you?"

Quint sighed. "Alex, it depends on her frame of mind. If she's angry, there's no reason for you to face her anger. I'll just put her up in the hotel and see that she gets on the stage tomorrow."

Alex wanted to ask what he would do if the stage was already booked full tomorrow but decided to leave it alone.

Moments later, all three siblings watched Quint drive the buggy out of the yard and head down the street.

"Gina, I'll go ahead and start doing the dishes while you take Missy up for her nap," Alex said.

"Okay. I'll get her settled, then I'll be right down."

"Before you go let's ask the Lord to work in Miss Taylor's heart and fix it so she's not mad at us, and that she'll take Dad's offer to stay and be his housekeeper."

A very nervous Quint Roberts walked into the lobby of the Bozeman Hotel and up to the desk. He smiled and said, "Hello, Tim."

"Hello yourself, Dr. Roberts. Say, I want to thank you for that salve you gave my mother. It's really helped ease the arthritis pain."

"I figured it had, since she hasn't been back in."

"What can I do for you, Dr. Roberts?"

"I want to make a reservation for your nicest room. It's for a young lady who's coming in on the 2:30 stage."

Tim picked up a pen from the desk and said, "Her name, Doctor?"

"Miss Annamarie Taylor. 'Annamarie' is spelled just like it sounds."

"All right. And how many nights will she be staying?"

Quint rubbed the back of his neck. "Well . . . that's kind of up in the air right now. It'll be tonight for sure, and if our plans change she'll need the room a little longer. I'll let you know as soon as I know for sure about the plans."

"All right. I'm putting Miss Taylor in room 301. It faces the street on the south side. It's furnished elegantly and gets sunshine most of the day."

"Sounds fine, Tim. I'll be back with the lady in a little while."

Moments later, an even more nervous Quint Roberts hauled the buggy to a halt at the hitching rail in front of the Wells Fargo office. He took out his pocket watch and checked the time. 2:23. He moved to the front of the building and leaned against the wall by the door to wait for the stage's arrival.

Main Street was experiencing its usual Sunday quietness. There was no traffic at all and no one was on the boardwalk.

Suddenly the peaceful quiet was disturbed by the sound of pounding hooves and the rattle of harness. The stagecoach was just rounding the corner a block away. Quint's stomach lurched and his hands went clammy. In spite of the cool air, sweat beaded his brow. He lifted his hat and sleeved away the moisture.

He heard footsteps inside the office, then the door opened and Fargo agent Will Hankins stepped out.

"Well, howdy, Doc," Hankins said. "You waitin' for somebody to come in on the stage?"

"Ah . . . yes, I am."

"Well, according to my records, only one passenger's getting off here. The rest are goin' on to Butte. I hope that one passenger is the person you're goin' to meet."

"If her name is Annamarie Taylor, she is."

Hankins grinned. "That's her name, all right."

Quint's heart was banging his ribs as the stage rolled to a stop.

Will Hankins looked up to the box and said, "Howdy, Mitch, Buck. Have a good trip?"

Both men were swinging their legs over the side as Mitch Bannister said, "Uneventful, Will. The kind we like."

Quint took a couple of steps closer to the

stage, his heart in his throat and his breath coming with difficulty.

Hankins stepped up to the stagecoach door and opened it to look inside. "Which one of you ladies is Miss Taylor?"

A sweet voice said, "I am, sir."

"I'm Will Hankins, ma'am. The Fargo agent here." He offered his hand to help her out.

Quint took two more steps toward the stage, tried to swallow the lump lodged in his throat, and painted a smile on his face.

20

"Thank you, sir," Annamarie said as Will Hankins took her hand and she stepped out of the coach with her black wool coat draped over her other arm. When her feet touched ground, she saw the tall doctor standing close by. He was smiling at her. She told herself he looked exactly like the photograph from the newspaper clipping, which she still carried in her purse.

When their eyes locked, an indescribable attraction rushed through Annamarie. Her lips formed a winsome smile against the smoothness of her face, and the ivory color of her features turned to pure rose. In those few seconds she thought of all the years of loneliness and emptiness, and the words God had spoken to Abraham echoed in her mind: "Is anything too hard for the LORD?"

The same attraction to Annamarie was rushing through Quint. Though he had studied her pictures from the newspaper clippings, seeing her in person did something to his heart. There was a strange magnetism between them that he had never experienced before. He could see it in her eyes and feel it in his heart.

Her eyes. Yes, there was something in her eyes that went even deeper than the magnetism the two of them were feeling . . . something Quint could not put into words. Suddenly it was as if the Lord said to him: "There she is, Quint. I chose her for you and she's all yours." Words from the Bible ran through his mind: "Isaac took Rebekah, and she became his wife; and he loved her."

"Annamarie . . ." Quint said as he stepped up to her.

Her smile warmed his heart as she offered her hand and said his name.

He took her hand gently in his. "I'm so glad you're here."

"Me too."

"How many pieces of luggage do you have?" he asked.

"Two trunks and an overnight bag."

"Let me take you to my buggy, then I'll see that your luggage gets loaded as soon as the crew takes it down from the rack."

"All right," she said softly.

"I have a room reserved for you at the

Bozeman Hotel. You'll find it quite comfortable."

"Thank you." She ran her gaze over the buggy, then looked around. "The children didn't come with you?"

"Oh . . . ah . . . no." Quint read the disappointment in Annamarie's eyes. "Missy had a cold a short time ago and was a bit feverish when we got home from church today. She may be coming down with another one. I had Gina put her down for a nap. And, of course, if I'd let Alex come by himself and he got to meet you before the girls did, that wouldn't have gone over well at all."

"We wouldn't want that, now, would we?" she said with a grin. "So Melissa is called Missy?"

"She was given that nickname when she was just a baby. My brother, Philip — her real father — gave it to her."

"I see. Well, it's a cute name. And I imagine she's a cute little girl."

"Oh, she is! And she's looking forward to meeting you. Alex and Gina are too, of course."

"I'm sorry Missy's not feeling well."

"Well, at least we have a family doctor who can give her the right care."

Annamarie chuckled.

Quint helped her into the buggy and told

her he would be right back. She watched him take long strides toward the stagecoach where Mitch Bannister and Buck Patton were now lowering her luggage from the rack. A moment later, Quint and the crew arrived with the trunks and overnight bag and loaded them in the rear of the buggy. Bannister and Patton bid her good-bye and headed toward the Fargo office.

When Quint climbed in beside her, he noted that she had put her coat over her shoulders. "Looks like we've got some snow headed this way," he said.

"Mmm-hmm. I was surprised to find it so warm when I arrived in Montana. I mean, for late November."

"It was rare, believe me. Are you hungry?"

She warmed him once again with her smile. "I haven't had anything to eat since breakfast, so I could use a meal."

"There's a nice restaurant at the hotel," Quint said, putting Ranger into motion. "I'll see that you have a good meal, then I'll get you situated in your room."

Annamarie was pleased to see that the hotel was indeed quite nice.

Quint guided her into the dining room, where the host met them and smiled at Quint. "Hello, Dr. Roberts. How nice to see you. And who's this lovely lady? I don't believe I've seen her before."

"This is Miss Annamarie Taylor from Atlanta. Annamarie, this is Leo Genova, the finest restaurant host this side of the wide Missouri."

"Pleased to meet you, Mr. Genova."

Leo did a slight bow. "The pleasure is mine, ma'am."

As Leo led the couple to a table, Annamarie noticed that he had a decided limp.

Quint noticed the direction of her gaze, and when they were seated, he said, "I did surgery on him a few months ago."

"Oh?"

"With the Lord's help I was able to save his left leg when it appeared at first that it would have to be amputated. He was crossing the street one day when a couple of gunfighters squared off and began shooting at each other. The noise of the guns spooked a team of horses hitched to a wagon. They bolted and Leo couldn't get out of the way. The wagon was loaded with grain, and it ran over his left leg and crushed it pretty bad."

"Oh, how awful. I've heard about the gunfighters here in the West. Does this happen a lot in Bozeman?"

"Not real often. Maybe four or five times a year. It's just too bad that Leo happened to be on the street at that particular time on that particular day."

"I'm glad you were able to save his leg. It must be very satisfying to be a physician and surgeon."

"Probably no more satisfying than the volunteer work you did in Atlanta at the orphanage plus teaching that Sunday school class for so many years."

"They were both very satisfying, but what it appears the Lord has for me here in Bozeman will be even more so."

Quint felt a cold ball settle in his stomach, and with it a strained expression etched itself on his face, which he instantly tried to hide.

However, it did not escape Annamarie's notice, and a shiver of apprehension traveled down her spine. *I must be imagining things,* she thought. *I'm just nervous. This is a monumental, life-changing decision for both of us, and it will take time. Annamarie, just try to relax and let God have control.*

She picked up her menu and turned back to Quint as he was saying, "I've already eaten with the children, but I'll have coffee while you eat."

Annamarie nodded and opened the menu.

The waitress appeared a moment later,

pencil and pad in hand. "Hello, Dr. Roberts," she said, smiling warmly. "And good afternoon, ma'am."

"How are you, Darlene?" Quint said.

"Just fine, Doctor, but if I wasn't, I know where I can find the best physician in these parts."

Quint grinned. "Darlene, I want you to meet Miss Annamarie Taylor. She's from Atlanta, Georgia."

"Welcome to Bozeman, Miss Taylor," Darlene said. "Now, what would you folks like to order?"

When they had given Darlene their order, Quint said, "I imagine the trip has tired you out."

"Well, yes, it has been quite wearying, but I enjoyed it very much. I've never been west of the Mississippi River."

"Really?"

"Mmm-hmm. But I've already fallen in love with the West. I find the wide, open spaces and those magnificent mountains absolutely fascinating."

"Same thing happened to me when I came here. It's wonderful country."

Darlene appeared with cups for both of them, poured the coffee, and was gone again.

Annamarie let her gaze take in the other

customers in the restaurant. Once again she caught the strained expression on Quint's features when her eyes came back to him.

"Tell me about each of the children, Quint," she said. "I want to know as much as I can before I meet them."

He spoke briefly of each one, telling her their basic traits and the things he loved most about them.

Annamarie then asked what had happened to his brother and sister-in-law. An expression of deep sadness hovered in his eyes as he explained how Philip and Elaine were drowned. He then told her of his Christian mother dying young, and of how he had the joy of leading his father to Christ just before he died only a short time before Philip and Elaine drowned.

Annamarie's meal arrived, and Quint led them in a prayer of thanks for the food and for Annamarie's safe arrival.

"You've had some heart-wrenching tragedies in your life too, Quint," Annamarie said. "I'm glad to see that you haven't let them embitter you, as often happens."

Quint looked down at his hands resting on the table and said, "It's been an emotionally rough time, Annamarie. But God, in His wisdom, doeth all things well. I'm so thankful that Papa got saved. Now I know he and Mama and Philip and Elaine are together in heaven."

A glimmer of unshed tears glossed her eyes. She dabbed at them with her napkin and said, "I'm so glad the children had you to take them in when they were orphaned."

Quint took a sip of coffee and managed a smile. "I love those kids with everything that's in me. There isn't anything I wouldn't do for them."

Again, there was a long moment of silence. After eating several bites Annamarie eased the tension by saying, "Tell me more about the children."

A slow grin spread over his face. "Well, all right. I'll start with the oldest. Alex. Well, what can I say? Alex is just Alex. He's all boy. Loves fishing, climbing trees, pushing the girls in the backyard swing till they scream, and just teasing his sisters in general . . . especially Gina. Of course, he has a compassionate heart, a willingness to help in the home any way he can, and he has a gentle spirit."

Annamarie smiled. "I know I'm going to love him. Now, tell me more about Gina."

"Well . . . she's a lovely young lady of thirteen, going on twenty-one."

Annamarie laughed. "Oh. One of those."

"The queen of them all! Really, she's already beginning to show attributes of what a fine woman she'll be one day. Bless her heart, she's stepped in and been mother to both Alex and Missy, all the while needing a mother herself. Gina is quite calm and easygoing, but occasionally her big brother can ruffle her feathers a bit. She has a great capacity for love and she has a gentle, caring nature."

"Sounds like the ideal young lady."

"I couldn't ask for a better one. In fact, I couldn't ask for three better ones. Philip and Elaine did a beautiful job of teaching and training them. And then there's the little one. I'd have to say Missy is the apple of everyone's eye. There's no doubt that she's been affected the most by the loss of her parents. Day by day she's doing better, and she cries less and less for her mother as time passes."

Annamarie's brow furrowed. "Poor little thing. It's so sad, especially for children her age to lose their parents. We had many such cases at the orphanage."

"I'm sure. And little Missy's so cute. She loves to do whatever Gina's doing. She follows her around devotedly. Missy is rather sensitive. She definitely has a mind of her own, but she's such a loving little girl. She wouldn't intentionally hurt any living thing.

Why, last summer when the houseflies were thick, she even got upset whenever we swatted one."

Annamarie chuckled. "Bless her tender little heart. I have to say, Quint, that just hearing about those children makes my heart fall in love with them already."

Quint smiled, silently thinking, *And I'm falling in love with you already, beautiful lady.* His blood chilled as he thought again of what he must tell her soon. "They're easy to love, Annamarie." He paused, then said, "How about filling me in on your background? The letters gave the information asked for in the ad, but I'd like to know some more now, if I may."

Quint listened intently as Annamarie told him of her upbringing in Atlanta and of being raised in a wonderful Christian home. She related briefly once again, as she had in her first letter, about the day she was saved. She then told him of the fateful day in September 1864, when General Sherman's army shelled the city, hitting the Taylor house. Tears misted her eyes as she went on to tell him that her mother was killed and that her father was wounded so seriously that he was an invalid.

Quint recalled that he had been right there on the outskirts of Atlanta when the

Union forces attacked the city. He figured that no matter what, he should tell her about it.

When Annamarie learned that Quint was a Union army doctor and was there when her family's house was shelled, she was a bit stunned.

"Annamarie, does this make you bitter toward me?"

She shook her head. "Not at all. The War is over, Quint, and you had no part in shelling the house, anyway. You were there to tend to wounded Yankee soldiers. Since you were brought up in the North, it was only natural that you serve with the Union army."

"Well, for many people, the War still isn't over . . . especially for Southerners."

"I know. But it's better that we Americans forget the ugly past and look to a beautiful future. I believe I have one." With that, she picked up her cup and took a sip of coffee.

Quint felt as if a lance had been driven straight through his heart and he fought to keep it from showing.

For a long moment, Annamarie explored his face, her eyes reading him with sharp care. There seemed to be a haunted shadow behind his eyes. "Quint, is something wrong?" she said, cocking her head. "You seem on edge."

"Annamarie," he said, meeting her gaze with his own, "there . . . there is something I need to explain to you. But before I do, I want to say very sincerely that I'm glad you're here. Your letters impressed me very much. But now having met you in person, I'm even more impressed with you."

"Thank you," she said in a whisper.

"Before I go on, I want to say it again. I'm glad you're here. Will you keep that in mind?"

"All right."

"You're a wonderful lady. I already know that and I'm superbly happy that you're here."

Her smile showed him a set of white, even teeth. "I'm glad you feel that way."

Quint cleared his throat. "Annamarie, I — well, you see —" He could feel the pulse pounding in the sides of his neck.

Annamarie cocked her head, frowning.

"Annamarie, there has been some deception in all of this and I must tell you about it."

She nodded, waiting.

"It all started when I hired a live-in housekeeper not long after the children came to live with me."

Annamarie listened intently as Quint told her of the desperate need the children had for a mother figure in their lives and how he had hired Mabel Ritter. He went on to explain how it didn't work out with Mabel, for she had no heart for the children.

Quint paused in his story to tell her about Susan Bedford jilting him and of the determination he had at first that he would never allow another woman to have the opportunity to break his heart.

"You mean you were a confirmed bachelor?" Annamarie said.

"I told myself I would never fall in love again. I would never even get close enough to a woman to let that happen."

She held his gaze. "But somewhere along the line you changed your mind."

"I discarded that foolish idea within a year or so after Susan tore my heart out. I really did want to find the right woman, but as time passed she never came along. I prayed earnestly year after year, asking the Lord to bring her into my life, but she never came."

Annamarie held his gaze and waited for him to go on.

Quint took a deep breath. "After I brought the children here and adopted them, Alex and Gina saw my loneliness and decided that I needed a wife and that they needed a mother. So they prayed about it. I mean, just the two of them . . . alone. They prayed about it and felt that the Lord could provide that woman through the mail order bride system. They had known a woman in Illinois who became the mail order bride of a rancher in Arizona. Well, Alex and Gina sent the ad to the *Atlanta Herald Tribune* as if it had been sent by me."

Annamarie felt a sudden cold sensation in her chest.

"You see, Alex and Gina pick the mail up at the post office for me every day, so they were in a position to get their hands on your letter when it came. It was Alex who penned the letter that came to you. I knew nothing of this, nor of your second letter until this morning, just before time to go to church."

Suddenly Darlene drew up to the table. "Is there anything else I can get for you folks? More coffee?"

Quint looked up at her and forced a smile, then set his eyes on Annamarie. "Would you like some more coffee?"

"That would be fine."

"All right. Be right back with some fresh brew."

"I'll wait till after she comes with the coffee before I go on," Quint said.

Annamarie closed her eyes and gave a nod, her face a pale mask.

Darlene returned and poured fresh,

steaming coffee in their cups. "There you are. If you need anything else, just holler."

"We will. Thank you."

When he looked back at Annamarie, she was staring blankly into his troubled eyes. She felt weak all over.

"Annamarie, remember what I told you a few minutes ago — to keep in mind that I'm glad you're here? Remember?"

Stunned into silence, Annamarie's blank stare remained on him.

21

The enormity of what Quint had just told her finally broke through to Annamarie's disbelieving mind, and unwanted tears rushed into her eyes. She blinked rapidly, trying to dispel them, but the tears spilled unheeded down her smooth, pale cheeks.

Quint prayed silently for wisdom. He thought how very beautiful she was, even then, as her cheeks glistened like damp marble.

Annamarie didn't make a sound. Her head was bent and her trembling hands were folded on top of the table as she sat and watched the droplets splash on them.

Quint reached out his own trembling hand and covered both of hers. One of her tears fell on his hand.

At his touch, she looked up into his kind, troubled eyes and made a concentrated effort to stop crying. With his other hand, Quint took a white handkerchief from his hip pocket and offered it to her.

"Annamarie," he said softly, "I'm sorry. I must have gone at this all wrong. But please listen to me. I am very glad you came to Bozeman. I really mean that."

Lips quivering, she sniffed and said, "How can you say that? This whole thing can be nothing but a nightmare for you. It had to be terribly hard for you to tell me the truth."

"It was. I would rather have taken a beating with a horsewhip than to have to tell you the truth of this whole thing. But something has happened since I learned of this at breakfast this morning. May I tell you about it?"

She dabbed at her eyes and looked at him with a tentative smile tugging at the corners of her mouth. "If you wish."

At the Roberts house, Gina tiptoed to the door of the girls' room, opened it quietly, and looked at her little sister who lay on her bed asleep. Missy's fever seemed to be lessening, for which Gina whispered a prayer of thanks to the Lord.

Closing the door behind her, Gina made her way down the hall to the staircase and let her hand slide on the banister as she descended slowly to the ground floor. She made her way to the parlor and found her brother sitting on the couch by the front window, staring at the yard out front.

His dull glance settled on her as she sat down beside him. "Wind's picking up, Gina. Clouds coming in. Looks like we might get snow. Missy asleep?"

"Mmm-hmm. Her fever's going down. That's why I stayed with her so long. I wanted to be sure."

There was a long silence, punctuated only by Alex taking a couple of deep breaths. At the second one, Gina laid a hand on his shoulder and said, "Alex, we were trying to do the right thing."

"Yeah."

"We really felt that the Lord was leading us to put that ad in the Atlanta paper. We wanted Daddy to have a wife and we wanted a mother for ourselves. That wasn't wrong. He does need a wife. We do need a mother."

Alex nodded. "But it sure looks like we did wrong. Dad looked gray in the face when he left here."

"But we were simply doing what we thought was the only thing possible to solve the problem."

Alex turned to his sister. "She looks like such a nice lady in her pictures. Maybe she won't be so mad that she'll head back to At-

370

lanta tomorrow. Maybe when Dad offers her the housekeeper's job, she'll take it." He paused. "That is, if she's not so mad at us that she never wants to lay eyes on us."

Gina began sniffling and tears ran down her cheeks. "Oh, Alex, I so much wanted it to work out. I need a mother so very, very much."

Alex slipped an arm around her and tugged her close. "I know, sis. Boys need mothers, too, but maybe girls need them more. We've prayed a lot about this. We just have to leave it all in God's hands. I just hope the Lord knows we really didn't intend to be deceivers. I hope He won't punish us for it."

Quint took a deep breath and said, "Annamarie, something happened deep inside me when I first laid eyes on you as you stepped out of the stagecoach."

"What do you mean?"

"I told you I've prayed so hard for all these years that the Lord would send the woman He had picked out just for me, but she never came along. I told the Lord not so long ago that when He brought her to me, he would have to let me know, 'There she is, Quint. I chose her for you and she's all yours.'"

Annamarie gave him a tentative smile. "You really told Him that?"

"Yes, I did. And you know what? When you stepped out of that stagecoach, it was as if the Lord spoke those very words to me."

"You're just trying to make me feel better."

He squeezed her hands and said, "No, no. I'm telling you the way it is. Annamarie, I . . . I already feel something very strong toward you in my heart. I really do. I know all of this has to be a terrible shock to you, and I can't blame you if you say you want to get back on that stage when it comes through here tomorrow. But I really do want you to stay."

Annamarie was staring at him through misty eyes. She wiped a tear and drew a shuddering breath. "Quint, this has been such a blow. I need a moment to clear my head. Would you excuse me while I go to the ladies' room?"

"Of course." He rose to his feet and took hold of her chair to help her up. "I'm so sorry for all this. But I mean it with all my heart when I say I want you to stay."

Annamarie dabbed at her tears with the handkerchief Quint had given her and hurried away.

Darlene saw Annamarie walking away, dabbing at her eyes, and came up to Quint's table, looking in the direction Annamarie had gone. "Dr. Roberts, is something wrong? It looked to me like the lady was crying."

"She is crying, Darlene. This has been a hard day for her. But she'll be all right."

"I could get one of the other girls to fill in for me while I go talk to her."

"It really won't be necessary. She'll be back in a moment. But thank you."

Darlene nodded and moved on.

"Lord," Quint whispered, "please work in Annamarie's heart so she will stay. Even . . . even if it's only as housekeeper. Maybe in time she would come to love me."

Annamarie stood at the long table in the ladies' room and looked at herself in the mirror. She took several deep breaths, trying to calm her shaking body. When her nerves had begun to settle, she picked up the pitcher and poured water into the basin. She splashed the cool liquid on her face and dried it with one of the small towels on the rack at the end of the table.

After removing her hat, she smoothed her glossy hair, then leaned forward and placed her palms flat on the table. Bowing her head, she said in a whisper, "Dear God, I need Your guidance and Your grace right now. You know what I felt in my heart toward Quint when I first saw him. And now, it seems he felt the same thing toward me. I'm so confused, Lord. What a shock to learn that this whole thing was done by Alex and Gina. And yet, was this Your way to get me here? Help me, Lord. I'm in Your hands. My future is in Your hands. Please help me. Give me wisdom. Show me what to do. I'm committing this whole mixed-up situation to You."

Annamarie looked at herself in the mirror again. She pinched her cheeks to redden them and said, "All right, Annamarie. You've committed the entire situation into God's capable hands. Let Him work it out."

Quint saw Annamarie emerge from the ladies' room and head his direction. He rose to his feet, and there was concern in his eyes as he said, "Are you all right?"

"I'm better," she replied, trying to smile.

Quint seated her, then took his own chair and leaned forward. "May I go ahead and tell you what's on my heart?"

"Of course."

"Annamarie, I had a battle within myself while I was bringing you here to the hotel. I . . . well, I even entertained the idea of not telling you about Alex and Gina's deception. I had read both of your letters and thought maybe since I was having strong feelings for you, I would just go on and pursue the idea of making you my mail order bride. But Annamarie, I had to be honest with you. I couldn't let this situation go on without telling you the truth."

Her cheeks were pale again as she said, "I very much appreciate your being honest with me, Quint. It has been a real shock, but it's always best to know the truth, even if it hurts."

He took a short, sharp breath.

"Let me go on before you say any more, Quint. Please."

"Of course."

"I want to say that in no way do I have any bad feelings toward Alex and Gina. They —" She choked up, tears filling her eyes once again. "They've been through a terrible ordeal. I can't blame them for making that desperate a move to obtain a mother. Had I been in their place, I'm sure I would've gone to similar lengths."

"I'm so glad to hear you say that, Annamarie. They are precious children. You'll love them on sight. I guarantee it."

"I already do." She used Quint's handkerchief once again to dab at her eyes.

Quint grinned slyly and pulled at an ear. "Of course, they're hoping and praying that you will become my bride and their adoptive mother."

There was a brief silence as she studied his face. Then she looked him square in the eye and said, "Since we're being honest with each other, I need to tell you something."

Annamarie started to speak, then choked on her words. Closing her eyes, she took a breath again then met his gaze squarely. "Quint . . . you said something happened in your heart when you first laid eyes on me there at the stage station. Well, I had the identical experience, at the same moment. That still, small voice in my heart seemed to say, 'Annamarie, there is the man I have chosen for you.'"

Quint swallowed with difficulty, unable to pull his eyes from her gaze.

"You seem amazed," she said with a smile. "Quint, dear, you shouldn't be so shocked. Since the Lord told you I was the one He had chosen for you, why wouldn't He tell me the same about you?"

His eyes brightened. "He would, wouldn't He?"

"He did."

Quint closed his eyes and said, "Thank You, Jesus! Thank You!"

Still smiling, Annamarie said, "Since the Lord has spoken to both of our hearts in such a clear manner, I would be wrong to leave. I'll stay. I want to give the Lord the opportunity to work His perfect will in our lives."

Quint leaned across the table again and took her hands in his. "That's what I want too, sweet lady. That's what I want too!"

Darlene drew up with a steaming coffeepot in her hand. "Can I warm up your coffee for you?" She filled both cups, smiled down at Annamarie, and walked away.

"Annamarie, let me tell you what my original plan was as I drove to the Fargo station to pick you up. If, after you'd been told the truth about what Alex and Gina had done, you weren't so angry that you wanted to turn right around and go back to Atlanta, I was going to offer you the job Mabel Ritter vacated . . . as our live-in housekeeper. In fact, it was Gina's idea. She figured if they couldn't have you as their mother, they could at least have you as their mother figure."

"Then it appears that we need to discuss our plans from this point on."

"Yes. What are your thoughts, Annamarie?"

"I think it would be best that I not be your live-in housekeeper. Is there a way I can live elsewhere and just come to your house during the day to take care of Missy while the other two are in school? Of course, I'll do the housework, including the washing and ironing. I could even stay and cook the evening meal and eat it with you and the children, then have you take me to wherever I'm staying. Is this a possibility?"

"Yes, it most certainly is possible. I've secured you the nicest room here in the hotel, as you will see. I'll just keep you in that room until we get to know each other better. Then in God's perfect time we'll marry and you'll move into the Roberts house for good."

Annamarie's heart was at perfect peace as she said, "Sounds good to me."

"And something else . . . As long as you work as housekeeper, I'll pay you well, even as I did Mabel Ritter. And I want to know the amount of your travel expenses so I can reimburse you."

"Really, Quint, that's not necessary."

"No arguments, sweet lady. What did it cost you?"

"Fifty-seven dollars, but you don't have to —"

He pulled out five twenty-dollar bills and laid them in front of her.

"But that's more than —"

"You'll need some extra. Take it, please."

Annamarie thanked him and put the money in her purse.

"Well," Quint said, "I'll escort you up to your room and get you settled."

After paying for the meal, Quint guided Annamarie to the desk in the hotel lobby. He introduced her to Tim Gibson, obtained the key, and arranged for the hotel's porter to bring the baggage up to the room from his buggy.

Annamarie held on to Quint's arm as they climbed the stairs to the third floor, then moved down the hall to the corner room on the south side.

"Here we are," he said, inserting the key into the door of room 301.

When he opened the door and gestured for Annamarie to enter ahead of him, she gasped at the sight of it. "Oh, Quint! This is the most beautiful room I've ever seen! You shouldn't have gotten such a fancy one."

He smiled. "Not even for my potential mail order bride?"

The baggage was brought in and Quint helped the porter put the trunks where Annamarie wanted them. When the porter was gone, he said, "If you're ready, I want to take you to the house so you can meet the children."

A shaky hand went to her mouth. "Now

I'm getting nervous. What if they decide they don't like me? What if —"

"There isn't any way that could happen. The Lord has prepared Alex, Gina, and Missy for you, just as He prepared you for them. It's going to be a wonderful and beautiful thing, this family of ours."

Her eyes seemed to dance. "Oh, Quint, that sounds so marvelous. 'This family of ours.' Let's go. I can't wait to hug those three!"

As they rode through Bozeman's streets, the wind grew stronger and colder. The sky was now heavy with clouds.

"We're going to get some snow," Quint said. "I can smell it in the air."

"I'm glad I got here when I did. They warned me at Atlanta's railroad station that Montana gets winter weather early and that I could get stuck in Billings for a good stretch if one of those famous blizzards hit before I got there."

"I'm glad you're here safe and sound. This may not be a bad storm, but it's hard to tell at this point." A warm smile spread over his face. "I'm glad you're right here beside me, Annamarie. You're doing strange things to my heart."

She matched his smile and said, "My heart feels like it's going to burst, Quint."

"Well, as a practicing physician, Miss Taylor, I would say that we both have heart trouble . . . *good* heart trouble."

Annamarie laughed gaily. "If we're going to have heart trouble, Dr. Roberts, this is the best kind to have!"

Missy's brow was now cool to the touch, and Alex and Gina were entertaining her in the parlor. Missy was laughing and having a good time when movement through the parlor window caught Alex's eye.

"Gina, it's Dad! Look, he's got Miss Taylor with him!"

Gina let out a joyful sound and hurried to the window as little sister said excitedly, "Mama? Papa?"

Missy bounded off the couch and ran toward them, repeating, "Mama? Papa?"

"Alex, let's go to the door so we can meet her right there!" Gina said.

They hurried into the hall with Missy on their heels and took up positions in the foyer.

Missy tugged on Gina's skirt. "Mama? Papa?"

Gina hugged her and said, "No, sweetie. It's not Mama and Papa. They're in heaven with Jesus. But Daddy has a special lady that he's bringing to see us."

The four-year-old was studying Gina's lips. "Special lady?"

"Yes, honey."

"Special lady comin' to see us?"

"Yes."

"Mabel?"

"No, Missy," Alex said. "Not Mabel. This lady is special 'cause she will love us."

"Oh, Alex," Gina said, "she just has to love us. She just has to."

"We've prayed that way, haven't we? Then, sis, we have to trust God."

"I'm sorry, Alex. I don't mean to be a doubting Thomas."

"Special lady," repeated the little one.

Gina took hold of her tiny hand. "Yes, this is a very special lady."

22

When the Roberts children heard footsteps on the front porch, Alex looked at Gina and said, "My stomach is jittery. Is yours?"

Gina grinned. "What's the matter, brother dear? Aren't you trusting the Lord?"

He made a mock snarl. "I'm supposed to preach to you, sis, but you're not supposed to preach to me!"

Even as he spoke, Alex reached for the doorknob. Gina picked Missy up into her arms and adjusted the little girl's weight on her hip.

Missy's eyes were large and round as she watched her brother open the door.

Alex gave a big smile and said, "Hello, Miss Taylor. I'm Alex. Welcome!"

"I'm very glad to meet you, Alex," Annamarie said, smiling warmly as Quint guided her through the door.

Gina waited until they had stepped inside

and Quint had closed the door behind them, then stepped up with Missy in her arms, and said, "We're glad to see you, Miss Taylor. This is Missy, and I'm Gina."

Annamarie already had her coat unbuttoned and Quint removed it. Smiling broadly, Annamarie said, "Thank you, Quint. I wanted to get the coat off before I start hugging, because this is going to take a while!"

Annamarie wrapped her arms around Alex, hugged him tight, and laid her cheek on top of his head. "Oh, Alex," she said, "I've been so eager to meet you and your sisters."

Alex slid his arms around her and squeezed hard. "We've sure been looking forward to meeting you."

Gina ran her gaze to Quint with a quizzical look in her eyes and mouthed, *Does she know what we did?*

"And now the girls," said Annamarie before Quint could give Gina a nod.

Annamarie embraced both girls at the same time, kissed Missy's cheek and the top of Gina's head, and said, "Such sweet girls! Oh, Quint, what darling children!"

Suddenly Missy reached for Annamarie and said, "Mama . . ."

Annamarie opened her arms as she

stepped toward the girls. "Is it all right, Gina?"

"Sure," said Gina, lifting Missy from her hip and into Annamarie's arms.

Missy said, "Mama," again, and laid her head on Annamarie's shoulder.

Fresh tears sprang up in Annamarie's eyes. "Oh, Quint, look!"

Quint chuckled. "You've won her over already, that's for sure!"

"Let's take Miss Taylor into the parlor, so we can sit down and talk," Quint said. "I want to tell you children some things."

When they sat down in the parlor, Missy clung to Annamarie, making herself right at home on her lap, then laid her head back on Annamarie's breast.

"Kids," said Quint, looking at Alex and Gina, "I've told Miss Taylor the whole story. She knows who put the ad in the *Atlanta Herald Tribune*, and she knows who wrote the letter and signed my name. She also knows whose idea the whole thing was."

Two young faces crimsoned. "Please forgive us for deceiving you, ma'am," said Alex, biting his lips.

"We didn't mean to do anything wrong," said Gina, tears appearing at the corners of her eyes. "We just wanted Daddy to have a wife and the three of us to have a mother.

Please forgive us. And please forgive me, especially, since it was my idea."

Annamarie's head canted to one side and a look of compassion etched itself on her face. The compassion was also in her voice as she said, "I understand, Gina, Alex. I'm so sorry for the loss of your parents. I know how that feels because both of my parents are dead. I wasn't as young as you are when I lost my parents, but I know how it hurts. It has to be even harder to lose them at your age. And I forgive you for deceiving me. The subject need never arise between us again."

Gina bounded off the couch and leaned past Missy to hug Annamarie's neck. "Thank you for forgiving me," she said.

Alex did the same.

Quint looked on with a lump in his throat, then had to fight tears when Alex stepped away from Annamarie and Missy raised up on her knees to fling her arms around Annamarie's neck and said, "Thank you for forgiving us, Mama."

When the two older ones had returned to the couch and Missy was once again sitting down, Annamarie looked at Quint and said, "Can I tell them now?"

Quint thumbed a tear from the corner of his eye. "Sure."

Annamarie explained to Alex and Gina

the feelings she and their father had for each other on first sight. The eyes of both children lit up at her words and their expressions grew brighter as Annamarie said, "Because your Daddy and I strongly sense that the Lord has chosen us for each other, we know that if we're right about it, we'll fall in love. If this comes to pass, we will eventually marry."

"Oh yes!" Gina said. "Yes, I know it will! I just know it!"

Alex bounced up and down on the couch. "And if you do fall in love and get married, you'll be our new mother, Miss Taylor!"

"We both believe that's going to happen, Alex," Quint said. "But we must give the Lord time to work in our hearts so that we know we have the proper love for each other to make a good marriage."

"Now, let me explain something else," Annamarie said. "Your daddy and I talked about the housekeeper situation. We agreed that I should be your housekeeper until the Lord showed us differently. However, since a possible marriage is in the offing, we agreed that it's best for the sake of our Christian testimony that I not live here in the house while I'm the housekeeper. Alex and Gina, I believe you're old enough to understand what I'm talking about."

"Of course," Alex said.

"I understand, Miss Taylor," Gina said. "Pastor Morgan preached a sermon just a few weeks ago about Christians keeping a good testimony before others by abstaining from even the appearance of evil. I don't recall at the moment which book in the New Testament he preached from, but it was a really good sermon."

"It was 1 Thessalonians 5:22, Gina," Alex said. " 'Abstain from all appearance of evil.' "

"Well, the important thing," Annamarie said, "is that you understand why I'll be living at the hotel instead of here in the house. Now, I'll spend each day here. I'll get here in time to cook breakfast and I'll be here till we've had supper and the kitchen has been cleaned up. Then I'll go back to the hotel for the night."

"Oh, I'm so glad you'll be here to take care of Missy when Alex and I are in school," Gina said.

Missy twisted on Annamarie's lap and raised up on her knees again. Looking into her eyes, she said, "Mama will take care of me!"

Annamarie kissed the tip of her nose. "I'm not really your mama yet, honey, but I sure will take care of you." Then looking back at the other two, she said, "Of course, in addition to the cooking, I'll be doing the housecleaning, washing, and ironing."

"I'll help you with all of it," Gina said.

"I can help clean the house," Alex said, "and I can help with the washing. But when it comes to cooking and ironing, I'm not too hot."

Gina said, "Missy helps a lot too, Miss Taylor, if you know what I mean."

Annamarie looked down at the little one on her lap. "I'm sure she's a great help."

Missy smiled and nodded.

"I sure like this new arrangement," Alex said. "Dad, since it has worked out like this, do you believe the Lord led Gina and me to do what we did?"

"Well, son, the Lord does not approve of deceiving others, but I can see that behind all of it, He had planned for Miss Taylor to come here. Even though there was dishonesty in what you did, He took the bad and made something beautiful out of it."

"But the Lord did use my idea to bring her here, didn't He, Daddy?" Gina asked.

"Yes, darling, He did. If I hadn't been so stubbornly against advertising for a mail order bride, He wouldn't have had to use what you and Alex did, in spite of your deceit."

"But God knew all of this beforehand, right?" Gina said. "So even though Alex and I did wrong in making it look like it was you who put in the ad and wrote the letter inviting Miss Taylor to come, He still used it to bring her to us."

"I can't argue with that. The Lord often has to work out His will in our lives in spite of our wrongdoings."

Gina swung her gaze to Annamarie. "I sure am glad the Lord brought you to us, Miss Taylor. I already feel like I've known you all my life."

"Thank you, Gina," Annamarie said, smiling warmly.

"I feel the same way, ma'am," Alex said.

"Me too," piped up Missy.

Alex chuckled. "You too what, Missy?"

Looking stumped, the little one shrugged her shoulders. "Whatever you said."

Everybody laughed.

"Daddy," Gina said, "is it all right if we ask Miss Taylor some questions? I mean about her life in Atlanta?"

"Well, honey, she's probably pretty tired. Maybe you can ask these things some other time."

"It's all right, Quint," Annamarie said. "I'm not that tired. I want them to get to know me as soon as possible. I'd love to answer their questions."

After a while, Quint glanced at the clock on the mantel and said, "Hey, everybody, it's almost five-thirty. Church is at seven. We'd better eat whatever we're going to before it gets too late." He turned to Annamarie. "Would you like to go to church with us tonight, or have we worn you out by now?"

"I'm fine. I'd love to go to church with you."

"I'll go to the kitchen and fix us some sandwiches," Gina said. "That's what we usually have on Sunday evening before church, Miss Taylor, since we eat our big meal right after the morning service."

Giving Missy a big hug, Annamarie stood her on the floor and rose to her feet. "I'll help you."

"I help too," Missy said.

"Sure, honey. Come on."

Missy took hold of Annamarie's hand as Gina led the way to the kitchen.

In the parlor, Quint and Alex listened to the chatter coming from the kitchen and grinned at each other. When they heard Missy say something funny and the laughter that followed, Quint said, "Isn't it wonderful, son? We haven't heard such happy sounds in this house since you came here."

"You've made us as happy as you could, Dad, but a home is supposed to have a wife and mother. God has given her to us and our happiest days are ahead."

Quint nodded, smiling. "Yes. Our happiest days are ahead of us."

The sky was clearing on Monday morning as Quint walked Annamarie out of the hotel onto the snow-covered boardwalk. He gripped her arm tightly to keep her from slipping. Some two inches of snow had fallen during the night.

She drew a deep breath of the frosty air and turned a glad face toward Quint. "I love the look and the feel of the snow! Only on rare occasions did we get snowfall in Atlanta. And even then, it was only a few snowflakes and they melted within minutes. This is wonderful! A perfect beginning to my new life."

When they arrived at the house, Annamarie received a warm welcome from the children. Quint was pleased at how the children were attaching themselves to her, especially Missy.

As the days passed, Quint saw the attachment growing stronger, not only on the part of the children toward Annamarie but also on Annamarie's part toward them. Quint had never seen the children so happy. On the days when Alex and Gina were at school, Annamarie and Missy spent countless hours doing tasks around the house together. The four-year-old was well behaved, and once again was a joyful, contented little girl.

Annamarie purposely planned time each day to play with the child. They also baked cookies side by side and had them waiting with mugs of hot chocolate or hot apple cider when Alex and Gina came home from school.

The older children commented often to each other that coming home from school was so different than when Mabel Ritter was there. Miss Taylor truly loved them and showed it all the time. In return, they made sure she often heard from them that they loved her.

It made Annamarie exceedingly glad that she had come to Bozeman, not only for the love she and the children shared but also for the deepening of the relationship she was finding with Dr. Quint Roberts.

On Wednesday, November 29, the big Baldwin 4-4-0 locomotive raced across the flat Wyoming landscape toward the scarlet and gold sunset. They had left Douglas ten minutes before and were running on schedule. If they kept it up, they would arrive in Casper an hour after dark.

Far in the distance, a dim blue line of mountains could be seen on the horizon — mountains that marked the eastern beginning of the Rockies.

The engineer held the throttle wide open while the fireman threw wood into the roaring flames of the firebox.

In the dining car, Paul Peterson sat with Kent McClain, who had joined him in the coach when boarding at Chadron, Nebraska. As they talked, they both learned that the other had fought in the Civil War on the Confederate side. A friendship was quickly established, and after learning that McClain was a married man on his way home to his wife and children in Casper, Paul told him of being wounded in battle and of the years cut out of his life by amnesia. He told him about the plans he and Annamarie Taylor had made to marry, and how he had missed her by just a few days when he returned home to Atlanta after being gone for over twelve years.

Kent McClain looked across the table at his new friend and said, "But even if you make it before she marries this doctor in Bozeman, Paul, don't you expect a fight from him? If she's to be his mail order bride, he isn't going to just pull back and say, 'Well, Mr. Peterson, since you really had first claim to her, I'll just get out of the way.' "

"Well, if it's a tussle he wants, I'll have to handle him. But I know when Annamarie lays eyes on me, realizing that I'm still alive, she'll tell him that I'm her first love and she wants to marry me."

Kent frowned. "But you told me you're a Christian."

"I am."

"Then why don't you just leave well enough alone and go back to Atlanta and find yourself another girl? You're going to damage two lives, Paul. She has promised this doctor she will marry him, and your showing up from the dead — so to speak — can't help but seriously interfere with their plans. She might fool you and tell you she doesn't want you now; their happiness is at stake. I have no right to give you advice, but I'll say it anyhow. Go back to Atlanta and let them have their happiness, Paul."

Paul set his jaw. "I can't. I love her too much. I've got to get her back."

"But what if she had married years ago? What then?"

"Well, then I'd have to back away. But there's a chance that she isn't yet married to this Dr. Quint Roberts."

"But if you get there and find that they are married — what then?"

Paul closed his eyes and shook his head. "Then I'll have to stay out of it. But if they're not married, I'm going to do my best to take her home with me."

Kent looked him square in the eye. "You really think God could bless you for doing such a thing?"

Paul was silent a moment. He took a sip of coffee, set the cup down, and said, "Kent, the Bible says in the last chapter of the Song of Solomon that love is strong as death and many waters cannot quench it. I love Annamarie and I want her for my wife. If she hasn't married Dr. Roberts, I'm taking her home with me to be my bride."

Suddenly there was a loud roar, followed by an upheaval of the dining car. Passengers, tables, dishes, and food went sailing as the car began to overturn.

Paul felt like a giant hand picked him up and threw him through the air. His head struck something hard. He saw a shower of lights, then a powerful, swirling vortex sucked him into a pit of darkness.

Paul Peterson's first clue that he was still alive came when he felt the vortex reversing itself and swirling him upward toward a vague light. He heard a groan from close by, then realized it had come from his own mouth as he heard a voice say, "He's stirring, Helen; go get the doctor! Sir, can you hear me?"

The light hurt his eyes and he closed them quickly. He rolled his dry tongue around in his dry mouth, groaned again and said, "Water."

Soon cool moisture was trickling into his mouth.

The voice came again. "Sir, can you hear me?"

Paul winced at the pain the light brought but saw a kind face hovering over him. "Wh-where am I?"

"You're at the Casper Clinic, sir. Do you remember being on the train?"

"Yes."

The nurse smiled. "Good! Now I must ask you this: Can you tell me your name?"

"C-could I have some more water, please?"

"Of course."

When she had given him almost a full cup of water she said, "Can you tell me your name?"

"Paul . . . Paul Peterson."

"Oh, wonderful! Dr. Haltom, he's awake and he knows his name. He remembers being on the train."

A moon-shaped face came into Paul's view. "Mr. Peterson, I'm Dr. Kenneth Haltom. You're at the clinic in Casper. Do you recall what happened before you went unconscious?"

"Well . . . it was very sudden. There was a noise like loud thunder, and suddenly I was flying through the air. I felt pain in my head, and that's it, Doctor. Until I came to a couple of minutes ago. How . . . how long have I been unconscious?"

"Three days."

"Really?"

"Yes, sir. Can you tell me where you're from?"

"Of course. Atlanta."

"And where were you headed?"

"Bozeman, Montana. Why all these questions?"

"Because we know about your head wound in the Civil War and your twelve years of amnesia."

Paul's brows pinched together. "How do you know about that?"

"You were dining with a man you met on the train when it wrecked, remember?"

"Kent McClain. He told you? Then he must be all right."

"Banged up some, but he's home now.

He'll be fine. You've got some bruises other than on your head. You'll know where they are when you try to move."

"But I'm okay?"

"As far as I can tell. You took a real blow on your head. If you have friends you want to wire in Bozeman, I'll see that the message is sent. We're going to keep you here for a few more days for observation. I want to make sure you're all right. Especially because of your amnesia history."

Paul's mind went to Annamarie. "Doctor, I can't stay here any longer. I've got to get to Bozeman."

"You're not up to that yet. You've got to have more rest before you go anywhere."

"No, Doctor, you don't understand! I've lost three days already! I have to get to Bozeman!"

"Please, Mr. Peterson," said the nurse, laying a hand on his shoulder. "You mustn't exert yourself. Besides, there are no trains running between Casper and Billings right now. They have crews working to repair the tracks, but from what we're told, it will take them another couple of days to get it done."

"I'll buy a horse and ride to Bozeman, then. I've got to get there as soon as possible!"

"You'd never make it on horseback," the doctor said flatly.

Paul met his gaze. "Do you know what caused the train wreck?"

"Indians."

"Indians?"

"Sioux and Cheyenne are on the uprise again. They've been attacking stagecoaches, trains, farms, and ranches all over Wyoming. They tore up a stretch of track about thirty miles east of here, right on a bend, so the engineer couldn't see it in his headlight till it was too late. They dug a deep hole where the track had been and the engine plunged into the hole. That's why your train came to a sudden stop."

"Are you feeling any hunger, Mr. Peterson?" the nurse asked.

"Come to think of it, I am."

"Good. I'll go get you something to eat. Broth will be best to start with."

When the nurse was gone, Dr. Haltom said, "I've got to look in on a couple other patients who were in the train wreck, Mr. Peterson. You just lie there and rest. I'll check on you again later."

"Doctor, listen — I've got to get to Bozeman. How about if I buy a horse and buggy?"

"That would be better than trying it on horseback, but you're in no condition to try even that, yet. Give it a few more days. The track will be repaired by then."

With that, the doctor left the room.

"O Lord," Paul said, "please don't let Annamarie marry that doctor. Let me get there in time."

Even as he spoke, he sat up and swung his legs over the side of the bed. Pain lanced through his back and legs, and his head began throbbing. "Got to get to her . . ." When his feet touched the floor, the whole room seemed to be spinning. "Got to get to her . . ."

He staggered to the closet and opened the door. His clothes and shoes were there. If only the room would stop whirling around him. As Paul reached out to take the hangers that held his shirt and trousers, his legs gave way and he crumpled to the floor.

At the same moment, he heard a gasp, followed by quick footsteps and the nurse calling his name. Her voice seemed to come and go, then darkness descended over him like an ocean wave.

23

On Wednesday night, December 6, Annamarie returned to the Roberts home with them after church and showed Gina how to braid Missy's hair in a style the little one had seen that evening on a girl who was visiting the church with her family. Even Quint and Alex were in the girls' bedroom to watch.

When Annamarie had carefully guided Gina's hands and Missy saw it in the mirror, she clapped her hands and said, "Yes! That's the way I want it!"

"Good," Gina said. "Now when I fix your hair in the mornings before Miss Taylor gets here, you can have it braided this way anytime you want."

Missy dabbed at her hair, looked at Quint, and asked, "Do you like it?"

"Looks good on you."

"I like it too, Missy," Alex said. "It makes you look older."

"Really? How old?"

"Oh, I'd say at least five."

"Then I really like it!"

"Well," Annamarie said, "I guess it's time for my chariot to take me to the hotel."

Everybody followed Quint and Annamarie downstairs. After Quint helped her into her coat and she had tied a scarf on her head, Annamarie hugged Alex, then Gina. When she picked the little one up to hug her, Missy kissed her cheek and said, "I love you, Mama."

Annamarie told her she loved her too and squeezed her tight, then put her down and said to Quint, "Should I discourage her from calling me that just yet?"

"No, it makes me happy to see that she looks at you as her mama. But maybe since she called her mother that, we ought to encourage her to call you 'Mommy' instead. When I adopted them, we decided since they called their father 'Papa,' they would call me 'Daddy' or 'Dad.'"

Annamarie bent down to Missy's level and looked into her eyes. "Sweetie, I love it that you've been calling me Mama. But Daddy's right. It's best that you keep that name for your mama and call me Mommy. Would you do that?"

The little one looked a bit puzzled but said, "Okay. I'll call you Mommy."

Gina said, "Daddy, would it be all right if I call her Mommy too?"

Quint rubbed his chin in thought, then said, "I think it would really be better if you wait on that. Missy's quite young and doesn't understand, but it would be best to hold off for right now. We're not married yet."

"Sure, Daddy," she said, smiling. "I'll just keep on calling her Miss Taylor until you two get married. Then I'll call her Mommy."

"Yeah," said Alex. "But I'll call her Mom, since I'm a big teenage boy."

Tears were in Annamarie's eyes as they stepped outside and Quint helped her into the buggy.

There was a full moon in the cold, starlit sky as Quint drove the buggy toward downtown. From the corner of his eye, he noticed that Annamarie was dabbing at her eyes with a handkerchief.

"You all right?" he asked.

"Quint, I've never been so happy."

He reached over and took her gloved hand. "And I have never been so happy — in all my life."

Soon Quint pulled the buggy to a halt in front of the hotel. When he turned to look at Annamarie, the silver moonlight was reflected in her eyes.

Quint's gaze seemed to be devouring her face, and she found herself wanting to press her lips to his.

As if he could read her mind, he leaned closer, until they were only inches apart. His breath fluttered warmly on her upturned face as his hand closed protectively over hers where it rested on the seat.

"Oh, Annamarie," he said softly.

She lifted her lips toward his. The kiss was brief but sweet and tender. Annamarie touched his cheek gently with her gloved hand. "Quint, have you really never been as happy as you are right now?"

"A few minutes ago when I said I had never been happier in all my life, I meant it. And now, after what just happened, I have to say that I'm happier than I was a few minutes ago."

"Oh, Quint," she said in a whisper, and they kissed again.

When their lips parted, he looked into her eyes and said, "I just got happier."

She smiled. "So did I."

Caressing her cheek, he said, "I'd better get you inside before you freeze to death."

Quint helped her from the buggy and she held on to his arm as they walked into the hotel together. They greeted the night clerk at the desk as they passed through the lobby.

When they reached room 301 and stood at the door, Quint kissed her again.

"Good night, Annamarie," he said. "I hope you have a restful night."

"I will. Good night, Quint."

He waited until she had closed and locked the door, then walked toward the stairs.

At the Roberts house, Gina was helping Missy into her nightgown. "You really love Miss Taylor, don't you, sweetie?" she said.

"Mmm-hmm," said the four-year-old. "Love Mommy."

Gina hugged her. "I do too. I love her very, very much. She's going to be a wonderful mother to us."

Missy's lips curved in a wide smile. "And she loves us too."

"I think she probably loves us even more than she did those children in the orphanage."

Annamarie closed her hotel room door, leaned her back against it and sighed, closing her eyes. She stayed there for nearly a minute, then moved to her bed and sat down on it.

"Dear Lord," she said aloud, "I know in my heart that I'm in love with that man. And I really believe he's in love with me. And

406

those precious children, Lord, they have each found their place in my heart, as You well know."

She felt warm tears trickling down her cheeks. "And that little Missy, Father. She's been calling me Mama since the day I got here."

Annamarie wept for joy, thanking God for bringing her to Bozeman.

Quint drove toward home, reveling in the sweet taste of the kisses that was still on his lips.

A struggle was going on inside him as he said, "Lord, I'm positive that I'm head-over-heels in love with her. My problem is that I want to be right and proper but I also want Annamarie to know how I feel. My kisses told her that I'm in love with her — and best of all, she was kissing me back. But I just want to be sure I'm going about this in the right way. After all, we've only known each other a few days. Once I've declared my love for her and she declares the same to me, we're not going to want to put off the wedding for very long.

"Lord, if we marry too soon, it might hurt our testimony before the town and the church. I'm just not sure what's proper in this situation."

Quint's thoughts suddenly went to the one man in town who could tell him what was proper.

"Of course, Lord," he said as the buggy drew near his house. "I'll go talk to him right now."

When Pastor Dale Morgan opened the parsonage door, he smiled in surprise. "Well, hello, Doc. Come in. What can I do for you?"

"I'm sorry to bother you so late, Pastor, but I need counsel, and the sooner the better."

"Hey, it's not that late. Let's go into the parlor."

"If — if it's possible, I'd like to talk to both you and Loretta."

Morgan grinned. "Sure. She's in the kitchen." Turning his head toward the rear of the house, he called, "Sweetheart!"

"Yes?" came the reply.

"Dr. Roberts is here and needs to talk to both of us."

"Be right there!"

In the parlor, both men were about to sit down when Loretta appeared, smiling warmly at the doctor, and greeted him with a ladylike handshake.

"I must apologize to you, too, Loretta, for

barging in here so late," Quint said. "As I told Pastor, I need counsel, and the sooner the better."

"Doc, you don't have to apologize. That's what we're here for. Come, sit down."

When they were seated so Quint could look at both of them, he shared his struggle, explaining that he loved Annamarie but didn't want to rush things with her, nor did he want to hurt either of their testimonies by getting married too soon.

"Well, you know, Quint, Annamarie has a right to hear exactly how you feel toward her, and it should be done very soon," Loretta said.

"So I wouldn't be rushing things with her, even though I've only known her for eleven days?"

"Absolutely not. Nobody can put a time on how long it takes to fall in love. She needs to be told. And to quote a very famous physician's words spoken this very night — the sooner the better."

Quint smiled. "Thank you. That settles that part of my struggle. Now, what about if we should want to marry soon?"

"You two aren't exactly a pair of youngsters, Doc," Morgan said. "You're both responsible Christian adults. If you agree about and declare your love for each other, then what's to stand in your way?" He turned to his wife and looked at her with adoring eyes. "Doc, Loretta and I knew almost immediately upon meeting that God meant us for each other. And we were youngsters. I was twenty-one and she was nineteen. Although we fell in love at first sight, we gave it a little time for our love to deepen and mature. But to you and Annamarie I will say, when God gives you peace about it, why wait? Because you're responsible adults, getting married a few weeks after you've met is not going to hurt your testimony before the people of the church or before the citizens of Bozeman."

"Thank you, Pastor," said a beaming Quint. "Life is so short on this earth at best. I've waited for a long time for God to send the right woman to fill my heart and life. And now that I've found her, I want to begin our married life as soon as possible."

Morgan looked Quint in the eye. "Do you have a date in mind?"

"After I make my official proposal of marriage to Annamarie, she and I will talk about it."

"Well, you just let me know and I'll be glad to perform the ceremony. Let me ask you, do you think Annamarie will want to join the church, now that things are on the verge of being settled?"

"I'm sure she will. She already loves both of you, and the church too."

"Good. I'm needing a Sunday school teacher for the girls' class that Gina is in. The Wilmers are moving to California next month, and with Annamarie's experience, she'll make the perfect replacement for Ethel. No one else in the church knows they're leaving yet, so just keep it to yourself for now, will you?"

"Of course," Quint said. "I know it will be a real blessing to Annamarie for you to offer her the class. I have no doubt that she'll accept it. She talks a lot about the class she had in Atlanta."

"Then she and I will both be happy," Morgan said.

Quint rose to his feet. "Thank you both for talking to me. I'm going to spend some time with Annamarie tomorrow night and tell her how I feel toward her. If she says she feels the same way toward me — which I believe she does — I'm going to propose. She and I will then come to see you, Pastor, and we'll set up the wedding date."

"Sounds good," said the pastor as he and Loretta stood up. "I'll be waiting. Loretta and I will be praying for both of you."

Quint thanked them as they walked him

to the door. He put on his hat and coat and hastened out into the cold Montana air.

When Quint arrived home, he was surprised to find Alex and Gina sitting at the kitchen table, waiting up for him.

"You two having a hard time getting to sleep?" he said.

"No, Daddy," Gina replied. "We just wanted to talk to you."

He took a seat at the table. "About?"

Brother and sister grinned at each other, then Gina said, "Alex and I both have noticed that you and Miss Taylor are looking at each other differently than you did at first."

"Oh? What do you mean?"

Alex grinned. "C'mon, Dad. You know what we mean."

"Daddy," said Gina, "have you fallen in love with her?"

Quint's features tinted. "Well-l-l . . ."

Gina giggled. "Out with it!"

"Okay. Yes, I've fallen in love with the lovely Miss Taylor. But I haven't yet put it into those exact words to her. I plan to do so tomorrow night. So when she's here tomorrow, don't either of you say anything to her about it, understand?"

"We understand," Alex said, "and we'll keep it to ourselves."

"Daddy, has Miss Taylor said that she

loves you?" Gina asked.

"She hasn't come right out and said so. It isn't considered proper for the woman to say it first. But I know in my heart that when I tell her I'm in love with her, she's going to say she's in love with me too."

"Yes!" squealed Gina, popping her hands together. "It's going to happen, Alex! They're going to get married!"

Quint chuckled. "Well, not tonight anyway. I want you two to get to bed."

They doused the lanterns and climbed the stairs together. Alex and Gina gave Quint good-night hugs at his door and headed on down the hall toward their rooms. Quint smiled to himself as he noted the lilt in their step.

When he finally lay in bed, he reflected on God's blessings and prayed for guidance as he planned to take the big step tomorrow night.

When Quint picked Annamarie up at the hotel the next morning, she was very happy and cheerful. At the house, the children welcomed her with hugs. After breakfast, the doctor left for his office, and shortly thereafter, Alex and Gina left for school.

Annamarie and Missy waved to them from the parlor window, then Missy looked up at her and said, "I love you, Mommy."

Annamarie picked the child up and held her close. "I love you too, sweetheart."

That evening, when it was time for Quint to take Annamarie to the hotel, the hugging ritual began. Then the children watched through the parlor window as Quint and Annamarie drove away.

It was a cold night, and Quint had warm blankets in the buggy to cover their feet and legs. The sky was clear and the stars twinkled like diamonds against black velvet beyond the bright silver moon.

As Quint drove the buggy through Bozeman's streets, Annamarie said, "I've come to love those precious children as if they are my own. I'm so glad they're now a part of my life." As she spoke, her breath formed white clouds in front of her face.

"I assure you, they feel the same way about you. They are vastly different children than they were before you came."

When the buggy reached Main Street, Quint turned it the opposite way from usual.

"Where are we going?" Annamarie said.

"To a favorite spot of mine just outside of town," he said softly. "There's a small creek that flows near the road, even this late in the year."

414

When they were a half-mile or so south of town, Quint veered the buggy off the road and stopped it beside the gurgling, ice-edged creek where they could see moonlight dancing on the water. On the opposite bank, skeletal branches of tall cottonwood trees arched across it overhead.

"Are you cold?" Quint asked her.

Annamarie's cheeks were bright red and her eyes were glistening. She pulled her coat collar a little tighter around her neck. "No. I'm fine."

Quint's heart was pounding as he took hold of her hand beneath the blanket. He leaned close and kissed her tenderly.

Looking into her eyes, he said, "Annamarie, I can't hold it in any longer without exploding. I know we've only known each other twelve days, and I don't mean to be rushing this, but I have to say it. I am head-over-heels in love with you."

She reached up and touched his cheek with a gloved hand and said in a whisper, "And my darling Quint, I am head-over-heels in love with you."

Quint's heart was now thundering in his chest. He silently thanked the Lord for sending Annamarie into his life and giving her such love for him. This time he kissed her soundly.

They embraced for a long moment, then he looked into her eyes and said, "Those two letters you wrote me, not knowing about Alex and Gina's deception —"

"What about them?"

"You signed both of them: sincerely yours."

"Yes?"

"Annamarie, more than anything in this world I want you to be sincerely mine. Will you marry me?"

For a moment, Annamarie could hardly breathe. Tears bubbled up in her eyes as she said, "More than anything in this world I want to be sincerely yours! Yes, I will marry you."

They sealed it with a warm, tender kiss.

Quint then told Annamarie about going to the Morgan home after taking her to the hotel last night and filled her in on his conversation with them and what their reaction had been.

"Oh, I'm so pleased that they think it will be okay if we marry soon. Certainly Pastor Morgan ought to know all about that."

"He does. He's a fine man, Annamarie. And Loretta is a sweet lady. You'll love them more the better you get to know them."

"I'm sure I will."

Quint took a deep breath and felt the sting

of the frigid air. "Now, dear lady, let's talk about the wedding date."

"Gladly! Do you have a date in mind?"

"I thought about it before going to sleep last night, and I've had it on my mind between seeing patients all day. If we got married on Saturday, December 23, we'll have known each other exactly twenty-eight days. That's four weeks — almost a month. You know, just in case someone wouldn't understand our situation. For two responsible Christian adults, that ought to be good enough not to damage our testimony with any reasonable person."

Annamarie was smiling from ear to ear. "Oh, Quint, December 23 would be perfect!"

"Pastor told me to let him know just as soon as we talked about it and wanted to set a date. Let's go to the parsonage right now and tell him."

"Yes, let's!" Annamarie said, giggling like a schoolgirl.

The next morning, Quint picked Annamarie up at the hotel a little early as planned and had her at the house cooking breakfast when the children came downstairs.

Quint was sitting at the table drinking coffee when they came into the kitchen.

Annamarie was at the stove, pouring scrambled eggs into a bowl from a skillet.

"Miss Taylor, you're early," Gina said. "You didn't give me a chance to help you cook breakfast. How come you came earlier today?"

Annamarie looked at Quint. "You want to tell her?"

A sly grin was on Quint's lips. He scooted his chair back and rose to his feet, then opened his arms. "Come here. All four of you."

Annamarie put the skillet down and moved to the tall, handsome man, feeling the strength in his arms as he folded her and the children close to him. Missy was so short she could hardly see the faces of the adults above her. Annamarie released herself from Quint's grasp long enough to pick Missy up, then returned to her place.

Smiling down at the three young ones, Quint said, "I picked Miss Taylor up a little early this morning because we have an announcement to make to you and I figured we might want to talk about it together for a while. I didn't want Alex and Gina to be late for school."

Gina's eyes brightened. "Daddy, I know what the announcement is about!"

"I do too!" Alex said.

"Well, all right," Quint said, "you two are so smart. What is it?"

"You're getting married!"

Annamarie laughed gaily as Quint said, "You're right. We've already set the date with Pastor Morgan."

"Oh!" squealed Gina. "When is it?"

"Fifteen days from now, counting today."

"Fifteen days! Let's see — this is Friday, December 8. That would be —"

"Saturday, December 23," Alex said.

Gina clapped her hands and jumped up and down. "Oh, praise the Lord! I told you He would do it, Alex! I told you our God would do it!"

"Yes, you did, sis."

Missy clapped her hands and said, "Mommy and Unca Quint Daddy are gonna get married!"

"Yes, honey," Gina said, "and then I can call her Mommy too!"

Annamarie's eyes were filling with tears that spilled down her cheeks as Alex said joyfully, "And I can call her Mom!"

24

"There it is, folks!" called out driver Mitch Bannister as the Wells Fargo stagecoach topped the rise of the pass. "Bozeman!"

Because of the icy air, the leather curtains over the windows were down and fastened shut. Paul Peterson unlatched one side of the curtain at his window, took a quick peek as the blast of cold air shot in, and quickly latched it shut again. The other passengers glared at him.

"Sorry," Paul said. "Just wanted to get a glimpse of the town."

All was quiet inside the coach as it wound its way down the steep trail with a heatless sun shining from the afternoon sky. Paul let his mind go to his mission.

Lord, I've prayed hard that You wouldn't let me be late. They can't have gotten married yet. They just can't. All I need is to see Annamarie and let her know that I'm still alive. We knew each other a long time before we became en-

gaged. Our love was deep. When I see her and tell her I still love her, she'll forget this doctor she's only known for a few days. She'll go back to Atlanta with me, and we can get married.

The stage pulled into Bozeman five minutes early, at 2:25.

When Paul alighted from the stage, he took his overnight bag from shotgunner Buck Patton. The other passengers were going on to points west.

As he walked along the boardwalk toward the center of the business district, Paul saw a couple coming his way. As he drew abreast of them, he said, "Ah . . . pardon me, folks. I'm a stranger in town. Just came in off the stage. Do you happen to know Dr. Quint Roberts?"

"Sure do," said the man, "He's a member of our church, as well as being our doctor."

"Good. Can you tell me if Dr. Roberts and his prospective mail order bride have gotten married? I'm an old friend of Annamarie's." At those words, the man and his wife smiled and the man said, "No, they haven't tied the knot yet, but the date is set for December 23."

Paul smiled. "Oh. The twenty-third, eh? Well, since this is the eighth, I guess I'm not too late. Do you happen to know where Miss Taylor is staying here in town?"

"She's at the Bozeman Hotel," the woman said.

"And where would I find the hotel?"

The man chuckled. "You're practically there now." Making a turn, he pointed at the sign. "See? Right there."

"Oh, sure enough. Thank you."

Moments later, desk clerk Tim Gibson looked up from some papers he was working on when he heard the lobby door open and close. As the stranger approached the desk, he smiled. "Yes, sir. May I help you?"

"I need a room, please."

"Just yourself, sir?" asked Tim, picking up the register book.

"Yes."

"All right. And how long will you be staying?"

"Probably just tonight. It might be two nights, but I doubt it."

"Mmm-hmm. Well, I'll put you down for tonight, then you can let me know to-morrow."

"Fine. Uh . . . I need some information if you can give it to me."

"I'll try."

"Well, I understand Miss Annamarie Taylor is a guest here in the hotel."

"Yes."

"I'm an old friend of hers and I sort of

wanted to surprise her that I'm here. Would you mind telling me what room she's in?"

"Her room is 301, sir, but you wouldn't find her there now. Are you aware that she is getting married shortly to our town doctor?"

"Oh yes. December 23."

"Right. Well, you must know then that Dr. Roberts has three adopted children. Miss Taylor has been working days at the Roberts house since she first came here, as housekeeper and sort of a mother to the children. The two oldest ones are in school, but the little four-year-old girl, of course, needs someone with her during the day. I can tell you how to find the Roberts house."

"Oh no. That isn't necessary. I'll just wait till Miss Taylor comes to the hotel this evening and surprise her." As Paul signed the register, he said, "You won't tell her I'm here when you see her come in, will you?"

"I won't even be here, sir. It's always late in the evening when Miss Taylor comes in, and the night clerk is on duty."

"Good. Just don't want to spoil the surprise."

"Do you want a room near hers?"

"Uh . . . no. That won't be necessary. Do you have something here on the ground floor?"

"Yes. I can put you right over here in room 103. It faces the street. Is that all right?"

"Sounds fine."

When Paul entered his room, he was glad to find that the window gave him a full view of the area in front of the hotel. He would be able to see Annamarie when she came in.

It was almost nine o'clock when Paul saw a buggy pull up to the front of the hotel. His heart quickened pace when he saw Annamarie's face by the light of the lanterns that sided the front door of the hotel. A man jumped down and ran around the rear of the buggy to help her down.

Paul eased back from the window so as not to be seen and said aloud, "So you picked a tall, dark, and handsome one, eh? Well, he won't look so good to you when you find out I'm still alive and still in love with you."

When Annamarie touched ground, it was obvious that the doctor was going to escort her up to her room. Paul rushed into the hall, hurried through the lobby to the staircase, and ran up the stairs to the third floor. He darted past room 301 and eased into a slender niche two doors down.

Peering around the edge of the niche, he held his breath when he saw the couple top the stairs. They walked the short distance to Annamarie's door and stopped, holding hands.

Paul felt his skin crawl but told himself when he knocked on her door in a few minutes that she would never want to hold the doctor's hand again. *She's more beautiful than ever,* he thought, adoring the profile he had loved for so long.

Annamarie reached up and touched Quint's cheek, saying, "Oh, darling, I'm the happiest woman in the whole world. It all seems like a dream. I guess I won't get over the feeling that until we're actually married something might happen to change all of this."

"And I'm the happiest man in the whole world," Quint said. "And don't you worry. Nothing's going to happen to change our plans for the future." Then, bending down, he kissed her uplifted lips.

Paul felt sick to his stomach. It became worse as he heard both of them exchanging words of love, devotion, and adoration. His heart especially felt deep pain as Annamarie told Quint how very much she loved him, saying that she would never love anyone but him.

Paul pulled back into the niche. *No! No! You love me, Annamarie! You love only me!*

When he looked back, Quint and Annamarie were locked tightly in an embrace and kissing.

When Quint let go of her, he told her good night, and as usual waited for her to close and lock the door before he walked away. As he went, there was an obvious spring in his step.

When the doctor disappeared down the stairs, Paul's face was dark with anger. He made his way to Annamarie's door. Memories of what he and the beautiful brunette once had together raced through his mind.

He raised his hand to knock on the door.

Suddenly a voice seemed to echo inside his head: *You're going to damage two lives, Paul. Their happiness is at stake. Go back to Atlanta and let them have their happiness . . .*

Paul gritted his teeth and lowered his hand. He shook his head and raised the hand again. He started once again to knock but checked himself as Annamarie's words to Dr. Quint Roberts reverberated through his mind: *Oh, darling, I'm the happiest woman in the world. It all seems like a dream. I guess I won't get over the feeling that until we're actually married something might happen to change all of this.*

Paul drew a tremulous breath. He shook his head and thought of the happiness he saw on Annamarie's face a few minutes before. Suddenly he was biting the very knuckles that yearned to pound on the door.

Tears spilled down his cheeks as he turned and walked down the hall toward the stairs.

On the evening of the wedding, Pastor Dale Morgan stood on the platform, Bible in hand, and smiled as the pump organ played "Here Comes the Bride."

Quint and Annamarie had planned a small, informal wedding. Since it was just two days before Christmas, the church was already decorated with evergreen boughs. Red velvet ribbons wound among the sweet-smelling branches.

Annamarie had chosen a soft wool dress of deep green trimmed with ivory lace at the neck, falling into a ruffled jabot down the front. The color complemented her jet black hair and ivory skin. The flared skirt was plain in front and tucked subtly at the waist in back. Tiny fabric-covered buttons marched down the back bodice, ending at the gently gathered waist emphasizing the slender form and grace of the elegant bride.

On the floor at the foot of the platform, Quint stood, heart pounding, while watching Annamarie walk slowly down the aisle toward him.

The wedding guests were on their feet, with every eye fastened on the beautiful bride. Her face alight from within, Annamarie walked carefully down the aisle toward her smiling groom. The power of his love-filled eyes steadied her wildly beating heart.

Alex, Gina, and Missy were at the second pew from the front, standing with Dr. and Mrs. Obadiah Holmes.

As Annamarie drew near the front, she gave a special smile and look of love to the three children, whose faces were beaming. When she was moving past them, Missy waved to her and said loudly, "Hi, Mommy!"

There were stifled chuckles as Gina bent down and whispered something stern in her little sister's ear.

The pump organ continued to play as Annamarie moved up to Quint, whose face was radiant. Love light shone in his eyes as he offered her his arm. When she slipped her hand in the crook of his arm, she smiled up at him. Just before they mounted the steps to stand before the pastor and take their vows, she whispered so only he could hear, "Quint, darling, I am about to become sincerely yours."

The employees of Thorndike Press hope you have enjoyed this Large Print book. All our Large Print titles are designed for easy reading, and all our books are made to last. Other Thorndike Press Large Print books are available at your library, through selected bookstores, or directly from us.

For information about titles, please call:

(800) 223-1244
(800) 223-6121

To share your comments, please write:

Publisher
Thorndike Press
295 Kennedy Memorial Drive
Waterville, ME 04901